Praise for the Red Solaris Mystery Series

## THE RED QUEEN'S RUN (#1)

"Touching upon a very real subject, this author offers the perfect formula of suspects, mystery, and a handsome police detective to heat up Red's fire. The frightening part, however, is that the foundation of school violence has become just as angry and backstabbing as the political realm. This is a great read about what goes on behind those academic doors."

— *Suspense Magazine*

"Morris has crafted a suspenseful, thoughtful, sexy debut...Her hero, Red Solaris, is vulnerable but tough, complex but straight-shooting, a woman learning how to wield power by remembering what it's like to have little of it. I'll read about her adventures anytime. Long live the Queen!"

— Christopher Coake,
Author of *You Came Back*

"A psychological thriller that reveals the Ivory Tower to be a hothouse full of monstrous egos, where bullying thrives long past playground days and 'academic discipline' requires research skills of the detective kind."

— Kate Manning,
Author of *My Notorious Life*

"Morris proves herself a masterful storyteller in this compelling debut novel. *The Red Queen's Run* is compulsive reading as it takes on the ripped-from-the-headlines topic of campus violence. I can't wait to follow its smart new heroine, 'Red' Solaris as this trilogy continues."

— Alan Deutschman,
Author of *Change or Die*

**The Red Solaris Mystery Series**
**by Bourne Morris**

THE RED QUEEN'S RUN (#1)
THE RISE OF THE RED QUEEN (#2)
(December 2015)

# THE RED QUEEN'S RUN

A Red Solaris Mystery

# Bourne Morris

HENERY PRESS

THE RED QUEEN'S RUN
A Red Solaris Mystery
Part of the Henery Press Mystery Collection

First Edition
Trade paperback edition | December 2014

Henery Press
www.henerypress.com

ISBN-13: 978-1-940976-57-0

Printed in the United States of America

*To Bob.*
*May he make me laugh forever.*

# ACKNOWLEDGMENTS

No book is written by one person. It just seems that way when you're alone at the keyboard. But then help arrives from multitudes.

My original editor Marjorie Braman saved me from despair and drowning and taught me how to put a novel together. Victoria Sanders led her to me. My amazing friends and readers taught me patience and cleared up the confusing parts. I owe more than I can say to the late Phil Rose, Merle Rose, Nancy Bostdorff, Cece Pearce, Diane Seevers, Leah Wilds, Cindie Geddes, Kristin Felten and Joanne O'Hare. I learned from all of you.

Thank you Otto Penzler for recommending my agent, Kimberley Cameron, who gave me support, encouragement and a better title for the book. She also led me to wonderful editors, Kendel Lynn and Anna Davis, plus an eagle-eyed staff at Henery Press who made me see more clearly.

Art Molinares taught me how to begin using social media and Todd Felts, at the University of Nevada, and his brilliant student, Ryan Kelly, pushed me farther. Jeff Ross and Brent Boynton envisioned wonderfully. So did Bob Felten, good friend and great teacher, who assigned four students the task of advising me on marketing. What a job they did. My gratitude to Shaun Burgess, Josh MacEachern, Garett Rosenquist and Erica Williams.

Thanks also to many University of Nevada friends who taught me about the academy, especially Joe Crowley, Donica Mensing, Rosemary McCarthy, John Fredericks, Jannet Vreeland, the late Travis Linn and numerous faculty members.

My fellow writers, all more skilled than I, deserve praise and gratitude and many bottles of good wine. Christopher Coake, Alan Deutschman, Kate Manning, Lori Rader-Day, Ben Rogers and Heather Hardy, thank you forever.

I owe much to the writers of *The Chronicle of Higher Education*, especially *Academe Today*, and to the ever-reliable *New York Times* for keeping me current with events in higher education, especially the violent and scandalous. And, of course, my gratitude to the amazing Lewis Carroll.

And finally, my family has been putting up with my obsessions and me for years. I love you deeply daughters and readers, Miranda and Temple, and amazing stepson, Scott, for my website. And, sweet husband, you deserve much more than a dedication for all your love and understanding. You make my world.

# Chapter 1

Anyone who thinks a college campus is a haven of scholarship and civility hasn't been paying attention. Last year, I sat through a dozen faculty meetings with recurring visions of Dr. Amy Bishop flooding my mind. I could almost see Bishop seated in a 2010 faculty meeting at the University of Alabama, then see her stand, aim a nine millimeter gun at her friends and colleagues across the table and begin firing. Before her gun jammed, Bishop killed three people, wounded three others, and then left the building and headed home to her husband and children.

Madmen lurk among us.

I don't recall the day when members of my own faculty began to scare me, or when their normal academic debates turned to prolonged and vicious quarreling. It was as if trouble crept up on us, a slow-moving storm that turned the sky pewter just before the funnel cloud manifested. I began to worry about potential violence.

I clearly remember the faculty meeting last August when George Weinstein's hand came down on the table so hard it bounced the piles of paper in front of us.

"Larry Coleman doesn't deserve tenure," said George, breathing heavily. Sweat shone on his upper lip. "We should never have hired him in the first place. He's a lousy teacher and a third rate scholar. I move we request his resignation."

I could smell the fear around the room.

Larry Coleman's eyes turned dark. His hands closed into fists, his lips tightened over his teeth.

"George, shut the hell up," said Max Worthington from the other side of the table. His voice was low, almost soft, his face gray with anger. "You can't say that about a colleague. Not here, not now."

"I can say whatever I goddamn please," said George, not even bothering to look at Max.

Max's voice grew louder. "Tenure doesn't protect your right to slander."

George moved around the end of the table until he was a foot away from Max. Max stood up. The two men loomed over us—big, tall, muscular.

Here we go.

Partly hidden by my open laptop, I waited to find my voice but I was paralyzed by the idea that anything I said would further inflame the situation. Pain in my stomach ruled me. It made me ashamed to think I was scared of two angry professors, but I was. I said nothing.

Henry Brooks, our dean, sat morose and silent. Henry was the best boss I had ever known. He didn't just manage, he inspired. Usually, he helped us play to our strengths and overcome our weaknesses. His fine, handsome features rarely displayed despair. But that day he looked old and defeated. He was my hero, but I felt sorry for him.

"This school is in crisis," said Simon Gorshak, the oldest of the faculty. He twisted in his seat to face the dean. "Henry, what are you going to do about it?"

"There is a motion on the floor," said George at the top of his voice.

"But no second to the motion," said an obviously exhausted Henry, "and I don't think ad hominum remarks illuminate the conversation or our understanding."

George turned and went back to his chair. Max sat down and pulled his laptop toward him.

A message arrived on my screen from Max, fuming and banging on his keyboard: "Hold on tight, Red. Palace revolution coming up."

I typed a reply: "The revolution eats its children."

# Chapter 2

The telephone call that changed everything came three days after that faculty meeting. I had been drinking with Sadie in my living room, on a cold Sunday afternoon when the Nevada wind was up, promising snow all night and a black sky without clouds.

Sadie sipped a glass of dry sherry, her thin features softened by the light from the fireplace, and tugged at a strand of silver hair that had escaped from the bun at the nape of her neck. Sadie was the retired Dean of Liberal Arts at Mountain West University and my best friend.

"I know I encouraged you to take that job as associate dean, but don't keep it too long," she said. "Too much paper pushing and budgeting and personnel squabbles. It eats the time you need for scholarship and teaching."

"Tell me about it," I said. "I haven't touched my research for two months and I don't even want to think about my student evaluations this semester. I'm spending way too much time trying to help my dean cope with faculty disputes."

"I saw Henry last week," Sadie said. "He told me the quarreling was even more hellish now than last semester."

"I wish I could be of more help to him. He probably told you about our three senior professors who tear him up every chance they get. We get nothing accomplished at faculty meetings. These guys always blow up the agenda."

"That's the way of faculty fights." Sadie sipped on her sherry. "I've seen some dreadful power struggles disguised as debates about curriculum or budgets. Noses get out of joint, especially senior, tenured noses."

I knew Sadie was right but it didn't help. "What gets me is the fierceness. This quarrel has gotten so much worse and it brings out the schoolyard bully in each of them. They hurt each other—they curse, they pound the table, they humiliate anyone who disagrees with them. And it happens at every meeting. I keep waiting for someone to throw a punch."

"Don't be surprised if someone does."

"But these are grown men with advanced degrees and distinguished reputations. They should know better."

Sadie looked weary of the topic. "I think I'll have a little more sherry before I head home," she said, rising from her chair and walking over to the small table I use as a bar. She poured herself half a small glass and returned to the fireplace.

I lived in a two-story brick house I bought with money I earned from a book I wrote about the newspaper business. My house was small but enough for a single professor—well-designed kitchen, a living room with a fireplace, one large bedroom upstairs and a smaller one downstairs that served as my office and guest room. My primary indulgence was a stereo system that played in every room so Mozart or Grace Slick could accompany me through my chores.

Sadie picked up a framed picture from the mantle over the fireplace. In her firm pay-attention-I'm-changing-the-subject-voice, she said, "Beautiful" to the photograph of a slender woman with pale skin and dark red hair. My mother.

"A beautiful drunk," I said.

"So you've told me. But you do look very much like her."

"I try not to act like her. I only keep her picture to remind me not to behave as badly as she did."

"I know. But I've heard you say that often enough to think you loved her anyway." Sadie smiled and eased back into the armchair nearest the fireplace.

My golden retriever roused himself from a nap and walked over to Sadie. He put his head under her hand. "Have you named this splendid dog yet?"

"Not yet. I just call him 'dog' and he comes." On cue, the retriever left Sadie, came over to me and put his head on my lap.

Sadie leaned forward. "Your life is on hold, you know. You're a beautiful woman with glorious red hair, who lives alone with her dog and goes to movies with an old lady twice her age."

"Sadie, I love going to movies with you. Movies and booze make you so insightful."

"You're past thirty. You should be crazy about some man and yearning to have his child." Sadie tucked another loose strand back behind her ear. "You haven't had a serious man for ages, and you are overdue." Sadie has an irritating grasp of my vulnerabilities.

"I date sometimes." I focused on the dog's ears and avoided Sadie's eyes.

"What about the biology professor with the shining white teeth—what happened to him?"

"The third date happened," I said.

"No good in bed?"

"It didn't get that far."

Sadie leaned further forward, elbows on knees, and gave me her impatient glare. "My dear, you have to try."

I matched her with my elbows on my knees. "Sadie. At that point sex with him would have just been...obligatory."

Sadie sat back. "Obligatory sex, ugh. That's the worst kind.'"

We both laughed and then our laughs fell into sighs as we stared into the fire.

"I met an attractive guy a couple of weeks ago at one of Elaine's dinner parties. Elaine's brother," I said. Elaine Morgan Witter was an adjunct professor at the journalism school and the editor of our local paper.

"Elaine's brother? What's his name?"

"Josiah. But he's called Joe. Joe Morgan."

Sadie's eyes lit up. She loves to tease. "Joe Morgan is a baseball player. Is Elaine's brother a baseball player?"

"No more sherry for you, my friend. The man's a police detective."

"A detective. Is he attractive?" Sadie sat up straight, reinvigorated.

I flushed remembering how I'd stared at Joe Morgan during dinner. "He's good looking in a roughhewn sort of way. Strong face, tall, good build, the same green eyes that his sister has."

"A tall, green-eyed detective." Sadie polished off the last of her sherry. "Alas, in the literature, detectives usually fall for nurses or lawyers rather than college professors. But who knows? He sounds promising."

Sadie rose and headed for the coat rack by the front door. I got up to help her with her coat. Sadie is so thin I always worry I'll crack one of her bones when I hug her.

"I look forward to our next lunch," she said, as she opened the door and turned toward the darkness outside. "Thanks for the sherry. It warmed me up."

I stood on my front steps, shivering as she made her way to her Jeep parked at the end of my driveway. When I heard her engine start, I waved her goodbye and turned back into the house.

The phone was ringing. I picked it up and said hello. A few seconds later my heart almost stopped beating.

It was Edwin Cartwell, one of the bellicose professors I had just described to Sadie. He was calling, he said, because there had been an accident at the journalism school. A man had died after falling down the concrete stairs from the third floor to the landing of the second floor.

"It might be Henry Brooks," he said.

I didn't believe him at first. I knew Edwin to exaggerate and dissemble. But when I asked him to repeat himself, his tone was calm, appropriate.

"It might be Henry Brooks," Edwin said again, without emotion.

Might be my boss, my dean? How he had fallen Edwin didn't know. He hadn't seen it happen. Edwin told me he took the stairs, as always, and found Henry's body face down on the landing. He had edged down the steps, careful not to touch the sprawled legs, the one arm flung across the last step. When he had reached the landing, he had placed his fingers on the side of the man's neck, avoiding the blood and bone chips. The man was dead. He had checked the pulse, called 911, and then called me.

"I think you should be here," Edwin said and hung up.

I stood, the phone still in my hand, stunned, envisioning what had happened. In my mind I saw a body falling down the stairs to the landing below. Was it Henry? Why? Had he fainted? Henry was sixty. He had a minor heart problem a few years ago but it had taught him fitness. Henry was in good shape. Like Edwin, he took the stairs every day.

The phone rang again. The second caller identified himself as Detective Joe Morgan from the local police. The man I had met, the detective with green eyes.

"Dr. Solaris, I'm sorry to tell you your dean has died from a fall down a flight of stairs. We need you to come to the journalism school right away." That was all. No recognition we had met at his sister's, no expression of sympathy. All business.

The air in my hallway chilled. Even the phone in my hand felt cold.

I put on a wool hat and coat and headed for the car. Soft snow had started falling outside. Night had arrived and I knew the roads would be icy. Mountain West University is only ten minutes from my house, but there are two hills to contend with on the way. On warm days the trees form a shimmering canopy over the road. But in winter, the road is gray, the sky is gray, and the trees are barren. At night in winter, the road is dangerous. Snow and black ice are problems on the streets of Landry, Nevada. A town of 150,000 can only afford so many plows for its main streets. It was Sunday night—those plows would not be out until the next morning.

I felt as if I had swallowed broken glass. Henry Brooks had been my champion as well as my friend. I wanted to sit in the car and cry, but no tears came—just a deep throbbing inside me.

I had expected something awful was going to happen. The faculty arguing had ramped up, people refused to greet each other in the hallways. "It's a goddamned gang war," Henry had told me. "Please don't dignify it with terms like *academic dispute*."

The wool hat itched. I took it off. Then I took off the scarf I had thrown around my neck. My car smelled of the dog I had left at home.

The campus was dark. Falling snow softened the outlines of the classic brick buildings. Most of the major colleges on the fifteen acre campus were constructed a century ago and clustered together in the center. As I rounded the curve on the campus road, I saw one of the smaller buildings—the journalism school—was lit up inside and out. Three police cars were pulled up to the front of the parking lot, doors open, roof lights revolving.

I parked near the front door of the building. An officer appeared at my car window, asked for my identification and then offered to help me through the snow. He told me to go in and up to the second floor. I walked through the first floor lobby, a two-story room flanked on the right with a wall of graduation class pictures, and on the left with photographs of major donors to the school.

A woman officer stood at the base of the steps leading to the second floor.

"Sorry, you can't go up there," she said, adjusting the gun on her hip. She was pale and homely, hair pulled back in a tight bun, no make-up.

"I'm the associate dean of the school. The police asked me to come."

"Name?"

"Meredith Solaris."

The policewoman looked dubious, pulled out a piece of paper and a notepad, made a note on the paper, then shifted to one side so I could pass.

Blood had dripped down from the second floor landing to the top steps of the flight of stairs down to the lobby. I stepped carefully up to the landing and saw the body. The head was turned away from me so I could not see the face, but the form was familiar, long legs, slim hands with delicate fingers, thinning gray hair. It was

Henry. The smell in the stairwell was familiar too, sickly-sweet. It made me gag.

"Thanks for coming. Sorry to call you out on a night like this." Detective Joe Morgan stood two steps above where Henry's feet splayed. He was writing in his notebook and didn't look at me until I spoke. Another man knelt between the body and me.

"How did this happen?" I sounded raspy.

"We still aren't sure," Joe said. "I called you when I could only get voicemail for the provost and the president."

Joe Morgan was irritated, disheveled, not as sharply attractive as I'd found him when we first met. He looked down at the short, heavy man in a parka who was kneeling and examining the body.

"This is Danny Ranko, our medical examiner. Danny, meet Dr. Meredith Solaris. She's the associate dean of the school."

Ranko lifted his head and nodded at me, then returned to his work.

Joe Morgan still did not look at me. A click and Ranko started dictating into a small recorder: "The victim appears to be a white male in his early sixties. From the position of the body it appears he fell, or was pushed, face-forward down the stairs, cracking his ribs, breaking his nose. The mouth and cheeks are covered with blood and broken bone. From the look of it I think he was dead before his forehead hit the landing. I'll confirm that in the autopsy." Ranko clicked off the recorder.

I grasped the stair railing to steady myself. I wanted to cry out, but I couldn't make a sound. Henry Brooks was dead, sprawled on a concrete stairway. I could not weep. I could not believe it. I had just seen Henry the Friday before. He was laughing at something as he listened on his phone, his mouth open, the lines around his eyes creased. My throat closed.

"I'm going up to his office on the third floor," Joe Morgan said. "Why don't you go back down to the elevator and take it up? We'll leave Ranko to finish up."

The nausea hit me when I entered the elevator. Christ. Don't throw up in here. The minute the doors opened on the third floor, I raced for the women's bathroom and vomited in the toilet. I heard a second flush from the men's room next door. Joe emerged at the same time I did.

We walked to Henry's office and stood in the doorway. Nothing seemed out of order—no scattered papers, no lamps overturned. It was neat and tidy and cold.

"Did the dean usually work on Sundays?" Joe asked.

"Often. I suppose you've heard the faculty has been at odds this semester. Lots of arguing. No one volunteers for our school committees so the dean has had to do more work than usual." I was babbling, nervous.

"So I heard from my sister." His expression was softer. "You okay to talk?"

I nodded. "Did you know Henry?"

We entered my third floor office. I closed the door, sat behind my desk, and looked out over the quad. Snow was falling, heavier than before.

Joe Morgan took off his coat and draped it over the back of one of the chairs. I opened the small refrigerator next to my desk and offered him some bottled water.

"Never met Henry Brooks, although my sister spoke highly of him," said Joe, taking the water and sitting down. "I'm sorry to have to put you through this, but what can you tell me about him?"

Even though my eyes were dry, Joe must have sensed my distress because his voice softened and his eyes looked more sympathetic. "I know this must be a shock, Dr. Solaris. Do you need to be alone for a bit?"

"Please call me Red. You did at Elaine's house when we met."

"Sorry. I wasn't sure you'd remember me."

I smiled weakly, remembering my conversation with Sadie and sipped from my own bottle of water. I cleared my throat and leaned forward on my desk.

Joe leaned forward as well. "I know this is hard. But the sooner I know as much as I can, the sooner I can figure out what happened."

He produced a notebook and I began to talk about Henry. I got through Henry's background—a PhD from the top journalism school in the country, assistant professor at Illinois when he was hired by Mountain West. Winner of two national journalism awards, he was a tenured full professor when the old dean retired. At the urging of the faculty, Henry applied for the dean's position and was successful in spite of several distinguished competitors from other universities.

"We usually like to hire deans from outside, but by then Henry was a nationally known scholar and so remarkable, so special..." finally the tears broke.

Joe handed me a handkerchief but I pushed it back and reached for a box of tissues in my bottom drawer. Joe waited until I was more composed.

"Your colleague, Edwin Cartwell, told me Henry was a widower and lived alone. There's no girlfriend we should call?"

I shook my head and blew my nose. Actually, there was someone to call but I was not about to tell Joe Morgan—or anyone else—that I suspected Dean Henry Brooks had been having an affair. And I was certainly not going to say I was fairly sure the woman Henry had had been sleeping with was Edwin Cartwell's wife.

Then I remembered Edwin had called me before Joe did.

"Is Edwin Cartwell still here? He called me at my house. I should probably talk to him."

Joe got up and opened the door for me. "Cartwell should be in his office. He told me he needed some time to collect himself before I take him down to the station for his statement."

I walked down a long hall and around a corner. Faculty offices were all on the third floor. Most were small and windowless. But Edwin Cartwell was a tenured full professor; his office was large with windows facing a small garden.

I could hear Edwin's voice before I got to the door. He was talking on the phone.

No, he was singing on the phone.

"Ding, dong the wicked dean is dead," Edwin sang.

He repeated the phrase several times for the listener. I froze a foot away from his door and pressed against the wall. Who was he talking to? Was he actually happy about Henry?

"No I didn't kill him," I heard Edwin say. "I found him."

I moved into the light coming from his doorway. As soon as he saw me, his tone changed. "Yes, terrible," he said into the phone. "I'll call you later. I promise."

"One of the faculty?" I asked.

"No," he said. "Just a friend." His mouth curved into the suggestion of a smile. Smug bastard. Edwin is thin and wiry with a complexion so pallid it's almost ivory. He rose and adjusted the visitor's chair in front of his desk.

"Tragic, Meredith. Absolutely tragic."

"Yes, Edwin. It's a great loss for the school."

Edwin folded his hands neatly on his desk. His hands are always clean and manicured. He was wearing a dress shirt and a dull brown sweater vest. Formal, even on a Sunday. "I know you admired Dean Brooks a great deal. Please accept my deepest sympathies."

"And you mine," I said. I was not about to let him know what I had overheard. "You knew him longer than I did."

"Ah, yes. Many years." Edwin brought his hands up and patted what was left of his sandy hair. "And his children, too. Poor dears. Would you like me to call them?"

Not you, Ding Dong.

"No thanks. I'll call them in a bit," I said, watching Edwin try to compose a tragic expression on his sharp face. "Tell me, when did you find the body?"

"Around five forty-five," he said. "I called 911 and then I called you."

"Are you all right?" I asked—as if I cared. "Have you called your wife?"

"I haven't told Mary." He fiddled with a pencil just long enough to seem reflective. "I'll tell her when I get home from the police station. I have to give a statement, you know." His thin lips pursed, prissy, self-satisfied. With what? The death of a colleague?

"Yes, I know you have to go to the station," I said. I stood up and turned to leave. His eyes followed me to the door.

Great, I thought walking back to my office. Later tonight, Mary Cartwell will hear about the death of her perhaps-lover from her perhaps-deceived husband. How will she handle that? How long will she have to wait to get to the bathroom so she can throw up or break down?


Joe Morgan was on his cellphone but ended the conversation the moment he saw me. He moved closer to the door of my office. Closer to me. His hair was combed and his face was no longer strained. He looked like the attractive man I had met at Elaine's dinner party.

"You need me to drive you home, Red?"

"No, I'm all right. Snow is better than ice."

Too bad. It would have been nice to get a ride home with a good-looking cop, but I was too tired, too sad. I told myself I didn't want to leave my car overnight in the parking lot.

"I think Edwin Cartwell is ready to leave," I said.

"Okay. I'll retrieve him," said Joe. "But I do have a favor to ask you."

"A favor?"

"I'd like to meet with you tomorrow morning. I need to know more about Henry Brooks and whatever you can tell me about the others here. Would eight be too early to come by your house?"

"No, eight will be fine."

I left him and headed back to the elevator and then out to my car. Normally, I love the northern Nevada winters. Sun so bright you need sunglasses when snow is on the ground. Crisp, dry, high desert air so different from the wet, bitter Midwest chill I endured as a child. Normally, I loved the Mountain West campus, its graceful college buildings surrounded by wide lawns and gardens, all facing a quad that looked more like Virginia than Nevada. But that night I would have traded places with any professor at any other college to escape my sorrow, not to mention my dread of returning to the school without Henry Brooks to guide me.

# Chapter 3

As I drove home, I found myself thinking as much about myself as I was about my lost friend. I didn't know how the school would survive without Henry. On top of that, Joe Morgan's request to see me the next morning kept intruding on my grief, and it worried me. I have a history of meeting the wrong guy at the wrong time. Ask me why I never married, why I left a good university offer in Ohio and, sooner or later, if I am being honest, I'll stop talking about the career opportunities at Mountain West and start talking about the men in my life. I'll talk about the men who disappointed me, both good guys and troubled guys. I might talk about the father who disappeared into grief for a wife who didn't deserve him—and forgot about the daughter who did.

And, if I've had a few too many, I may even talk about my mother. She was born in the west. I wasn't, but it's my blood. I am attracted to the west for more reasons than I fully understand. Big Sky country gets to me. Nevada is more home than Ohio ever was. The town of Landry is in northern Nevada nestled in a gentle valley with views of the Sierra Mountains to the west. From here you can drive to Reno in less than an hour and to San Francisco in an afternoon.

My old Ohio friends used to call and tell me they were in Las Vegas and wondered if I could drive over for lunch. It delighted me to inform them that Landry is separated from Las Vegas by six hundred miles of desert and a nuclear dumpsite. "Oh," they would say and return to the blackjack tables.

What I didn't tell them is that northern Nevada is nothing like the low desert of southern Nevada. The few times I had flown to Las

Vegas, I had looked out of the plane window down at the huge desert landscape and wondered why the first fellow ever stopped there. Perhaps his horse died.

In contrast, Landry is quiet and green, evergreen in winter and lush with deciduous trees and lawns in summer. Outside of town, the landscape is harsher but still beautiful. High desert shrubs and rugged mountains surround us. Not just big sky, it's blue-sky country all year 'round where the sun shines almost every day and the air is always dry.

By the time I got back to my house, the snow was two inches thick on the ground and I realized I had been too lost in sadness and thoughts of Henry to be frightened of black ice on the drive home. I needed a cup of coffee and some time to reflect on what had happened. The answering machine was blinking, but I ignored it and went into the kitchen. The dog must have sensed I was unhappy. Instead of his usual excited greeting, he just ambled over and put his soft nose into the palm of my hand.

I was the one who had to tell the faculty that the dean of our school was dead. Only some would seriously mourn Henry Brooks' death. Nonetheless, every one of them would be in a state when they got the news, even those who hated him. A dead dean meant we'd have to search for a new dean and new leadership meant significant change. Academics don't care much for change.

We were already at swords' points about our journalism curriculum. One group wanted to shift the school's emphasis to new media, online journalism, computer assisted reporting, blogs. Their opponents wanted to stay with a traditional focus on reporting, basic print, and broadcast journalism. What should have been a lively academic debate had, over time, become a divisive name-calling fight, as painful as an outbreak of shingles.

I ignored the blinking light on my phone, poured a second cup of coffee, and sat down at the kitchen table. I wanted to remember Henry, to honor him in some way. The last time I'd seen him in his office, I'd asked:

"Do all faculty groups fight like ours?"

"No," he had said looking up from his computer and turning toward me. Henry was fine featured, elegant looking, and, I suspected, just a bit vain about his appearance. Always in cashmere and tweed jackets, Henry could have passed for a British aristocrat. His once blond hair was gray but his blue eyes were bright and his brow smooth. He had rubbed his temples and put his elbows on his desk.

"Many faculty groups get along very well. We are just going through a very bad patch, Red. Sadly, it's not unusual on a university campus."

"But why? Before I went into teaching, when I worked at the newspaper, we knew if you started any serious inter-office trouble, you could get canned. On the flip side, if you didn't like it there, you could leave and get a job somewhere else."

"That's the point Red. Once we are in place, leaving can be difficult. Most universities are located in small towns and the university is the only game in town. If you're a newly minted PhD, and you're married, you moved your spouse and kids to a new place where your employer is the only option. Your spouse finally finds a job, your kids make new friends at school. But then the worst can happen. If you get fired or fail to get tenure, you have to move again. Even if a move is good. Some years ago I was offered the dean's position at a school twice as large as ours. My wife had a fit, my daughter burst into tears, and my son looked like he wanted to poison my food."

"Okay, I get it. You get tenure, you keep your job, your family settles in and your reluctance to move becomes stronger. But why the anger?"

"Because, after a while, you dig in. You resist the challenge of ideas that threaten yours. And you indulge in games of passive aggression."

"The aggression I saw in the faculty meeting yesterday was hardly passive. I was waiting for a fist fight or a riot to begin."

Henry had sighed and folded his hands on his desk. "Things should get better. New course plans impinge on budgets and make faculty crazy sometimes. We just have to outlive the resentment for now. Meanwhile, please know how grateful I am for your help in all this. You're the one I trust most. You keep me sane."

That was the last time I had seen Henry Brooks alive.

God, I would miss him.


I was sitting lost in sadness when my phone rang again. A second cup of coffee in hand, I reluctantly answered on the fourth ring.

"Ah, Meredith. So good to get you directly," said Philip Lewis, the university president. "My dear, I appreciate how difficult this must be for you. Difficult for all of us. I am so sorry."

The president had seemed fond of Henry even though he once expressed dismay over the in-fighting in the school. "The students are aware of the faculty fights," he had said to Henry. "That's not good. You will have to find ways to ameliorate this situation."

"We will miss Henry greatly," Lewis said. "I hope you and your faculty will be able to rally to the needs of the school at this tragic time."

"I hope so too," I said.

"Have you talked to them yet?"

"Only to Edwin Cartwell who found the body and was at the school tonight. But my machine is blinking and I suspect the word is out."

"You'll have to call each one, you know," Lewis said. "A hard task but your leadership is important now. Let me know if you think I should talk to any of them tonight. Otherwise, I'll plan on coming over to the journalism school just before noon to meet with everyone. Of course, I'll need to see you and the provost beforehand. Can you be in my office at ten o'clock?"

"I'll see you at ten, President Lewis."

"After your calls, I hope you'll be able to get some rest. I know this is a particular blow for you, but we must remember, Henry Brooks did have that heart problem a while back, so perhaps his death was not totally unexpected. Good night."

Not totally unexpected? For God's sake, not expected either. Now what? What about the school, the faculty? What about me?

I started making calls to the faculty. My first was to Max Worthington, the easiest to talk to, and one of my confidants on the faculty. Max taught online journalism and became my first friend when I moved here. He and his wife Trudy invited me to dinner twice a week during my first semester. By the time I reached him, he had heard about Henry's death from three other faculty members.

"I feel terrible," he said. "How the hell did Henry fall down the stairs? He used those stairs every day."

"I don't know, Max. And the police seem uncertain. Tomorrow morning I'm seeing the detective who was at the building tonight. Maybe he'll have more information from the medical examination."

"How are you holding up, Red?"

"I'm exhausted, but I have to call the others so I'm drinking lots of coffee."

"Henry was such a good guy. I don't know how he put up with those clowns we work with. Terrorists, all three of them." Max seemed seriously upset. I tried to comfort him.

"Maybe Henry's death will make people start to behave," I said. "Maybe we will all see we should be engaged in mourning not combat. Besides, Henry was usually their primary target, maybe with him gone..."

"Red, do you think his fall was an accident?"

The implication of his question hit hard.

"Jesus, Max, what else could it have been? President Lewis seems convinced Henry had a heart attack. Do you think it might not have been?"

"No, Red. It's just that the last faculty meeting was so brutal on Henry, I wondered..."

"You see through a glass very darkly, Dr. Worthington."

"It's my nature. But listen, I'll let you go. You have more people to call. You might want to forget the coffee and switch to Scotch." Max's voice softened. "Take care of yourself, hon. I know how rough this is on you and it's going to be particularly hard for a while. Let me know what I can do to help."

It was after midnight when I finished phoning and got to bed. I lay, curled in fetal position, trying not to think about how much I missed Henry and trying to erase the image of his broken body.

It was not the first time I had seen a body on a staircase. One afternoon when I was nine, my mother drank an entire bottle of gin, then got up and pitched forward down the wooden stairs leading to our basement. I heard the sound of her fall from my perch on the window seat in the living room where I'd gone to avoid her. I raced to the basement door. My mother lay on the dark stairs, feet facing me, one shoe off. Out cold. I ran for help. The neighbors came and telephoned my father, who raced home from his classroom. They carried her up the stairs and put her on the couch. She had vivid cuts and bruises on her face and forearms. Her hands were bloodied and full of splinters. When we opened her shirt, we found more bruises on her breasts and belly. My father broke into deep, heavy sobs. "Oh Emmy. Oh Emmy. What have you done to yourself?" He looked up at me. His eyes fixed on me as his sobs continued. The neighbors watched me—their stares sympathetic but clearly horrified. Was I supposed to have stopped her? Was I supposed to have prevented her fall? Even then, people expected too much of me.

# Chapter 4

I got up early the next morning, showered and washed my hair. I stood naked in front of the full-length mirror as I dried my hair. Long legs, full breasts, pale skin marked by a narrow cape of freckles on my shoulders. My hips seemed wider than the last time I had looked. I turned sideways. Another few pounds and my butt would be too big. But, on the whole, my body looked good. Except it felt empty. I was thirty-five and single. I was a virtual orphan. My mother was dead and my father so lost in senility he rarely recognized me. Sadie was right. I did need a man in my life. Particularly now that I had lost Henry, I needed a broad shoulder, arms around me, someone to cradle me in bed when I wept.

Thirty minutes later, I was still in my bedroom when the doorbell rang at exactly eight o'clock. I took one more look in the mirror before I went downstairs. I had tried on a black dress, but decided Henry would have hated me in black so I put on a red wool suit. Red was my best color. It set off my hair. Red was a positive color. And I didn't want anyone —especially Joe Morgan—to see me looking washed out and dreary.

Joe stood on my doorstep in a heavy leather jacket, khakis creased so sharp I wondered if he had been military before joining the police force.

We sat in my living room drinking coffee. I told him I had to see President Lewis at ten but I would tell him everything I could before then.

"How does the journalism school fit into the university? I am more familiar with the term college than school," said Joe.

"The journalism school is just like a college," I said. "It's an independent unit and the dean reports to the provost."

"That's Fred Stoddard, right?" Joe was writing notes. "So Henry Brooks reported to Stoddard and Stoddard reports to President Lewis?"

"Yes."

"And you are the Associate Dean who reported to Brooks?"

"Yes."

"Tell me about your relationship with Brooks"

"Henry hired me, helped me get tenure, and then called me into his office a year ago and told me he wanted to groom me for administrative responsibility. I thought the senior faculty might resent me in that job. But Henry said I would be good and he needed me. There had been a lot of fighting among the faculty about the curriculum and he wanted someone objective. He was also...a wonderful friend." I fended off tears.

"Did any of the faculty object to your promotion?"

"A few thought they should have been asked to vote on it, but Henry said he could exert the dean's prerogative and promote his own choice. A few complained, but most of them went along. Some began to lobby me to get on their side of the dispute about what courses we should teach."

"And did you take a side?" Joe's eyes were as green as seawater and fixed on me.

"No, I didn't. Henry's decision to promote me to associate dean allowed me impartiality."

Joe sat back in his armchair, turned the page in his notebook and looked at me for a long minute. "Tell me about the faculty, particularly the dean's major opponents in this argument you all were having—those who would have been on his enemies list."

I started with George Weinstein, a former editor whose family once owned a large metro newspaper. George taught advanced reporting, editorial writing, and editing courses. After college, he edited his family's newspaper. After the paper was sold, he went to grad school. He inherited a great deal of money.

"So he doesn't have to work?"

"I think he likes being in charge of a class. It reminds him of running a newsroom," I said. George is a big man with broad shoulders and a loud voice. He hates to be interrupted but consistently interrupts others.

Next, Simon Gorshak, who taught news writing and loved traditional journalism and first amendment issues. Seventy-five years old but not inclined to retire. A perpetual grouch, Simon was once dean of the school years ago, long before Henry, long before Henry's predecessor.

"What Simon never mentions is that he lost the confidence of his faculty and was forced to resign as dean."

Joe looked up from his notebook. "Resign?" Green eyes widened. "If he resigned, why is he still here?"

"Because when a dean resigns he often just goes back into the faculty as a tenured full professor. He doesn't have to leave the university, just the dean's position."

An ironic smile looked good on Joe's strong face. "And how does that work out?"

"Sometimes the old dean can be a real pain in the ass, especially for the new dean."

"I'll bet," said Joe, stretching his arms. "Okay. Who else?"

"Edwin Cartwell, whom you met last night. Edwin's a journalism historian who teaches freshman and sophomore writing classes and a graduate class in journalism history. History is also his research subject. Yale graduate, wrote for a literary magazine, then got a PhD from Georgia."

"Yeah, I heard a lot about Yale and the magazine last night at the station."

"Edwin's very proud of his eastern heritage," I said. "Edwin's also a snob. A traditionalist and a snob. Still disapproves of *The New York Times* going from black and white to color photos on the front page."

"Hmm. I read the *Times* online edition every morning. It's always been in color."

How about that. A Nevada cop who read *The New York Times*.

"So, those are the three who fought with the dean," said Joe, resuming his note taking. "Did Henry Brooks have any strong supporters besides you?"

"Oh yes," I said, thinking fondly of Max Worthington. "Most of us actually supported the dean. Max Worthington and Phyllis Baker were very vocal at meetings."

"And the rest of the faculty?"

"They mostly observed," I said, noticing the clock read twenty past nine. "I could say more about them, but I think I should be leaving for my meeting with President Lewis."

We stood up simultaneously and he reached out his hand. A warm, strong handshake. "Thank you, Red. I appreciate the background information."

"Why are you so interested in the faculty dispute? Does it have anything to do with what happened to Henry?"

"Maybe, maybe not," said Joe, reaching for his jacket. He stuffed his notebook into his pocket and turned toward the door. "But any accident resulting in death requires investigation."

I felt a chill in spite of my warm wool suit. "Do the police think...?"

"The police don't think anything yet, Red. Except for me. I personally think I'd like to know a lot more about the journalism school if you can tolerate my curiosity."

"You'll find I'm very tolerant, Detective Morgan."

"Joe, please. We did meet at Elaine's," he said, this time with a broader smile. He walked into the hall to my front door. "May I call you?"

"Please do."

Please do.

# Chapter 5

The day was crisp and cold, the campus covered with blinding bright snow. I walked from the journalism parking lot to the central quad. Huge elm trees lined the snowy lawn, their branches bereft of leaves, stout long-armed guardians of the center of campus marking the paths on either side of the quad leading to the administration building. A bell tower chimed, assuring me it was just ten o'clock as I climbed the stairs to Philip Lewis's large office overlooking the quad below.

"Good to see you, Meredith," said Lewis, extending his hand. Lewis was in his late seventies, his skin as thin as tissue paper, but his grip firm. "Although I would have preferred happier circumstances." He motioned me to a chair at the large oval table in the center of his office. The provost, Fred Stoddard, sat on the other side shuffling through some papers. He looked up.

"How you holding up, Red?" Stoddard said. Did everyone think I was going to fall apart?

"It's going to be a hard day," I said. I liked both of these guys, but I was still preoccupied with the image of Henry lying dead on the staircase, and not quite ready to engage in political niceties with university brass.

"Well, at least you look well. I'm glad you're not wearing black." I felt like a bug on the table. Stoddard was a big, bald man and the morning sun was reflecting off the top of his head.

"Did you reach all the faculty?'

"All of them. I finished at midnight."

"How are they taking this?"

I took a beat and smoothed my skirt. "They're in shock and a few seem truly grief-stricken." I thought of Edwin singing Ding Dong. "Others seem resigned to the loss and worried about the future."

"They will all need your leadership, Meredith. I hope you're up for this," said Lewis. "We cannot put a hold on things while we mourn Henry. We are close to Finals Week, and the faculty and students need the journalism school to keep functioning."

Naturally, that's what this meeting is about. Maintenance work. Student needs first, personal grief second.

"And the major donors and alumni need to be reassured that all will keep going without Henry."

Oh yes, donors and alums second. Grief third.

"And you have an accrediting committee visiting next semester," said Lewis.

"All of which means we'll need to appoint an interim dean," said Stoddard.

"Of course," I said.

Please God, appoint a good one. This change is bound to scrape the wounds. I looked away from them toward the window where the sun bounced off the snow and reflected white light into the room.

"We think it should be you," said Lewis, pulling his chair closer to mine.

Oh, God.

I should have seen this coming, but the thought of managing that cage of tigers made my stomach ache. "Thank you both. I know I am the Associate Dean, but I think the faculty might prefer someone a bit older, more senior."

"Some probably would like an old turkey," said Stoddard. "But the fact is, you are the best qualified to get everyone through this semester and next semester's search for a permanent dean. Henry was very high on you." He indicated the papers he had been shuffling. "I've been reading last semester's evaluations and, Meredith, you are clearly the best choice."

I felt my face redden. "What about Simon Gorshak?" I said, pretending humility and hoping they would not take the suggestion seriously. "He'll expect it." Gorshak was, in large part, responsible for some of the more venomous statements in faculty meetings. But, he was also the most senior of the faculty.

"Not a chance. Simon never learns. He is too contentious," replied Lewis, much to my relief.

"Too committed to his own dammed agenda," said Stoddard. "Bad enough he's tenured and we have to keep him on the faculty."

Interesting. I didn't know Stoddard had been watching us that carefully. I started to appreciate the provost.

"How about it Meredith? The school really needs you."

I nodded. I was flattered, even excited in spite of my sadness. "I may need some help from you," I said. "Larry Coleman is going up for tenure and is terrified some of the senior faculty will sabotage him."

"I've got your back," said Stoddard. "And Philip can help, too."

Lewis smiled and patted my hand. He made me feel like a little girl rather than an associate professor about to be interim dean.

"I'll be grateful to both of you," I said, just starting to grasp the idea that I would be the top management of the journalism school until we hired a new permanent dean. George Weinstein would be furious. Edwin Cartwell would plot treason. Simon Gorshak would get up early to slash my tires.

"When do you want to announce this?"

"Today, when we meet with the faculty in the school. Did you set up a noon meeting?"

"I did."

"Good. Now, Dean Solaris, before that meeting, we should chat a bit about a service for Henry, and how you would like my office to help his children when they arrive."


The journalism school was across the snow-covered quad from the president's office. Three stories tall and brick, it had been built in the 1970s on a small plot of land between two older colleges. Although no ivy covered its walls, it was constructed in the Colonial style of all the academic buildings.

The school was full and noisy when President Lewis, Provost Stoddard, and I arrived shortly before noon. Mondays were always lively but this one seemed particularly crowded. Media people were everywhere. Conventional TV cameras jostled with laptops and shoulder cameras held by the younger journalists. I spotted Joe's sister, Elaine Morgan Witter, across the entrance hall.

"Red," she called, waving. "Can we get an interview with you and Philip Lewis?"

"We'll have a press conference after we talk to the faculty," murmured Lewis.

"Later," I called back to Elaine, hoping Lewis would follow Stoddard and me quickly into the elevator before the reporters began to badger them. Too late. One reporter with a handheld camera squeezed into the elevator with us. Stoddard stepped between the reporter and Lewis. Stoddard weighed at least two hundred and fifty pounds and stood over six feet.

"We have a meeting with the faculty upstairs," said Stoddard, his face close to the young reporter's. "We'll have a press conference when that's over, so why don't you go back downstairs and tell the others. No comments for now."

We reached the third floor and walked to the room at the end of the hall. The faculty lounge was large and comfortable, with upholstered chairs placed by tall windows overlooking the quad. In the center, a long table was surrounded by modern swivel chairs. The table seated twenty for faculty meetings.

All the chairs were filled when we entered. It was clear the regular faculty had all arrived early, as had several members of the adjunct faculty, some of whom could not fit at the table and perched on the edges of the upholstered chairs.

Joe's sister, Elaine, slipped in by a back door and sent me a small, sympathetic smile. She joined the other adjunct professors in the back of the room.

Edwin Cartwell offered his chair to Lewis, who waved him away. Lewis and Stoddard stood at the head of the table. I went over to the windows and sat on the sill. The room felt uncomfortably warm and I was glad to be near the large cold glass overlooking the snowy landscape outside. I slipped off my coat and waited.

"This is not a good morning," President Lewis began, "but I am grateful to see so many of you here in spite of difficult weather and even more tragic events." Lewis had been a literature scholar. He was known for his careful and fluid language. I was comforted by the grace of his delivery. I was not ready to say anything. I was still grieving for Henry. Moreover, I was nervous about what Lewis would say after he finished acknowledging the apparent cause of the death of the dean—"heart attack, we think"—and the several minutes of praising Henry.

The first question came from George Weinstein who narrowly missed interrupting the president as he cleared his throat. "Aren't we going to cancel classes today?" It was more of a challenge than a question. That was George's manner.

"I think not today or tomorrow," said Lewis. "The students are going to need to see and hear you today. Don't underestimate their sense of loss. I know this may be difficult, but you need to be good leaders and good teachers, especially today. We'll probably close the school in memoriam on the day of Henry's service but that depends on the date his children choose to have it."

"When are Henry's children due?" asked Edwin.

"Late this evening. The son, Michael, had to fly from Paris. He's meeting his sister in Chicago and then flying here. The provost and I will meet them at the airport..."

"When will we start a search for a new dean?" George interrupted again. Lewis paused and looked steadily at George. The room went completely silent. Lewis was not used to rudeness and certainly no one expected anyone to bring up the subject of a new dean while the old dean still lay in the morgue. The president said nothing, allowing silence to be reproof.

After several awkward seconds, Provost Stoddard spoke. "We won't begin a search until after services for Dean Brooks."

"So who's running the school in the meanwhile?" George said again, oblivious to criticism.

"George, for God's sake," said Phyllis Baker.

"Well," continued George, defending his question and now standing on his feet and buttoning his jacket over his considerable stomach. "Don't we need to know? I mean, we are too small to have department chairs, so, if we're not closing the school down, we need to have someone to cover the bureaucratic nonsense." George cleared his throat again, his method of punctuating for emphasis. "And, importantly, we need to form a committee to choose an interim dean, and a search committee for a new dean." George's voice was loud and his face tended to flush when he was insistent or upset and he was both. More than once I had seen George shoot his cuffs to establish his importance to the audience.

"The provost and I have already chosen an interim dean," said Lewis. The room was hushed again. "And later this semester, we will get together with her to set up a search committee."

"Her?" said Edwin, now on his feet.

"You mean you're not going to give the faculty a chance to choose their own leader?" said Simon.

Oh shit, here we go. I'd warned them hadn't I? This was going to be a disaster. Across the table I saw Larry Coleman lean back in his chair, his fingers steepled in front of his mouth to help conceal a smile. Phyllis Baker's dark brown eyes looked a bit brighter. Max Worthington looked expectant.

Lewis remained calm. "The journalism faculty will have an important role to play in the search for a new dean. But meanwhile, the provost and I have chosen a highly qualified administrator to be the interim dean. And, no Simon, we are not going to put this to a vote. I make interim choices. Faculty are only advisory." Lewis smiled at Simon who glared back.

Another moment of silence. "And your choice is?" Edwin's mouth purses up when he's irritated.

"Dr. Meredith Solaris," said Stoddard with a slight smile and nod to Edwin. "Your very capable and experienced associate dean. She has our complete confidence."

The room began to buzz.

"Great," said Max audibly above the buzz. Elaine's smile grew wider. A bit of tentative applause followed.

"Ah," said Edwin, sitting down and letting out a conspicuous sigh. "The Red Queen rises."

I wondered how long it would take for me to start loathing Edwin Cartwell.

How do you get over that awful feeling you've just been promoted beyond your level of competence? Look at your resume, my father used to say. Look at what you've already done and look particularly at what you've already accomplished. Especially if it was arduous. How did you get through grad school? How did you get to be associate dean?

What was bothering me?

The faculty quarrel.

The fights of children are terrible. I remembered the red, sweaty face of an eight-year-old opponent in grade school. Behind him I saw the cruelty in the faces of his conspirators. They twisted my arm and stole my lunch money. That was one of the few fights I lost. For weeks afterward I hated them all and wanted to make them bleed and cry and plead for mercy.

Grownups presumably have their passions under control—in particular sophisticated, well-educated grownups. But not my faculty. Somehow their feud had awakened hatred. And now a man was dead because of it. Perhaps hatred had always been there, a snake sleeping at the bottom of a basket.

I remembered how my father combed snarls out of my hair. He'd tug and pull and demand courage in spite of the pain. He said courage would give me the strength to be virtuous. Since he was the only parent I had who gave a damn about me, I inhaled my tears and promised courage would become my strong suit. For most of growing up, I was sure I had the guts of a prizefighter. In elementary school, I tackled blood-boiling debates and playground fights. I was the tough chick. Willing to take a punch and give a better one back. No one messed with me.

And, because of what happened when I was thirteen, I thought I'd always be able to stand up to anyone.

It was Ohio in midsummer. I was walking home from music camp. The air was heavy and moist, scented with cut grass. I was several blocks from home when I heard the distant squealing of brakes. The driver must have turned on to the side street where I was walking because I saw a car go by in a blur and I figured he was still going fifty when his fender struck a small blond boy and sent him head-first into an iron fence.

I saw the whole thing. I know I was shouting as I ran across the street because, by the time I reached the car, people had come out of their houses and surrounded the boy. Even before a woman's voice started wailing, I knew from the way the kid's body was angled away from his neck that he was dead.

As I approached the car, I could see the driver's face, white and sweaty. I don't know why, but I opened the car door and leaned in. "Get out," I said. "You're going to be sick and throw up all over the upholstery."

And the guy got out. He had arms like a wrestler. Black t-shirt with a Marlboro box folded into the sleeve. I guessed him to be in his twenties. He steadied himself and walked toward the crowd.

I looked around. Everyone was focused on the boy's body, even the driver who was standing well back of the others. The muscles in his back moved with his heavy breathing.

I reached into the car and took his keys. I stuffed them in my pocket and then headed toward the edge of the crowd, trying to stay out of the driver's line of sight.

"You bastard. You bastard. You killed my baby." I'll never forget the anguish in that mother's voice. I saw the driver stop, turn and head backward toward his car. An old man in the crowd came after him and clawed at the driver's arm. "You can't leave," the old man hissed.

The driver spun around and slammed his fist into the old man's face. Then he ran to his car and climbed in the front seat. I saw him bend down and search the floor. "Where the hell are my keys?" he said. "Who took my keys?" He got out of his car and looked around in a panic. His eyes were wild. I couldn't stop staring at him. His eyes landed on me.

I looked down, tried to focus on the root of an elm tree pushing its way up through the concrete sidewalk. I knew I should run, but my legs wouldn't work. One quick stride over the chunk of broken sidewalk and I would be clear to run. The crowd would stop the driver. Wouldn't they? The old man had tried and gotten punched and the crowd had done nothing. Sweat poured off my neck and down my back.

"My keys, kid. My keys." The driver was maybe three feet away.

I found my voice if not my legs. "Mister, look around you. There are twenty people here."

The driver cocked his head to one side. His hand shot out, palm toward me, threatening. "The keys, kid. Or you'll get hurt."

The crowd muttered. I sensed the crowd was shifting toward me, some even behind me. The old man was near and two younger men were behind the driver.

"You lay a hand on me and you'll be sorry," I said in a voice that did not sound like my own. "You've already killed one kid."

The muttering became a growl. The driver's head swiveled. His arms came up with both fists clenched.

The sudden whoop of the ambulance made him stagger. A police car moved silently into his view, red and blue light flashing across his face.

His arms dropped to his sides. His head fell forward as his legs buckled, forcing him to kneel on the hot pavement.

As the first policeman reached the driver, I reached into my pocket and threw the keys into the street.

"Good girl," I heard a man say. "Brave girl," said a woman nearby. A large woman with long white hair stood in front of me, blocking the sight of the driver and the policeman. A cigarette was planted firmly between her thick lips. Her face was framed in chins and greasy with the heat. She spoke softly to me.

"Child, you are never going to be this afraid again."

I ran all the way home to my father. When I told him about what had happened and what the white-haired woman had said to me, he said, "Red, my love, take that as prophecy."

But the prophecy was wrong. My courage seemed to fade with adulthood. I had been frightened for more than a year. It started when George Weinstein gave a party at his ranch, several miles outside of Landry, I didn't want to go, but went because Henry wanted company. Lunch was an elaborate barbeque with imported beers and wines from small labels in Napa.

"Can't be shipped out of California," said George, beaming over the loaded table. "You have to know the winemakers to buy for your own cellar."

After lunch, George took those of us interested in riding to the stables behind the house. "All former mustangs," he announced, "rounded up and auctioned off every year. They go for dog food if guys like me don't buy them."

A "gentled" Palomino was assigned to me. "You sit her well," George said as we cantered out across the meadow that surrounded his ranch. The day was glorious, bright blue sky that went on forever.

On the way back, George rode ahead of us toward the barn. I followed him, guiding the mare into the dimness. As I attempted to dismount, my foot caught in the stirrup. I started to fall, but George was there, hands under my armpits, his face inches from mine, large, sweaty, and grinning. He freed me from the stirrup and held me above the ground. His thumbs dug into the flesh above my breasts. "I'm okay," I said, but still he held me, my boots inches away from the floor of the barn. He seemed to be laughing but made no sound.

"Planning to count her teeth, George?"

Henry was behind me.

George released me.

Henry drove me back to Landry. It was dusk and I could only see his profile. "You all right?" he said without taking his eyes off the road.

"Was that about sex?" I was still tense.

"No. That was about power," said Henry. George had once been Henry's friend and his firmest supporter. But once Henry became the dean, he ignored George's advice. Hired people George didn't like. Cardinal sin. George had never forgiven Henry. "Suspending you in the air was to show you how strong he is and to show me he was still in charge even if I'm dean. George likes to control. And he likes to scare people. He's irritated because he can't scare me, so he went after you."


When I became aware of the animus between Henry and George, Edwin and Simon, the three faculty members were still talking like grown-ups, couching their attacks in the high-toned linguistics of professional dispute.

They began their diatribes with such phrases as, "in the interests of improving the school," or "recognizing the needs of American journalism." I wondered if they were scripting their remarks before the meetings.

The root of their anger was simple and ugly—not really about the school. No, it was personal with these folks. All three had been on the search committee that recommended Henry for the job of dean. And, then, when two teaching spots opened up, instead of hiring the traditional newspaper and magazine candidates George and Edwin favored, Henry had hired two "new media" guys: Max Worthington, a specialist in online writing and, then, a year later, Larry Coleman who had been an online editor and a well-known blogger. George, Simon, and Edwin were outraged. The old guard closed ranks.

In Larry's case, Henry had said, "We need his online skills. Trust me, this hire is essential for the future of the school."

"Bullshit," Simon Gorshak had said, addressing the entire faculty at the August meeting. "We have a power-drunk despot on our hands. When I was dean this kind of totalitarian hiring decision would have been unheard of. "

"Oh really," said Max. "Is that why you were forced out?"

It was downhill from there.

Now Henry was dead. Probably murdered. Would whoever killed him come after me?

"Hell is a tenured professor with hurt feelings," Henry had said.

# Chapter 6

Even before Henry promoted me into administration I had heard him say the job of dean was the most difficult in a university. "It's about money and people, people and money. Forget scholarship, forget the pleasures of teaching. Deans don't have enough time. Sometimes I even forget why I applied for this post."

"Why are faculty so difficult to manage?" I had asked, not just thinking about George, Simon, and Edwin but about others with complaints, requests, and unreasonable attitudes toward colleagues.

"Because they are people who think otherwise," Henry had said.

"People who think otherwise," I repeated.

"You got it. Professors are known for differing, for holding opinions outside of the norm, even unpopular opinions. The ethos of the university encourages dissent and higher levels of discussion. But sometimes one of them just indulges in argument for its own sake, rolling around in contentiousness like a dog in bird shit."

"They have so much freedom. Why aren't they more loyal to the university?"

Henry had looked thoughtful. He folded his hands behind his neck and stuck his elbows up in the air. "Some professors are primarily loyal to their disciplines. For some, loyalty to a college or university comes in third."

"What comes in second?"

"For the good ones—students. Thank God."

\*    \*    \*

The Tuesday after Henry's death was my first full day as the interim dean. By ten o'clock I had endured visitations from six members of the regular faculty and calls from two alumni. Most of the conversations began with some variation of "You may not be aware of this, but, before he died, Dean Brooks and I had agreed that..." followed by a predictably self-serving request:

"...I would teach only on Tuesdays and Thursdays so I can have a block of time for research."

"...we would resolve this at the faculty retreat in January. No later. He promised."

Two more phone calls from worried alum and then one of the lecturers was in my doorway.

"Dean Solaris?"

"Call me Red. Everyone else does."

"Yes, I heard the Red Queen joke. It's making the rounds. I trust you are more even-tempered than the original."

"I'm doing my best. How can I help you?"

"Well, before he died," he said. Ah, yes. The lecturer had large brown eyes and a habit of talking too fast when nervous.

He began again. "That is to say, you probably know I was denied tenure at my previous university."

"I'd heard that, but perhaps you should fill me in."

Six years after you are hired by a university, you go up for tenure. You are either successfully tenured, or you are given a year to look for another job. In university speak it's called "up or out."

"I did everything I thought was expected of me," he said. "I was a good teacher. I got the second highest student evaluations in the department. I developed new courses for the grad program. I published a dozen articles in good journals." He was talking faster and stopped to take a breath.

"My book was almost finished. I..." His voice thickened. "I thought tenure was a slam-dunk. And they turned me down. I don't think anything has ever hurt as much."

I sympathized. "Tenure is never a slam dunk. Did they tell you why?"

"Not really. Vague references to my research, but I know I had some enemies in the senior faculty of my department. I mean I was always civil but not particularly deferential. I stupidly thought academic freedom meant I could speak my mind whenever I chose. I thought that was what tenure is supposed to protect?"

"For the tenured, yes. But, it can still be a crap shoot." My breath became shallow. Amy Bishop was denied tenure at Alabama.

The lecturer was watching me cautiously. I still wasn't sure what he wanted. "What did you and Henry discuss before he died?"

"Well, when he hired me, I asked if I could apply for an assistant professor position and for tenure before the sixth year. I mean I have already..."

"What did Henry say?"

"He said he would review my work here early next year and decide."

"I'll honor the deal you had with Henry."

He exhaled loudly. "Thanks, Dean Solaris."

"Red," I said.

But he was out the door.

I wondered if Henry had truly made a deal. Should more people be on Joe's list of suspects?


Henry's assistant was Nell Rogers, a small and tidy gray-haired woman who had worked for Henry and the dean before him. Nell knew university procedures cold and where all the academic land mines were buried. She knew how to keep a dean out of trouble. I was thankful she had said, in the midst of her grief for Henry, that she looked forward to helping me. Nell came in a moment after the lecturer had left.

"You have a call waiting for you. He's been on the line for several minutes—that Detective Morgan."

"I'll take it, thank you Nell."

"You might ask him when they'll take the tape down from Henry's office door so you and I can get in there," she said as she turned away.

I picked up the phone.

"I heard that," said Joe. "Tell her we hope to finish up at the school tomorrow."

"She'll appreciate that," I said. "What's up?"

"First of all, congratulations. I hear you've been named the new dean."

"Interim dean."

"Well, Interim Dean Solaris, I do need to talk further with you and wondered if you had any time this afternoon—either at your office or here at the station."

I felt a slight flush. Joe Morgan seemed to have that effect on me. "I can't see you this afternoon because I have to teach a class in fifteen minutes," I said, "but if you could stop by the house this evening..."

"That'll be fine. I'll see you at your house. How about sometime after 5:30?"

I said yes and then he asked me, "What class do you teach?"

"Media Ethics. It's my favorite class and, even if I have to give up teaching full time so I can do this dean's job, I hope I can continue teaching this one. My students are terrific."

"Ethics. Hmm. I'd like to know more about that. I'll see you this evening."

For the first time since I heard of Henry's death, I felt a small moment of optimism. There was something about Joe Morgan I wasn't quite ready to define, but his curiosity—or perhaps what I hoped was his interest in me—gave me confidence. My step was lighter as I headed for class.

Teaching is the most joyous profession of all. There are few things more satisfying than watching a group of students engage in debate, change their minds in light of someone's convincing argument, or just finally get it. It makes everything else I struggle over worthwhile.

Media ethics is an optional course in my school and I've never had more than thirty students a semester.

Many have remained good friends long after the course and their graduation was over, and some still call me when they face ethical dilemmas in their professional lives.

Several write letters telling me how useful my course was to them after they graduated.

If I had my way, we would start teaching ethics in fourth grade, not wait until junior year in college. My afternoon class in media ethics was the only good part of my first day as dean of journalism.

"I'm sorry to hear about Dean Brooks but I'm psyched you're our new dean," said Samantha, usually the first to speak.

"Sweet," said the sloe-eyed young man next to her. Peter leads his own rock band.

"Thank you," I said. "I'm sure you've already talked with your other professors, but do any of you have questions about the dean's death? Or feelings you would like to talk about?"

"Oh my God, it's so sad," said Olivia, tugging on a lock in the center of a thicket of curly brown hair. Ever thoughtful, often nervous. "His kids aren't much older than we are. I can totally imagine how they feel. My dad died two years ago."

"So did mine," said Eric, star halfback.

"How did the dean die? Was it really a heart attack?" came from Tammy across the room.

"That's what we've been told," I said.

"I'm so sorry about it. Will there be a funeral?"

"I'm not sure. The provost says his children may prefer a small memorial gathering."

"That's better," said Eric. "Funerals are barbaric."

"Oh, I don't agree," said Samantha. "Some people need the rituals of the funeral to help them begin to grieve. They need to see their loved one honored."

"And some would like to avoid the pompous ass kissing from people who never gave that much of a damn for the guy in the first place," said the halfback.

"How should we cover this in the student paper?" I said.

"Short and simple," came one reply. "I heard the details were pretty gory."

"But," said Peter, "as journalists aren't we obligated to be specific? I mean what if the fall in the stairwell turns out to be what really caused his death rather than a heart attack..."

"We also have an obligation to the readers and the family not to gross them out," said Samantha next to him.

It was hard for me to teach that day, but I was grateful for my students' thoughtfulness.

The dog knew. Just a quiet lick on my hand when I came through the door. Animals are so in touch.

I fed the dog and poured myself a glass of wine. The television news was boring and then a reporter came on with an interview of Elaine Morgan Witter about Henry and what he'd done for the school. As a local editor, colleague, and friend of Henry, Elaine provided a respectful, even tender obituary. She looked good on television, with the dark green eyes and the thick hair she shares with her brother. I couldn't help but watch the clock, knowing Joe would arrive soon.

At the end of the five o'clock news, the doorbell rang and there stood Joe Morgan. This time the dog jumped up and down. A bias for alpha males I reasoned, but I did have to admit Joe looked very attractive in a black cashmere turtleneck.

"Is this a good time to talk?" he said.

"Good as any," I said leading him into the living room. "Wine?"

"Thanks." He sat down. "Red wine if you have it."

"I do. I take it you're not on duty."

"I sort of am on duty, but I'll take the wine."

"Bad day?"

"You might say so," he said.

I brought him a glass and sat down opposite him.

"How are you holding up?" He looked sympathetic.

"I'm sad but managing."

"Meredith...um, Red." He looked down at his shoes. "Much as I would like to know more about the faculty and more about your ethics course, right now I have to ask you where you were Sunday?"

Where I was? "Joe, do I need an alibi? Henry died of a heart attack, didn't he?"

"Please just answer my question." Joe's green eyes were fixed on me. His was by far the best-looking face of the day.

"Okay, Detective. I went to a late afternoon movie with Sadie Hawkins."

That got a smile. "Sadie who?"

"Seraphim Hawkins, former dean of liberal arts and a good friend. Everyone calls her Sadie."

"What time did you leave the movie?"

"I'm not sure, but Sadie and I had some drinks here and, just as she left, the phone rang. It was Edwin Cartwell telling me about finding Henry."

"And Dr. Hawkins can vouch for you, for the late afternoon and early evening as well," Joe said.

"She can. Now tell me why she needs to?"

"Because troubling stuff came up in the autopsy," said Joe, sipping his wine. "There were injuries on Henry Brooks' body that are inconsistent with a heart attack or a fall forward down a flight of stairs."

"Meaning?"

"Meaning more investigation into his death."

"To determine...what?"

Joe looked very uncomfortable. "Other contributing factors."

"That's bloody vague."

Joe looked away from me, got up and went to the window. The dog followed him and he scratched behind the dog's ears.

"I have to ask you to stop by the station sometime tomorrow and give a statement," he said with his back still to me.

"Is that why you seem uncomfortable?" I walked over to stand beside him.

"In part."

"What's the other part?"

He turned from the window toward me. "The other part is I wanted to ask you out to dinner and this makes it awkward."

I smiled up at him. I admired a good chiseled face with a firm jaw line and a straight nose, not to mention those eyes. Dinner? Yes, indeed.

"So ask," I said attempting to sound casual.

"Tomorrow night," he said. Not quite a question.

"*After* I've given my statement?"

"Yep."

"And after you've confirmed my alibi."

He handed me his wine glass and moved to the front door. I held it open. For a moment he leaned toward me. I thought he might kiss me, but he raised his hand and very lightly touched my shoulder.

"I'll be here to pick you up at 6:30 tomorrow," he said, and left.

I spent the evening wondering whether or not Joe Morgan had wanted to kiss me but backed off. Later in bed, I decided the gentle touch of his hand was even better than a kiss. A kiss is over and done with. Everyone kisses everyone. The touch of his fingertips was more intimate, more promising.

# Chapter 7

Seraphim "Sadie" Hawkins was a handsome hawk. Her sharp eyes darted. Her nose was a beak. The deep vertical lines on either side of her mouth completed the look of the raptor. She had mentored me through every crisis since I came to the university. She pored over my tenure application even though she was not on my committee. One time, when she found me weeping in my office over a piece of lost text, she had taken my hands in hers, handed me her handkerchief, and taken over the computer to find the missing research. We had lunch twice a week.

She was deep in a manuscript, her latest book, scribbling away. Her head was close to her work in the inadequate lighting of Gormley's Bar and Grill. She didn't look up as I sat down.

"You're on time for once," she said, still reading.

"I couldn't wait to get out of that school. It's a zoo."

She looked up from her manuscript, pen poised in her hand.

"The pleasures of academic management." She tapped her lip with her pen and smiled. "I miss them not."

The man who always waited on our table brought Sadie an iced tea.

"Congratulations, Dean Solaris," he said.

"Thanks, Wilson. I'll have a stiff Pinot."

The corners of his mouth twitched. Was everyone having a good time at my expense? Although he wears the same shirt and apron as all the waiters, Wilson owns Gormley's and does not suffer fools. He adores Sadie and I suspect he likes me. "Best wishes, Doc," he said, moving to the bar.

"Your cop called on me at home at dawn," Sadie said.

"At your house at dawn?"

"Well, dawn for a woman who now sleeps until nine. He wanted to know if I saw you on Sunday. I told him we went to the movies."

"Sadie, we did."

"Of course we did. And then we had drinks at your house afterwards. That's what I told him. He's very attractive—remarkable eyes—but he asks a lot of questions. Especially about you. Does he suspect you of something?"

I had stopped at the station before school and given my statement to a junior detective who seemed only mildly interested in compiling information on my whereabouts Sunday. Joe Morgan needed to confirm my alibi but hadn't he trusted me? The Pinot Noir arrived in time to cover my reaction. I told Sadie about the questions raised during the autopsy of Henry's body. I probably was supposed to keep that a secret but, what the hell, Joe was asking questions about me, checking up on me after I had talked to him, after he asked me out to dinner.

Sadie folded up her manuscript. Her hawk eyes narrowed. "Do you think Henry was murdered?"

Ding Dong.

"Some of those guys get pretty worked up, but I find it hard to believe they're that violent. A fistfight maybe, but not murder."

"That's because you haven't received your first death threat," she said. Her lined face was solemn.

"My first what?" One Pinot Noir might not be enough.

"Sometimes deans get death threats," she said. "I received two during my time. One from a disgruntled candidate who flunked his interview, another from the lesbian lover of a secretary who was certain I had made advances toward her partner."

"Jesus."

"The Dean of Engineering once got a note in a box with a dead rattlesnake. It was from an assistant professor who had been denied tenure and promotion."

I twirled the wine glass, wondering if I would have much appetite for lunch. "Are death threats commonplace in this university?" Sadie had never mentioned death threats before.

"Not commonplace," she said, "but they happen."

"Any of the threats made good?"

Wilson was back, hovering and eavesdropping.

"Only one I know of and not at this university. It was a decade or more ago at one of our community colleges. And that particular lunatic took out the dean and two colleagues with a twelve gauge."

Holy shit.

"Our special for lunch today just might be steak tartar," said Wilson.

Back at the journalism school, chaos greeted me. Students milled about the hallways and the entrance. Nell Rogers met me at the top of the stairs with a wild look in her eye. Her usually neat gray hair was sprouting tendrils around her face. She pulled me into her office and closed the door.

She spoke in a whisper. "The police came at noon. They asked me to set up time with everyone —*everyone*—on the faculty and staff for interviews with detectives."

"It's all right, Nell. They have some additional information on Henry's death and they need to check it out."

She was still breathless and agitated. "And, they've cordoned off the hall to the dean's office, I mean your office, with even more of that yellow tape."

"Nell, sit down. Let me get you a drink of water."

"I'm all right, Dean Solaris, but you—you have to stay in your old office. That's what they said. Until they have finished with the dean's office."

Poor Nell.

She was beside herself with concern. This was her school, her responsibility, and there were cops all over and faculty calling my office every five minutes demanding to know what was going on.

"Nell, I can handle this. Why don't you go home and get some rest," I said.

"Oh, I can't go home. No one can go home." She was frantic again. "The police were very firm about that. Everyone has to stay and be interviewed. There was no way to warn you about all this."

"You could have called my cellphone. I was at lunch with Dean Hawkins at Gormley's."

"They were very specific about that. No outside calls."

No outside calls. No going home. What the hell was going on? Joe had said they were concerned about the cause of death, not sure of anything. Had they found more evidence? Had Henry been murdered? Christ. I practically ran to my office. No outside calls indeed. No one told me that. This was my school, now. How dare Morgan and his gang just take command?

I picked up the phone to call Stoddard. Or Lewis if need be. This was an unwarranted invasion.

Joe appeared in my doorway. I hung up.

"What the hell is going on?" I said.

"An investigation of a possible homicide. I told you last night."

"But did you have to quarantine the whole journalism school? You can't do that."

"I'm sorry, Red. I'm afraid I can do what I need to do. We need to move expeditiously to preserve evidence that might be destroyed if we wait."

A woman appeared in the doorway behind Joe. The blonde, disinterested detective who had interviewed me. She had loosened her hair since the morning and the top button of her blouse. Because she was working with Morgan? She was wearing gloves and holding a carved glass award in her hand. "We found this in a box of books behind his desk," she said to Joe.

"Red, do you recognize this?"

The chunk of polished glass was about eight inches high on a solid base. It was a large rough triangle with a sharp pointed top. A university symbol was etched in the center of the triangle. The base was engraved with Henry's name.

"It's an award Henry got from the alumni association at his alma mater. He kept it on his desk," I said. "It's been there for several years."

"It wasn't on his desk when I found it," said the woman detective, still speaking only to Joe. "It was under some books in a box."

"Nell may have put it there," I said. "She's been packing Henry's things up to give to his children."

"Let's check it out," said Joe to the woman, who slid the glass award into a large plastic bag in her other hand. "See what the forensics guys think."

The blonde detective turned away and almost ran into George Weinstein who pushed his way past Joe and stood in front of my desk.

"This is outrageous. I am told I can't leave the building until some cop talks to me at 4:30. That's too late. Margaret and I are driving to Reno. We have dinner reservations and theater tickets. I have to leave now." George was in full bluster.

"Detective Morgan, do you know Dr. George Weinstein?"

Joe nodded. "Yes, Dr. Weinstein. I appreciate this is an inconvenience. I will get to you as soon as possible but I do have others to interview."

"Well, I can tell you right now I did not have a goddamned thing to do with Henry's death and I don't know anything more than what was in the papers. So your appointment is a stupid waste of time." George's face was reddening and he glared at Joe.

"Nonetheless, I will see you in your office at four thirty," said Joe, who I noticed with pleasure, was taller than George.

George wheeled around and headed for the door. "This outrage gets reported to President Lewis, Red. You can be certain of that."

Max Worthington's was the next face in the door. He leaned in. "Detective Morgan, I have a 3:30 appointment with you but I wonder if you could see me earlier. I've just gotten a text from my wife who isn't feeling well."

Joe looked at his notebook. "I'll see if I can get to you earlier, Dr. Worthington. I'm seeing Dr. Cartwell in ten minutes, perhaps he'll swap with you."

"Not likely," said Max.

After Max left, I slammed the door closed.

I exploded. "What is all this high-handed crap? Earlier today, you wake up an old lady to ask her a bunch of questions about me when I had already told you everything I could. Now you insist people stay in the building. No outside calls. Apparently you have trust issues, *Detective* Morgan. Or, do you just have some kind of hard-on for academics?"

The moment I spoke the last words, I turned away from him, knowing he was smiling. I put my hands over my face. Then I felt him near me. I could hear the amusement in his voice. "That depends, Dean Solaris. Are we still on for dinner?"

There was a knock at the door. We turned as Nell opened it. "Detective, Dr. Cartwell seems very anxious you not be late for his appointment," she said.

"On my way," said Joe, stepping away from me. "Cartwell is the one person we know was in the building the day Henry died. I need to talk to him again. I'm sorry about the ruckus here, Red. Really. But investigating a possible homicide is..."

I took a deep breath. "I know. Just your job."

His head cocked to one side. "Listen Red, I really appreciate your insights into the faculty disputes and all the academic processes. I want you to know that. It does help us."

A thought occurred to me. "Wait, Joe, I may have an idea about Cartwell that could be useful. I need to talk to his wife."

"Unofficially?" His eyes narrowed.

"Unofficially, but soon."

He looked doubtful. "If it's about this case, may I remind you that you're not a cop."

"I know and I won't try to be one. But I think I could get some of that insight you need into Henry's relationships."

Again, eyes narrowed. "Relationships with someone's wife?"

"She won't talk to you about it. And I'm not even sure I know what I think I know."

"Okay. But I want you to tell me whatever you find out tonight at dinner."

Tonight at dinner.


Mary Cartwell was exquisite to look at. And she looked at herself often. Mirrors decorated the house. She was fifty and looked thirty. Full-lipped, full-breasted, long-legged. Perfect. She'd agreed to let me in, but she was not happy about it. However, I knew it was the best time to talk. Edwin would be out until late evening after talking to Joe and then teaching his graduate seminar.

We settled at her kitchen table over cups of coffee.

"What's up?" She looked down at her cup and then up at the ceiling.

"I am thinking of a poem," I said, "part of a poem by T. Cole Rachel: 'we are governed by rules of avoidance, narrowly scraping past, unavoidable pains'..."

"You didn't come here to recite poetry," she said. She pushed back her hair.

"No, but I did come to talk about something you would probably like to avoid talking about."

"Like?"

"You and Henry Brooks."

She rose from the table and walked over to the kitchen sink. She turned on the water full blast and splashed her face.

"What do you mean?" She patted her face with a dishtowel. Creamy skin, gorgeous with no make-up.

"One afternoon last summer," I said. "I was buying garden supplies at the nursery and I saw you coming out of a room at the motel next door. Two minutes later, I saw Henry come out of the same room. You left in separate cars."

She leaned against the sink, her hands gripping the edge of the tile on the counter. "Does everyone on the faculty know?"

"No, I honestly think I'm the only one."

She let out a deep breath.

"And you have kept it to yourself."

"Yes."

"Thank you."

"But now I need you to talk about it," I said.

"Why? He's dead. Who cares anymore?"

"The police care. They are investigating Henry's death and I offered to help. I thought it might be easier for you to talk to me."

She opened her mouth but only a sigh came out.

"Mary, didn't Edwin call you about all the interviews at school today?"

"No. Edwin and I don't talk much anymore."

"Did he know about you and Henry?"

"No. He didn't." She said this with emphasis and a shake of her head. "Edwin and I live in the same house and occasionally pass each other like ships in a harbor. We eat together. We sleep in the same bed. Once in a while, we have sex. Usually after we've both had a lot to drink."

She sat down again. She rubbed her eyes.

"The police are bound to find out about you and Henry. I have a friend who's the detective on the case and I persuaded him to let me talk to you first."

She folded her hands and gazed out the kitchen window. Her eyes filled with tears. She wiped the tears away and took a deep breath. After what felt like five minutes, she started. At first just minimal information, but then, perhaps to justify her affair with Henry, I got the story of her life.

Cartwell had never been enough for her. Not at graduate school before they were married. Not at Georgia where he taught a full load of courses and worked nights on his research, while she lay naked with one of his grad students in the spare room over the garage. Not in Illinois where Cartwell hoped to get tenure and Mary hoped to get pregnant, if not by her husband then by the lean-limbed instructor from her art class.

But Cartwell did not get tenure and Mary did not get pregnant. They moved west, hoping this place would satisfy both their ambitions.

As she grew older, Mary came to accept her infertility, kept her body slim, and decided the yearnings of her lovers would be her fulfillment. According to Mary, Edwin Cartwell, consumed with his teaching career and his research, remained oblivious to her sexual adventures. By the time she was forty-nine, Mary had engaged in several affairs, but none had lasted more than a few months.

She told me she knew passion but not love. "Until Henry," she said, her voice catching. With Henry, she was painfully in love, but frustrated by not being able to see him on weekends. She always had to wait until Monday afternoon. That was their rule. Even though Henry was widowed and lived alone, they had to keep their affair a secret. Monday, late in the afternoon at the motel, they would meet and he would make her laugh and kiss her and she would tell him not to worry about the troubles at school. Mary ached for Mondays.

"How did it begin?"

"One night a year or so ago, at that fall party Lewis gives for faculty at the beginning of the semester. It was stuffy in the alumni hall, so I went out for some air. On the terrace, I ran into Henry. He was alone. He always complimented me about something whenever we met. I looked forward to seeing him. That night, he just watched me. I walked down the steps onto the lawn and kept on going toward the trees at the edge of the lake. I knew he was following me without even turning my head."

Mary paused and sipped coffee. "I was looking at the lake and I felt him come up behind me. He didn't say anything. He just put his arms around me. He kissed the side of my cheek and said, 'you have been unhappy long enough.' That's how it began," her voice caught again.

"Over a year ago?"

She nodded. "As soon as he touched me, I knew that was exactly what I wanted him to do."

"By now, were you considering a divorce?"

"Oh," she almost laughed. "Let me tell you, I was ready to divorce Edwin the first time Henry made love to me. But Henry said we had to wait. He didn't want a scandal. We had to keep it a secret until we could figure out a plan. He didn't want people to know."

That would be Henry, I thought. Dean Henry Brooks wouldn't want to be caught seducing a faculty member's wife. Especially the wife of a faculty member who fought with him.

"And you're sure Edwin never knew?"

"Never. Edwin never knew about Henry and me. Believe me, if he had, I would've heard about that. *That* we would have talked about."

I was no longer sure how much I could expect of her, but I worried about how she'd handle the police inquiry. We both stared at the table and the coffee cups. After some moments of silence, I said, "Mary did you and Henry ever make a plan to be together permanently?"

"Not really, Henry wanted to wait until summer. He didn't want school to be in session when I told Edwin I was leaving."

"And you're certain your husband doesn't know."

"Absolutely certain."

"One last question."

Mary got up again and leaned against the kitchen counter, stretching her elegant legs. "Where was I on Sunday?"

I nodded.

"I was here alone, cooking supper for Edwin and thinking about next summer." Her pale cheeks colored. She turned to me, her remarkable face now taut, her eyes flooded. "If I had been with Henry or anywhere near him last Sunday, he would be alive. If he had a heart attack I would have gotten him to the hospital. I would have done anything to save him—anything."

"I believe you," I said.

"Will the police?"

"I hope so."

# Chapter 8

That night, Joe Morgan arrived on my doorstep promptly at 6:30, dressed in dark wool pants with a pale blue cashmere sweater over a shirt. He looked almost professorial. He drove me in his newly washed car to the best restaurant in Landry and ordered an excellent wine with dinner.

The restaurant was dark and crowded, but Joe had reserved a small table in the corner where it was quiet and no one was within earshot. I sipped on the wine, wishing I had not promised to tell him about my conversation with Mary Cartwell.

I must have looked tense. Joe leaned across the table. He spoke softly: "A college professor goes to the doctor's office. The nurse asks him what's wrong and the professor says, 'I think I am disappearing.' So a few minutes later, the nurse comes back and says: 'the doctor can't see you now.'"

Okay, a cop who tells corny jokes. I pretended I hadn't heard it before. But I was grateful for his sensitivity. Clearly he was going to let me avoid discussing Mary for a while. The conversation got easier after that. Joe talked about his love of basketball and his time playing on the team at Mountain West.

"NBA ambitions?" I asked.

No, he said he wasn't NBA material and Mountain West is too small to make it to the top of college ball. He studied hard and graduated. "Pre-law."

"But you didn't become a lawyer?"

"No. I went to Chicago to go to law school but left after the first year and joined the police force."

"Why didn't you stay in law school?"

"Too cerebral, I guess. I liked action. I liked the men and women on the force. I liked the training. I loved getting bad guys. Also, I'd rather investigate than prosecute. And I'm sure I'd rather investigate than defend."

"What brought you back here?"

"A suspect in a murder case in Chicago took off and ended up here. I was sent because I know the area. The chief here liked the way I worked and recruited me away from the big city with the offer of an enormous fortune and the chance to save my hometown from criminals and terrorists."

Okay. I relaxed.

"Do you miss Chicago?"

"Not right now."

"Surely they have women in Chicago."

"Not women with red hair like yours."

That felt good. It had been a while since a man had flirted with me. Joe had a wide smile that made me feel warm and he had strong, long-fingered hands that made me want his touch. Basketball player, ah yes, he could hold the ball forever in one of those hands.

Over coffee, I learned Joe had a shelf of books on China and Russia. "The cultures fascinate me," he said.

Also a shelf of poetry. "Fredenson, followed by Gerard Manley Hopkins are my favorites."

"Yeats?"

"Absolutely. 'And pluck 'til time and times are done, the silver apples of the moon, the golden apples of the sun.'"

He said he went to San Francisco for the opera if it's Rossini or Puccini. He liked Dvorak's New World Symphony. And, of course, read *The New York Times* online.

"I thought cops were mainly interested in sports," I said.

"College basketball," he said. "When North Carolina is in the Final Four, you can't get me out of the house. I take unpaid leave if I have to."

"How do you feel about dogs?"

"I had a dog in Chicago, up until two years ago. But after he died, I've had a hard time thinking about a new dog."

"Tell me about him."

"Big beautiful shepherd. Best dog I've ever had. Died of cancer when he was twelve."

"It's so hard to lose them," I said.

"What's your golden's name?"

Oh dear. My first weakness showed up. "I haven't been able to give him a name," I said. "I tried a few times, but nothing stuck. He didn't answer to any of them. So now I just call him 'Dog' and whistle for him."

"What name did you try?"

"Thaddeus. My dad's name."

"Good name for a dad. Lousy name for a dog. No wonder he ignored you. Dogs need short two syllable names. The best ones end in y or ie. My dog's name was Smiley."

I laughed out loud. "Smiley. What a great name."

Joe laughed, too. "He had a funny expression he used to get around his mouth—like a grin—when he was hungry. Ergo, Smiley. Also George Smiley is my favorite literary spy."

By then we were both laughing. His fingers were near enough to the back of my hand to touch me. But he didn't. Neatly trimmed fingernails. Hands browner than his face. Hands that worked outdoors and played indoors. Oh my.

Yet, on the second cup of coffee I finally brought up the subject of Mary Cartwell. I knew it might change the mood, but I had promised a full report. Looking back, I suspect I thought it would also be a chance to talk about a woman's need for sex without talking about this woman's need for sex.

"So you think her husband doesn't know about her affair with Henry?" Joe said when I finished.

"Yes. Mary has been married to Edwin for twenty-five years. Even though he's strange and reserved, I think she knows what he knows."

"You say she's a beautiful woman. A husband might kill for her."

"Might. But I think she's right. Edwin doesn't have a clue about her behavior."

"That's interesting. I came away from my interview with Cartwell also thinking he wasn't a likely suspect even though he was in the building. His whole story about finding Henry's body seemed credible. And why call the police and draw attention to yourself? Also, Edwin Cartwell doesn't seem like the type to get into a fight."

"So you think there was a fight?"

Joe looked troubled. "I need to know I can trust you, Red. This is police business—strictly confidential."

"Right. You can trust me."

"Forensics aren't complete, but the theory seems to be that Henry sustained a serious wound in his back from that glass award sculpture that was on his desk. And it's hard to wound yourself in the back so it's probable someone else was involved and there may have been a fight."

"And that caused the heart attack?"

"Maybe. We only know he had a heart attack at some point."

"So, how did he get from his office all the way to the stairwell and fall down the stairs?" I knew the answer before Joe spoke.

"It may not have been a fall."


I did not sleep well that night. Joe had walked me to the door. "You look tired," he said.

"I am." But I hoped he would say more.

"I'll call you," he said. "Even if I don't need more information. I'm not supposed to socialize with a source, but, if your alibi holds up and my chief doesn't blow a gasket, I'd like to have dinner again sometime."

Then he left me, still wanting the touch of his hands, still thinking about Henry and Mary's story. Late that night I awoke with Mary's erotic descriptions melding with my own fantasies about Joe Morgan. I finally fell into a deep sleep that ended at six o'clock the next morning with a phone call.

"We need to talk." It was Simon Gorshak. The tone was imperious.

"Simon, I have a terrible schedule today. We'll talk tomorrow." I tried to match his tone.

"The tenure and promotion committee meets at nine o'clock this morning," Simon went on. "You and I need to talk before then. Meredith, this is important."

Did I want to go to school early? Did I want Simon Gorshak to come to my home? I wavered just long enough for him to assume accceptance.

"I'll see you in your office. Will eight o'clock work?"

"I'll see you there," I said, and tunneled into my pillow.

I was in my office by seven, looking through Larry Coleman's file and his tenure application. Larry was due to go up this year. In our school a tenure application goes directly to the school committee of those faculty members who are already tenured. They review the candidate's teaching evaluations, outside letters from other university faculty in his or her field, and his or her own report on six years of research.

Once tenured, it's hard to be fired. A tenured professor can be fired if he or she commits a crime or some horrendous act, but just being disagreeable (like Simon) or bombastic and pompous (like George) or dyspeptic and difficult (like Edwin) is not reason enough.

So, it's important for the school to get it right. The process is demanding and fraught with anxiety. I didn't think Larry was the type to bring a gun to the faculty meeting, but I suspected he would file a grievance if he were denied.

"Morning, Meredith." It was Simon. It was also George and Edwin. An ambush. They settled themselves in chairs in a semi-circle in front of my desk.

"What's on your mind...um, minds?"

Simon cleared his throat to begin, but George couldn't wait. "Meredith, regardless of how the other members of the Promotion and Tenure committee vote, we will all vote against Coleman."

"Phyllis and Max are also members," I said.

"And it won't matter how they vote," said Edwin, "because it will be three against."

"I believe the dean has a say in all this," I said.

"That's why we're here," said Simon. "We don't want this to turn into another faculty brawl. The school's been through enough this year. We want you to think about supporting our decision so we can quietly end this and send Coleman on his way."

Oh do you? I leaned back in my chair. "And what will be my reason for denying tenure to Larry Coleman?" I asked.

"His research lacks rigor and originality," said Simon.

"And his students only give him good evaluations because he is popular and far and away the lightest grader on the faculty," added Edwin.

"How about the outside opinions?"

"Who cares?" said George. "New media experts are a dime a dozen and don't know much. I, for one, found nothing compelling in their letters. I doubt some of them even read Coleman's so-called research. At least not carefully."

I gazed steadily at the three of them. Edwin shifted in his chair. Simon cleared his throat again. Only George stared back, ready to raise his voice. Go for it, I thought. Make an ass of yourself and guarantee you won't have my support.

George went for it. "You're not going to put this school through some new horror show are you Meredith?" Accusation is one of George's favorite techniques.

"No, George, but you three might be about to do just that."

"Not if you support us," said Simon. "The administration will back your decisions. They made that clear enough."

"I don't think so. I think the administration will be appalled at your vindictiveness." I tried to keep my voice even. My stomach was starting to hurt. "None of you has a good reason to vote against Coleman. Your issue with him is about curriculum, not qualifications."

"Nonetheless, we will vote against him," said Simon.

"If you can't convince me he doesn't deserve tenure, how do you plan to convince a special committee?" I had to be cautious now. My anger was starting to overcome my fear of confrontation and might get the better of me.

"What special committee?" asked George.

"A university grievance committee," I said. "If you deny tenure to Coleman after all his work, he'll file a grievance. And..." I paused to make sure they were listening carefully, "and I will back him."

"Then so be it," said George as he rose up and headed for the door.

The pain in my stomach subsided. I continued, "By the time the grievance hearing is over, administrators and other faculty will see you as mean-spirited and bigoted because a colleague dared to disagree with you. You'll be seen as narrow-minded bullies."

That stopped them.

"Meredith, for God's sake," said Edwin.

The pain was almost gone. I hardened. "Look, gentlemen, the schoolyard bullshit has gone on long enough. I am willing to preside over a civil argument about curriculum. But this pissing contest has to stop."

"Or what?" This from George, one hand on the door.

"Or two things will happen. One, Coleman will be tenured by the university because his school is too dysfunctional to do it properly."

They waited a moment. "And two?"

"You'll discover whether or not I really am The Red Queen."

# Chapter 9

Later that morning, I got a lesson in Pyrrhic victory. The journalism school tenure and promotion committee met on Larry's tenure application and decided not to decide. Instead, as they put it in a brief memo, "given recent disputes in what is a small faculty, we think it best to have the whole of the tenured journalism faculty vote on this application."

Then in the afternoon, Ardith Trent, who teaches broadcast and does occasional work for local television, came to me with a problem. Ardith is a small, bird-like woman whose voice was raised to an unusually high pitch.

One of her students had found a clip on YouTube and appropriated the idea and most of the footage. One of the mantras of newspaper journalism was, "get it first, but get it right." And for God's sake don't steal it or invent it.

"She presented it in class as her original work," Ardith said. "No attribution whatsoever."

"How did you know it wasn't her work?"

"Dumb luck. It's a piece I used last summer when I was freelancing in Duluth."

"What did you say to her?"

"I called her over after class and told her I knew she had plagiarized it. And, you know what she said? I couldn't believe it. She said it was not plagiarism because she had not copied someone's writing. *Just their video*. And it wasn't that big a deal." Ardith sat down heavily. "Worst part? She's one of my best students. Absolutely on target for an A until now."

"Not unusual," I said. "My worst cases of plagiarism usually involved A students."

"Why is that?" Ardith looked close to tears.

"I think it's because A students always think of themselves as A students, people who never fail. So, when they run into a problem with an assignment, they cannot bear to screw up. They'd rather copy someone else's work and hope we won't suspect or that we'll be too tired to care if we do."

Ardith took a tissue from her pocket and blew her nose. She still dressed in the perfectly tailored jackets she wore when she anchored a news program.

"How do you want to handle this?" I asked.

"I plan to give her an F in my course," said Ardith. "Frankly, I'd like to see her expelled from the school. I don't want that young woman in journalism."

I sent Ardith off to Student Services to report her student. "See if you can find out from them if this is a first offense," I said. "If she's a recidivist, expulsion from the school may be the right remedy. But remember, I can't expel her from the university, just the journalism school."

Nell stuck her head in after Ardith had gone. "Two calls while you were meeting. One from that Detective Morgan and one from President Lewis."

Joe was the only one I wanted to talk to at this point. I dialed his number on my cellphone. I got the recorded message and left my name. Pity. I really would have liked to hear the sound of his voice, and I hoped he had some new information about the case.

Lewis was busy, too, but his assistant told me Henry's children were going back to their homes and thinking about a small family service after the body was returned to them.

No funeral to arrange. That was a blessing.

Joe called me early the next morning to tell me he had no news about Henry's case and he was going to be tied up on another incident involving a drunk nineteen-year-old ex-boyfriend who drove his truck through the wall of his ex-girlfriend's small house. The truck landed on the bed, pinning the ex-girlfriend and her new lover. It took firefighters an hour to rescue the couple as gas and oil leaked all over them and the bed. Fortunately, they both suffered only minor scrapes and burns. The driver was arrested and booked on drunk driving plus two counts of battery with a deadly weapon. I would hope so.

The afternoon snow turned into slushy rain bringing a sky of dull gray, unusual for Nevada, more like winter in Ohio. I turned on my desk lamp as much for its incandescent cheeriness as illumination, a counterbalance to the gloom outside my windows.

Nell stuck her head in. "A student named Celeste Cummings wants to see you right away," she said.

"About?"

"Something to do with a grade Ardith Trent gave her."

"Tell Celeste I'll see her at four. Then find Ardith. I need to talk to her first."

Nell's head disappeared and Ardith showed up ten minutes later.

"Celeste is a repeat offender, a recidivist as you called it," Ardith said. "Student Services say their records show she had one problem with her sophomore English class and another in anthropology."

"Plagiarism both times?"

"No, just in English. The professor let her off with a warning and made her re-write her paper. In anthropology, she cheated on a test. Got caught reading text messages from her roommate who was back in the dorm with a copy of the textbook. The professor gave her an F on the test but not in the course. The good thing is both reported the incidents to Student Services."

"Now what do you recommend?" I asked. In most cases of academic dishonesty, it's the professor's call.

Ardith's thin face looked fierce. "I've already told Celeste she flunked my course. She seemed arrogant and indifferent and said she'd just switch over to online journalism and forget broadcast."

"Do you still think she should be expelled?"

Ardith didn't hesitate. "Yes, I do. I wish you could expel her from the whole university. She cheats at everything."

"I can't expel her from the university," I said, "but Celeste Cummings will at least be out of the journalism school."

Left alone, I wondered if this was typical for a university dean or if I was just having an awful first week.


Celeste Cummings arrived at five past four. I recognized her from a freshman writing class I had taught.

A lovely face, fine featured, large blue eyes over a snub nose and a bright red mouth. She was tall and slim, had probably been pretty since she was a toddler. I invited her to sit at the small round table with me.

"I suppose you know Trent wants to give me an F in her broadcast class," she said. Long, manicured fingernails tapped my table.

"Yes, I know."

"Well, I'm sorry but Trent is a dried up old bitch who resents anyone in class who she sees as on-camera competition."

"Is that why you think she's failing you?"

"No." The lower bright red lip quivered. "She's failing me because I used a stupid little bit of video for one of her stupid class projects and forgot to provide attribution."

"You know providing attribution is essential in journalism, don't you?"

The blue eyes flashed. "Of course I know. You taught us that two years ago. I just forgot, that's all. It was a silly oversight and for that, she's flunking me."

I sat back and took a deep breath. "This is not your first problem with academic dishonesty is it, Celeste?"

Now the eyes were wary and the red mouth hardened. "I'm not sure I know what you mean." She pronounced each word precisely.

"There's the matter of the English paper and the anthropology test," I said.

Her jaw fell. Then anger. "What the hell do those courses have to do with this? I'm not an English or anthro major, I'm a journalism major."

"Not anymore," I said. "I am expelling you from the school."

Now she was standing. "You can't do this." She stamped her foot so hard I thought she would break one of her four-inch heels.

"Indeed I can."

"No, you can't. I've won awards in this school. Television station managers have told me I have a great future in television. You can't throw me out of journalism. You can't wreck my future career over a stupid mistake."

I remained seated trying to look calm. "Nonetheless, Celeste, you are expelled from the school of journalism. You will receive formal notification later this week."

"Bitch, I pay your salary."

Why do students think this is the ultimate weapon to use against faculty?

I rose and walked to my desk. "Celeste, your tuition pays a small portion of my salary. Most of it is paid for by the state which means that the people of the state, including the television journalists of this state, pay my salary."

Celeste's pretty face was distorted with rage.

I went on: "I have an ethical obligation to all those people, particularly those who might be tempted to hire you. You have no business in journalism, Celeste. Go find another career that doesn't require you to cheat."

"Go to hell."

Still brooding about Celeste, I picked up my cellphone on the first ring. Joe wanted to meet for a brief drink at a bar near the police station. A drink would be good after this day. Especially a drink with Joe Morgan.

Landry's main street is mostly bars, restaurants, and small casinos that try to skim off some of the tourists from Reno and Lake Tahoe. In winter, traffic is light.

"I'm sorry to drag you out again," Joe said, easing into a booth in the back of a nearly empty dive named Toots. The walls were covered with pictures of former prizefighters whose boxing bouts had taken place in Reno or Carson City. The walls had not been painted since the previous century and the leatherette seats in the booth were cracked and stained.

"And sorry I can't take you to a classier drinking joint, but I have to be back at the station in an hour."

Joe looked good. A bit harried, but good.

"How goes the investigation into Henry's death?"

He frowned and motioned the bartender to come over to the table. "A Heineken's and a..." he looked uncertainly at me. This was probably not the place to order wine.

"Ginger ale," I said.

We sat in silence waiting for the drinks. It was clear I wasn't getting any answers to my question while anyone could hear them.

After the bartender left our drinks, Joe took a pull on his beer. "I am reluctant to share a lot of this case with you, Red. Not because I don't trust you, or because I think you are a suspect, it's just that..."

"Everyone in the school is a suspect," I said. "But I do have a good alibi, don't I? Sadie Hawkins doesn't lie."

Joe relaxed. Then he said in his most serious cop-fashion, "and, Doctor Solaris, what was the name of the movie you saw last Sunday?"

"Gee, Detective. *Gone with the Wind*? I can't remember now. It was so long ago. Now tell me what's going on. I want to help and I do know all the suspects better than you do."

"What I can tell you now is that the forensics guys and Danny Ranko, the medical examiner you met, are all convinced the wound in Henry's back was caused by that pointed glass sculpture, that award. It punctured the skin on his back and created a massive contusion. And there's no way the fall down the stairs caused it."

"Did someone stab Henry with that thing? It's awkward and pretty heavy."

"We're still working on it. There was no blood in the office or the hallway but the wound did bleed some and stained Henry's shirt. Danny found traces of Henry's blood on the glass award, but no fingerprints, not even Henry's."

"So it was wiped clean?"

Joe's little half smile. "Yes, Detective Solaris. So it would seem."

"But doesn't that strengthen the idea it was murder rather than an accident."

"Yes. But Henry also had a heart attack. The back wound may have occasioned the heart attack, but the heart attack and the fall down the stairs are what killed him."

"So we know what killed him." I felt a chill even in the warmth of the booth.

Joe put his hand over mine. I noticed how strong it was and the warmth of it took the chill away. "We think so and I'm still investigating a probable homicide. But keep in mind—even though I am telling you all this—you are the dean. I am the detective."

I nodded. "Thank you for trusting me. I can't tell you how much it will mean to me to know what really happened to my friend and whether or not one of my faculty is homicidal."

He looked at his watch. "I've got about another five minutes to finish this beer. Tell me what you know about Simon Gorshak."

"Is he your primary suspect?" I was surprised and excited. Wouldn't it be great to be rid of Simon?

"No one is primary, yet," said Joe. "I just don't know as much about him as the others. He was very uncooperative during our interview at the school. I didn't get much out of him."

"Well, he's as mean as a trapped ferret and I wouldn't put it past him to kill Henry. He hated Henry. But Simon would have hated anyone who was made dean after he lost his position. All I know, is that he was a writer for *Fortune* a hundred years ago."

"Is he married? He refused to answer that when I talked to him. Said it was not relevant to my inquiry. Weird. Most people don't have a problem with that question."

"Hmm. I don't know if Simon is married or not. He never brings anyone to university events and I've never heard him mention a wife. I can certainly ask around. The faculty members who've been there longer than I have will probably know. Simon is so universally disliked, no one talks about him much."

Joe rubbed his chin. "So far, I found an old DMV record for a Doris Gorshak. But her license has not been renewed since 1997. And, whoever she was, she's never registered to vote."

"I'll see what I can find out," I said. I felt good. I got to help my handsome cop and, maybe, get the upper hand with Simon Gorshak.

Joe walked me to me car. "I like having you as my partner," he said. I could see the seriousness of his face. "But you are not to talk directly to any of these guys about Henry's death. Other stuff, okay, but not Henry. I don't want you confronting any of them."

"I know that," I said. "I promise, I'll be a good girl."

That brought another smile. "You know, Dr. Solaris, one of these days after this investigation, I am going to hope you don't want to be a good girl."

"I know."

He opened my car door for me and closed it after me. He stood by the side of the car, his hand on the roof looking down at me.

I started the engine. As I pulled out of the parking lot, Joe stood still, watching me until I was out of sight. My God, he was attractive. But I knew he had to be careful. And so did I.

As I turned toward home, the road looked dark ahead. The image of Henry's body flashed before me. I hated that I could no longer see a clear picture of my good friend, Henry Brooks, dean of journalism, distinguished scholar, still alive and laughing instead of cold and dead on those stairs.

# Chapter 10

The next morning, after a visit to the library, I encountered Philip Lewis. It was a crisp late morning, but the snow had melted. That often happens in Nevada. We'll get a storm overnight but the Sierras take most of the snow and often leave just an inch or two on the ground that melts away by ten in the morning.

"Beautiful day we're having," said Lewis, taking my arm. "How are you doing Meredith?"

"I think I'm doing well," I replied. "But I could use some historical information if you have a minute."

Lewis stopped and looked kindly. But then he almost always looked kindly. "What can I tell you, my dear?"

"I need to know more about Simon Gorshak than the personnel files tell me," I said.

Lewis lost his kindly look. "A difficult man, Simon. You know, of course, he was dean for several years, long before Henry."

I nodded. "I wonder if you know more about him personally, as a man?"

"More than I wish I knew," said Lewis. "Simon was a terrible manager as a dean—unsympathetic, irascible, so unjust he lost the confidence of his faculty. They came in a body and asked me to fire him, you know. But, he was tenured and the best I could do was dismiss him as dean and send him back into the faculty who despised him. He was devastated and angry and impossible to reason with..." Lewis paused and looked sad. "And then, of course, a few years later his wife left him."

"So he was married?"

"Oh yes," said Philip. "Doris was quite pretty, although rather too thin in my view. Dressed very fashionably as I recall."

"Did she leave him because he lost the dean's job?"

Lewis smiled, dropped my arm and took a step away. "I really don't know," he said. "I just know it must have been dreadful for Simon to lose his post, his reputation and, ultimately, his wife."

"President Lewis," I began. But Philip Lewis turned.

"Have to dash. See you later, Red." He waved his hand as he walked away.

I headed back to the journalism school and, without stopping to take off my coat, went straight down the hall to Simon's office.

His door was closed but I could see a light through the glass panel, even though the venetian blinds that covered the panel were shut tight. I knew he was there. I could hear his voice, louder than usual. "Goddamn it, I tell you, I sent that check in a week ago," I heard him say. "You stop harassing me or I'll call my attorney." Then I heard the phone slam down.

I knocked on the glass panel.

"What?" I heard Simon's voice, still angry.

I opened the door. Simon was seated at his desk. He turned his chair toward me, his face grim and grayer than ever. "What do you want?"

"I just wanted to say I know how distressing the police interviews were the other day and I am just making the rounds to see if everyone is okay," I said.

Simon turned back to the papers on his desk and put his hands on his pencil cup as if he was about to work. "I'm fine."

"Did you have a difficult interview?" I remembered what Joe had said.

Simon glanced up at me, "The police ask too many stupid questions," he said, voice low and calm.

I considered taking a risk. "Simon, are you in any sort of trouble?"

He looked up and then stood up and took a step toward me. His small eyes were shining with anger. "No, missy, I am not in any kind of trouble. You were listening outside my door, weren't you?"

He grabbed my arm. Simon is an old man but the strength of his grip surprised me. I looked down at his hand, old, bony; his fingernails were long and ragged and I could feel the pinch of them through the sleeve of my coat.

He put his face close to mine until I could smell his sourness.

"You and your damned cop can stay out of my private life."

"I'm..."

"Shut up, Solaris. You may be the appointed dean but I know you were just one of Brooks' whores and if you meddle with my private affairs, you'll wish to Christ you hadn't."

I stood stunned.

"Now get out of my office," he said, pushing me into the hall. He slammed his door so hard the blinds behind the glass panel rattled.

I walked back to my office in a daze. That old man was amazingly strong and, as far as I was concerned, he definitely had murder in him.

I collapsed in my chair and called Joe. My voice returned without shakiness. "I forgot to ask. How's your drunk driver?"

"Sober and incarcerated. His parents refuse to bail him out. How are you? I miss you. Please don't make any elaborate plans for next weekend. As soon as I know my schedule, I want to see you."

"I want to see you, too."

"How's it going?" It was clear he didn't want to end the conversation.

After a moment of silence, I decided I couldn't wait for later to tell him about Simon. "Joe, I found out more about Simon. He *was* married to a woman named Doris, but Philip Lewis tells me she left him a few years after he was fired as dean."

"That's useful to know," said Joe.

"That would have been years ago. When I went to his office this morning..."

"You what?"

"I wasn't going to say anything to him about your investigation or about Henry. I went to see how he was doing. When I approached his door, it was closed, but I could hear him yelling at someone about a check."

"And," I could hear Joe's voice harden.

"I stupidly asked him if he was in any trouble…"

"Red, stop. I told you to be careful around these guys."

"I know. I know you're right. Simon grabbed my arm and literally pushed me out of his office and said if either you or I interfered in his private life, we would wish we hadn't. Joe, he was angry and much stronger than I imagined."

I heard Joe's long intake of breath. "Red, promise me you'll stay away from him."

"That won't be hard. He scares the hell out of me."

Silence. We both know there was more we wanted to say to each other, but not on the phone.

Finally, "Can Nell and I clean up Henry's office now? I really want to settle in there."

"I'll check with my team. I'm sure it's okay but it will give me a reason to call you again."

"Do you need a reason?"

Pause. "No, I don't."


Still thinking about Joe, I didn't hear the knock on my half-opened office door. Max Worthington pushed it open. Max was tall enough to fill my doorway. He had a smooth, boyish face that probably was movie star handsome when he was younger. A look that certainly helped his journalism career. Ever since I had first met Max, he has always struck me as warm and intelligent and, while I sometimes wished he would control his temper with George, I admired his willingness to defend Larry Coleman. Other faculty members were all too likely to let a colleague take it on the chin from the elders. I found Max easy and comfortable and I was grateful for his support.

Max had been my friend from my first day at the school. "Let me know what I can do to help you adjust," he'd said. He became my steadfast cheerleader when I was on tenure track. He edited my papers before I sent them in to journals. Once, under the mistletoe at a Christmas party, Max's kiss had been a bit too wet and had lasted a little too long, but I forgave him. Max was an easy guy to forgive.

"How's Trudy?" I asked. Trudy was pregnant with their fourth child. I had not seen her recently but, whenever I saw Max, I thought of his wife's kindness to me when I first came to Mountain West.

"Still a trooper," he said. "She's big as a house but unfailingly cheerful."

"Please give her my love. What's up?"

Max did not sit down, but approached my desk and leaned on the edge.

"Red, I come to plead the case of one of the students I advise."

I leaned back in my chair and smiled. "You have the floor, counselor."

"She came to me in tears yesterday with your letter expelling her from the j-school."

Oh, crap. Celeste. Already maneuvering.

Max moved around my desk until he was on my side. He leaned against the wall. "She's a kid, Red. A smart kid who made a mistake. Don't you think throwing her out of the school is a bit heavy-handed?"

"Max, perhaps you don't know all of Celeste's history."

Max smiled slightly. "Well, she did mention some stuff about earlier infractions in other classes. But, honestly Red, we have a lot of students who struggle when they first get here. A lot cheated in high school and got away with it. Then they get into college, and we hammer them."

"Celeste Cummings is an unrepentant cheater. She's been caught three times, but God knows how many other times she's gone undetected."

Max stepped closer. His eyes were serious and he spoke quietly. "Red, you are a beautiful woman. Celeste is a beautiful woman. Do you think that could have factored into your decision?"

"Max, you are way out of line. Back off."

He moved back against the wall. His hands went up, palms facing me, in a defensive posture. "Just trying to help a friend, coach. Two friends, I hope."

"I've made my decision, Max."

He moved toward the door, then turned to give me a rueful smile. "You know how I tend to stick up for the oppressed," he said. A dark thought crossed my mind, but I dismissed it. I liked Max.

I went off to lunch worrying about Celeste but was pleased to see that Phyllis Baker was joining Sadie and me at our table. Next to Max, Phyllis was my best friend on the faculty, a good friend who made me laugh when I was down and told me I was unique and wonderful when I was feeling particularly ordinary. Phyllis was the physical opposite of Sadie. A dark brown perpetually plump face, a body shaped like a pouter pigeon set on top of long, thin legs. She was settled at the table in front of a martini. She greeted me with a cheery grin. "You look pretty good for a woman who has been beaten to a pulp and left to rot by vicious male faculty."

I sighed and fell into the chair beside her. Wilson appeared with the glass of the wine he knew I was about to order.

"Bless you," I said. "It's been hell."

"Heavy lays the crown," said Sadie, sipping her predictable iced tea. Sadie doesn't drink alcohol before five p.m. After five, she can channel Dylan Thomas.

"So tell us everything. We're dying to know exactly how awful it's been for you."

It's probably true in other professions, but I know with certainty that, in the academy, friendships can be solid and lifelong. If you are fortunate enough to find good friends across campus, as I did, you discover one of the great benefits of a university career.

Funny, smart, absolutely loyal, Sadie and Phyllis would keep my secrets and get me through no matter what. We ordered food from the attentive Wilson and I started in. As I had promised Joe, no mention of Simon, but everything else was on the table. When I described the expulsion, I didn't name Celeste. When I talked about Max's visit, it prompted an interesting comment from Phyllis.

"I've often wondered if Max Worthington doesn't have the hots for you."

"Me too," said Sadie. "I've noticed at faculty parties at Stoddard's house that Max seems very attentive when you're around."

"Max is married with kids," I said. But it set me to wondering. Max had come a little closer to me than was comfortable when we talked about Celeste.

"He has a reputation," said Phyllis. "Champion tennis player, newspaper editor, Berkeley PhD. And he's great looking. I can think of a few university ladies who wouldn't let a wife and kids get in the way."

"Red already has a man in her sights," said Sadie, turning back to the student-cheating episode. "Your decision was quite right. I wish more faculty would come down hard on cheating, especially plagiarism. I know it's hard to prove and a pain to document, but integrity matters. It's our cornerstone."

"I agree, but some faculty are afraid the student will file a grievance against them if they come down hard," said Phyllis. "Also, I'm afraid many of our overworked colleagues don't want the hassle and would rather forgive and forget."

"I still hate to see us tolerate cheating," said Sadie. "Ultimately, it means we're willing to grant degrees to people who haven't earned them. Sooner or later, we pay for that."

"How do we pay for it?" Phyllis asked. "Maybe their future employers pay for it when the students can't do their jobs, but how do we suffer?"

Sadie cleared her throat. "C'mon now. You ever run into lawyers who didn't know their stuff? You want an elementary school built by an engineer who cheated his way through college? Or your dear old mother cared for by a nurse who faked her credentials?" Sadie was now swaying with the energy of her argument. "And what about the bastards at the top who hurt thousands of people? You think Bernie Madoff learned to cheat *after* he graduated?"

"All right, point taken," said Phyllis. "But it's such a nice afternoon, the sun is out and I want to know more about this man Red has in her sights."

"A tall, green-eyed detective," said Sadie, sucking on the ice cubes in the bottom of her glass.

"Ahh, a detective."

"He's investigating Henry Brooks' death," I said knowing my cheeks were pink.

"And what else is he investigating?" said Phyllis with a wide grin.

# Chapter 11

The days dragged on. The following week arrived, but no call from Joe. Saturday afternoon, I came home from grocery shopping and found a note pinned to my door. "Stopped by to say hello. No news on Brooks. I'm still tied up, but I will see you soon. Joe."

Damn. Even his note made me feel warm. I wish I hadn't gone shopping when I did.

I put away my groceries and decided to call my father, the man my mother insisted had spoiled me for all other men. The accusation was unfair. If one of my parents was to blame for my failed relationships with men, it was my mother, Emily Solaris.

I stopped calling her "mom" when I was twelve.

She was stunningly beautiful and totally self-absorbed. When she wasn't shopping, she was drinking and then, as she aged, she was mostly drinking.

She had no time for me.

My father spent extra hours at his university in those days, to avoid her and, I suspect, the anger he felt. With his long work hours and her devotion to liquor, I was isolated and on my own.

By the time I was six, I was making my own breakfast. I learned how to wash my own laundry and braid my own hair. I had a few friends at school but never invited them to my house.

On weekends, my father tried to compensate. If my mother started her breakfast with a beer, he and I would go for a walk or to an exhibit at a museum or an early movie. Thaddeus Solaris was tall and blue-eyed and white-haired by the time he was thirty. My defender, my best friend, my rock.

The nurse who answered my father's phone said, "He's not having a good day, Dr. Solaris. Tomorrow might be better."

I asked for him anyway, always hopeful the sound of my voice would transform him from Alzheimer's patient back to the laughing, extraordinary man I cherished.

"Daddy?"

"Who's this?"

"It's Red, Daddy. Meredith."

"I don't know any Meredith."

I tried again. "I'm your beautiful red-haired girl." He had written that description on all my birthday cards and Christmas presents.

"Emily?"

"No, Daddy. Red...Meredith."

"I don't know any Red Meredith. This number is on the Do Not Call List. Don't call again."

The nurse came back. "Maybe tomorrow," she whispered. "Sorry. His good days are fewer and fewer."

She was being kind. The "good days" were gone. They had gradually faded away during the years after Emily had died. Now they were gone for good.

"The best science professor I ever encountered," Kenny Ross had said. Kenny was Dad's primary physician and had been one of Dad's favorite biology students. "I miss him terribly," Kenny had said the last time I visited my father in the Alzheimer's care nursing home. "I wish I could do something, but it's downhill from now on, Red."

Kenny discouraged me from moving my father from Ohio to a facility closer to Mountain West University. "At least he's physically comfortable here. He might not do well in new surroundings and, unhappily, it won't make his memory better. I'm sorry, Red, Ohio or Nevada, he still won't know who you are."

He only remembered her.

When I was little, I loved her. But she didn't love me. By the time I was mature enough to understand her alcoholism was a disease, I was conditioned to the distance between us. I had stopped hoping she would ever overcome her addiction. Had she lived, we might have worked out some sort of relationship. But Emily Solaris drank and drove and ended her life with her head and her beautiful hair smashed against a windshield.

My father never recovered. Two years after her death, he burned the research notes he was working on and resigned from the university. The man who had kept me company, told me jokes too raunchy for my age, critiqued my papers, listened to my stories, sat in the front row of all my school plays and cheered my soccer games, disappeared into senility. I changed my graduate school destination to Ohio so I could be with him. I got a job with an Ohio newspaper just so I could be home to care for him. But I was no more help to him than he had been to my mother.

"You cannot save your parents," a therapist told me at the time. "You can only save yourself." That was after my first broken engagement. After a second disastrous love affair, I put my father in the nursing home and left Ohio.

I went to bed uneasy, filled with sadness about my father and anxious about what disaster might occur next. And what might happen with Joe.


The next morning I lay in bed, relishing thoughts of Joe Morgan, when his sister called. Elaine's voice was strained. "Red, one of my reporters got several interviews with people on your faculty. Seems many of them came away from the police interviews thinking Henry might have been murdered, pushed down the stairs. The police won't confirm but they won't deny either. They just give me the ongoing investigation routine. Red, I'm sorry, I know this is still rumor, but it's already hit the blogs and I can't sit on this for long."

"Elaine. I know you can't. I just wish Detective Morgan and friends had more definitive information. If Henry was pushed down those stairs, I wish there was some evidence."

I called Joe on his cell.

"Red, I'm as frustrated as you are. We all are. But getting evidence in a situation like this takes time. Sometimes weeks. Only TV shows get evidence quickly."

"Simon Gorshak?"

"Nothing concrete yet but there may be someone up at Lake Tahoe at the Cal-Neva Casino who can help. The guy's away today, but I'm driving up there tomorrow afternoon when he's supposed to work a shift."

"Can I come along?"

"I thought you had a fulltime job of your own."

"I do. But it's been two weeks since Henry's death and finding out more about how he died is as important to me as it is to you. The school can do without me for one afternoon. And please don't worry, I'll wait in the car and stay out of your way."

A pause. "Okay, you can come with me. But you can't go near my informant."

"Agreed. I know a good place for dinner after your interview."

# Chapter 12

The top headline in Monday's student newspaper read, "Journalism Faculty Fears Dean was Murdered." With the blogs and the student paper pushing the story, Elaine would be hard pressed not to publish her reporter's interviews.

The TV stations showed even less reticence. Ardith was in my office waiting for me when I arrived at school.

"I just wanted you to know, I didn't leak this story and I didn't give any interviews to anyone," she said.

"It's all right, Ardith. I'm surprised it took the media this long. The police have been talking to everyone in the building most of last week."

"Have they come up with anything that substantiates murder?"

I shook my head. Joe had cautioned me about discussing the wound in Henry's back and anything he found during his investigation. I knew I had to keep my mouth shut.

"I appreciate your insights into the faculty, Red. But, you must be careful with what I tell you," Joe had said. "You can't ever seem more knowledgeable than anyone else. If someone on the faculty did kill Henry, I don't want them to be concerned about what you know or don't know."

Ardith had no sooner left than a ghost of Henry appeared in my office. I had never met him, but Michael Brooks looked so much like his father I knew who he was before he introduced himself. Tall, with fine fair hair that would someday gray and thin like his father's, and most remarkable of all, his father's voice. It was startling to hear him speak. Nell was standing behind him, her eyes wide.

"I'm on my way to the airport, Dr. Solaris. But I wanted to stop by before I left. My sister and I don't plan to be back until after the police investigation is complete."

I shook his hand and indicated a chair. I probably looked as stunned as Nell did. "I'm so sorry, Michael."

"It's been very hard," he said. "And Meg and I don't know what to make of this rumor that Dad was murdered."

"Neither do I. I do know the police are doing everything they can to bring this to closure, but so far...nothing."

"They promised to send Dad's body back to us after the investigation is done. We want to bury him at home. Here's my card and number, Dr. Solaris. I guess I should say, Dean Solaris. If you hear anything, I would appreciate a call."

He handed me the card and then reached for the small suitcase he'd brought with him. He rolled the suitcase toward the side of my desk. "Meg and I went through Dad's papers at home. We put all the journalism school stuff in this suitcase. We thought you would know better what to do with it."

"I'd be happy to look it all over. If I find anything personal, I'll be sure to send it to you."

"Oh, there's nothing personal in that case," he said. "Meg was pretty thorough about separating it out."

"Michael, just this morning I got permission to start cleaning out your father's desk and bookshelves. I'm not allowed to turn over anything today, but if there's something you or your sister would like, I could put it aside for you to make sure you get it."

Michael frowned. "There was one thing we didn't find at the house, but I'd like to have if it's around here."

"What would that be?"

"Dad and I went to the same university. A few years ago, the alumni association gave him a glass trophy, their Alumni of the Year Award. It was the same year his book was nominated for the Pulitzer. I remember going to the dinner and..."

Michael's eyes closed for a moment. A terrible sadness overcame his face. He looked exactly like his father, but there was none of Henry's cynical toughness in this man. This was a sweet, stricken son.

I looked down to avoid meeting his eyes. How best to answer him without lying? I leaned toward him and said, "Michael, I will do whatever is necessary to track down your father's trophy."

Joe and I started our trip to Lake Tahoe late Monday afternoon. The drive to Tahoe takes about an hour with Joe driving. It's more like an hour and a half for normal people.

In summer, when the landscape is not covered with snow, you can see what the high desert looked like to the first settlers—brown hills covered with mounds of fuzzy sagebrush, punctuated with rocky outcroppings. Where the tree line begins, the brown hills turn to green. In winter the snow blankets the lower trunks of the tall evergreens that cover the Sierra on this side of the mountains. The first "chains required" signs appear, although the day Joe and I drove up, the road was clear and the sky was cloudless.

"What have the police learned about Simon so far?"

Joe glanced over. "As I mentioned, Simon was uncooperative in the two interviews we had. Admitted only to the number of years he had worked at Mountain West and where he lived. No mention of a family. When I pressed, he gave me that arrest-me-or-leave me-alone routine. You know, we can't force people to tell us what they don't want to tell us, even if we do arrest them."

"I know. But you also said it was odd he wouldn't admit to having a wife."

"Our investigation reveals he lived in a nice house not too far from yours until a few years ago. Now, he lives alone in a small, cheap apartment in Reno and commutes to Landry. His bank account suggests he lives from paycheck to paycheck, plus Social Security, and has no outside source of income, so he may have a debt problem we haven't figured out yet."

Joe glanced over at me. "That might explain why Simon was so angry with you for eavesdropping on his phone call."

I remembered something Henry had told me. "I may be able to add something to the economic picture of Simon. Last year, Henry told me he'd finally had it with Simon. He called him into his office, told him his teaching was terrible and his behavior was worse. Henry said he was destructive to the school and demanded that Simon retire. Simon threatened to sue if Henry tried to get rid of him and insisted he couldn't afford to give up his position even though he was well past retirement age."

Joe worked his jaw. "Hmm. What we know is that Simon once lived pretty well and now he lives in reduced circumstances and may be in trouble. Also, his fear that Henry might actually find a way to get rid of him, tenured or not, might have provided a motive for murder. Might have."

Simon scared me. So did the Mt. Rose highway. There were too many serpentine curves and, when it narrowed to two lanes, the curves are so pronounced that car passengers could be rocked from side to side.

Past the ski resort we crested the summit at 8911 feet and the mountain meadows came into view. Even on a weekday, the skiers crowded the resort parking lot and the meadows were strewn with cross country skiers and families with kids on sleds.

We rounded a curve and there was Lake Tahoe, shimmering and huge.

At first a blue patch between the tall trees, the lake loomed larger and larger as we closed in on it. There were signs for bear crossings, then a few houses on the outskirts of Incline Village.

Joe and I stopped talking when the lake came into view. It was breathtaking. Vast, gleaming, intense blue surrounded by snow-covered mountains, Tahoe is the largest alpine lake in North America, twenty-two miles long and twelve miles wide. The border between Nevada and California runs roughly through the middle and just before hitting the border, we arrived at The Cal Neva Casino Hotel at dusk.

The man we were looking for was Terry Bingham, a blackjack dealer. Joe's source in Carson City told him that Bingham had been friendly with Doris Gorshak at one time.

Joe parked the car near the entrance—cops can do that—and came around to my side to open my door. "Red, remember what we discussed. You can sit nearby and eavesdrop, but no interruptions. I don't want him to know you're with me. Okay?"

"Yes, Joe."

The Cal Neva literally sits on the border, a fact graphically noted inside the larger rooms. One of the oldest casino hotels in Nevada, the Cal Neva was once owned by Frank Sinatra in the 60s and famous for appearances by members of The Rat Pack and Marilyn Monroe. But that was then.

The evening we walked in, only a few people were there. Only three blackjack tables were open and most of the slot machines stood unattended. Two women who must have been in their eighties were sitting side by side at quarter slot machines, chatting amiably and nursing generous glasses of whiskey. A younger woman with a pewter face and stooped shoulders slouched against an empty chair behind them, smoking a cigarette. Her eyes were dull and unfocused. I hoped she wasn't their caregiver; she looked as if she might not remain conscious long enough to get them home. The casino reeked of cigarette smoke.

Terry Bingham dealt blackjack with hands that darted faster than bird wings. He was slender and well groomed with graying, dark hair slicked back off a sharp-featured face.

As Joe approached his table, Bingham looked up. His dark eyes darted from side to side as if looking for an escape route.

Joe stopped and stood still behind one of the players seated at the table. Bingham finished the hand and motioned to the pit boss standing nearby.

The pit boss walked over to where Bingham stood behind the table. The two men whispered for a moment. Then Bingham told his table in a soft-spoken voice that there would be a brief pause while a new dealer came in.

"They told me you would come at the end of my shift," Bingham said as he approached Joe.

"Sorry, this was the only time I could make it," said Joe, extending his hand. "Detective Joe Morgan, Landry Police. Thank you for agreeing to see me."

"I don't know what help I can be," said Bingham.

"Let's go somewhere quiet," said Joe, indicating a group of bar tables. I strolled to another table near enough to hear but not be obvious and busied myself looking for a pad and pencil in my handbag.

Joe leaned forward, his elbows on their table. "Mr. Bingham, I am investigating a possible homicide in Landry and need to know more about someone you may have known a few years ago."

"Call me, Terry," he said. "I don't think I know anyone in Landry."

"I'm told you may have been acquainted with a woman who used to live in Landry, Doris Gorshak." Joe leaned in further.

"Doris? She in trouble?" Bingham's thin face became serious. He ran his fingers over his hair. His hands trembled just a bit.

"Not that I know of," said Joe. "But her husband, Simon, is a person of interest in an investigation at the university and I need to know more about him."

Bingham lowered his voice. "Look, I never met the guy. I knew Doris. She was a regular at my table. Nice lady."

"Please tell me what you can about her."

Bingham ran his hand over his hair again. His right eye seemed to develop a minor tic. "Doris was, like I said, a nice lady. Nice-looking, too, in a skinny sort of way. Always wore sharp clothes. Not a great blackjack player but polite, even sweet."

"Did she lose at blackjack often?"

"Yeah, she lost most of the time. But she came back every week, sometimes twice a week. Played from early evening until the boss told the cocktail waitress to stop bringing her drinks. Tequila was her favorite. Lots of it. All night."

"What happened when she ran out of money?"

Terry sighed. "She'd head for the bar. Sometimes she'd get some guy to buy her more tequila." He hesitated. "Usually she would leave with the guy."

"Different guys?"

"Always different guys. Probably guests of the hotel. Me, I didn't judge. She was usually too drunk to drive so maybe that was her way of getting a bed for the night."

A question crossed my mind and came out of Joe's mouth. "Were you ever one of the guys?"

"Hey Detective," Bingham bristled. "I got a good girlfriend in Reno. I don't need to get into any trouble about Doris. She was just a friend. I let her crash on my sofa a couple of times. But that was years ago and that was it. Nothin' between us."

"I'm sorry, Terry, I didn't mean to say there was. I do need to know if Doris ever told you about her life in Landry."

Bingham calmed down. "She told me she was married to some big shot at the university, that she lived in a nice house and her husband gave her money whenever she asked. At least he did until the last time I saw her."

"Tell me about that last time."

Bingham leaned back. Clearly he was tired and hesitant, but it was also clear he wanted to be rid of Joe. "The last time I saw Doris, she'd stayed at my place overnight. I made her some coffee in the morning and she looked up at me with tears in her eyes and thanked me for 'being kind,' as she said. Then she said she was meeting her brother at the Cal Neva that morning and her brother was going to take her home to Buffalo. I must have looked surprised because she said she was leaving her big shot husband because he wouldn't give her money anymore and he was talking about having her committed to rehab for gambling and for drinking. So she was getting out."

"Was that all she told you?"

"That was about it. I drove her back to the casino and, sure enough, some skinny guy who could have been her twin was waiting in valet parking with his car. She got out of the car, thanked me for being her friend and said to say goodbye to Nevada for her. Then she walked over to her brother's car and got in. That's the last I saw of her."

"And nothing more about her husband?"

"Just what I told you. I figure Doris was a real looker when she was younger, but I also figure her big shot husband ran out of patience. I mean once or twice a week she was up here drinking and gambling and whatever instead of being with him."

Poor Simon, I thought, forgetting for a moment that he scared the hell out of me.

Joe thanked Bingham and gave him a card, asking him to call if he remembered anything else. Bingham shook Joe's hand and returned to his table. Joe signaled me to head out. As we approached the front door, I glanced back at the casino section. The old women were gone, but the young woman with dulled eyes was still leaning against a slot machine, still smoking a cigarette. Television ads portray slot players as happy, surrounded by friends, nearly hysterical with the joy of winning. I'd never seen that.

It was dark by the time Joe headed out of the Cal Neva driveway. "I'll take you to that restaurant you like."

The place was in Tahoe City with good food and a view of the lake from a table by the window. A full moon illuminated the enormous lake; the waters were still and the mountains old and white in the distance.

"I hate Simon, but I sort of feel sorry for him," I said.

Joe looked at me intently, green eyes even darker than usual.

"I grant you his wife treated him badly, but who knows how he treated her. What we know now is Simon was probably broke because of his wife's gambling. We also know Simon was afraid he might lose his job and hated Henry. What we don't know is if all of this means Simon had motive to go to Henry's office, pick up that trophy and try to ram it into Henry's back, and then watch Henry stagger down the hall and maybe give him a push down the stairs...and then go back and wipe the trophy clean and leave Henry to die in that stairwell."

I was quiet. Joe was right. Tragedy may beget crime but doesn't excuse it. We ordered our dinner and ate slowly. We tried to talk about more comfortable topics, Joe's other cases, my classes, but the memory of what we had learned intruded and kept us sober and reflective.

"Red, there's something I want to tell you," Joe said. We were just starting our coffee. "I didn't leave Chicago purely because the Landry chief wanted me here."

"Joe, it's okay. I don't need to know everything about..."

"Let me finish, Red. It's important to me that you know this. So listen because this is hard." Joe swallowed and looked out the window at the lake, then back at me. "I loved doing police work in Chicago and I loved Chicago. But one very hot day in the summer, I walked into a store where there was a robbery in progress. I saw a short guy in a big, puffy coat with a ski mask on. The woman behind the counter was screaming her head off and the guy was pointing a gun at her. I called him out. He turned, aimed his gun at me and I fired mine. I shot right through his chest and killed him."

"That must have been awful, Joe. But he was committing a crime." I reached for Joe's hand but he pulled back in his chair and looked away.

"Yes, he was committing a crime. His first crime, as it turned out. With an unloaded gun." Joe's breathing was short and shallow.

"But you didn't know that the gun wasn't loaded," I said, wishing he would look at me instead of the lake.

"No, I didn't at the time. When I took off the ski mask, I saw he was a kid." Joe's gaze returned to me. His eyes were liquid. "Thirteen years old, no record and an old gun of his father's that didn't even work anymore and had no bullets."

"Oh, Joe. And there was an investigation and news stories I suppose."

"You suppose right. It was awful. The kid's mother had cancer and lost her job. The kid was trying to get money for his family."

His head was bowed and I sensed his sorrow. We stayed that way, silently for several moments. Then he lifted his head. "I was cleared, but I couldn't stay in Chicago. I keep seeing that kid lying on the floor in the middle of the heat with that big coat on. I should have figured out he was a boy trying to look grown-up. Now, I think about his mother and wonder if she's still alive. I wrote her a letter but I never had the nerve to actually see her."

Joe was looking directly at me. "If we are going to keep working together on this case, I want you to know why sometimes I get moody and distant. I'm not an easy guy to be with."

"I think you're a terrific guy to be with."

"I think you would have made a good cop."

"I don't want to be a cop. I want to be a cop's friend."

"Deal."

# Chapter 13

Eighteen days had passed since Henry's death, with no real break in the investigation. Yet I woke up Thanksgiving morning, surprisingly content, suffused in gratitude. My room was painted a soft blue and the windows had sheer curtains that let in the light. The window was always open at least a bit. In the summer, the morning came with the smell of the roses that climb the front of the house. In November, the spruce tree outside rustled in the wind.

Thanksgiving dinner was set for four o'clock at my house. I had invited Joe and his sister, Elaine, and her husband, Vince, with their kids and, as I did every year, Sadie. Elaine made homemade cranberry sauce. Sadie brought wine and her incredible pecan pie. Give thanks for good friends. Give thanks for my mother's big dining room table, the only furniture I'd brought with me from Ohio.

After dinner, Vince took the kids to see the newest Christmas movie.

"This was wonderful," said Elaine, yawning and smiling at her brother. Elaine was dressed in one of those full silk tunics plump women use to hide big hips and round bellies. Her dark hair was cut short and framed her face; she had no gray around the temples like her brother. She was a pretty version of Joe.

Sadie sipped her port. Joe put his arm across the back of the sofa, almost touching me but not quite, yet comfortably proprietary.

"I trust you all will have a lovely long weekend to get away from all the troubles of the school," said Sadie.

"Wouldn't that be wonderful? Except I have some work to do on a presentation to the Faculty Senate next week," I said. "And Joe still has the investigation."

"What are you looking for at this point, Joe?" said Elaine.

"I'm looking for more information. I can't seem to find out who might have been in or near the journalism building that Sunday."

Elaine shifted in her chair. "Joe, I know I'm not supposed to ask, but did the medical examiners find anything that suggested foul play?"

"They found what they found, Elaine."

"So, no murder?"

"Jesus, Sis. You sure do know how to ruin a nice holiday afternoon." His arm came away from my shoulders.

"Sorry, folks," said Elaine, "but my reporters and editors are after me. They think I'm covering for the cops because of Joe or for the school because I teach there. I get phone calls every day." She frowned and folded her arms across her chest.

"I get calls, too, Elaine, but we have to live with the mystery until Joe solves it," I said, hoping for a return of his arm near my shoulders. "For now, I would love a change of subject." I had managed not to think about Simon for an entire day.

"Aren't you worried for yourself Red? I mean if someone killed the last dean..."

"Damn it, Elaine. If you don't change the subject, I'm taking you home." Joe stood up, ready to go if needed.

"Okay. Okay, I'm sorry," said Elaine. She walked to the window. "Looks like the weather might change," she said. "I think it's probably time to go home and hear all about the movie Vince and the kids saw."

Sadie stayed seated while Joe helped a subdued Elaine into her coat, took her arm and walked her to the door. He put his arms around her and I heard her whisper one more "I'm sorry" into his shoulder. After Elaine left, Joe picked up the coffee cups and headed into my kitchen.

"Elaine's not entirely out of bounds on this," Sadie said, looking at the fire. "I worry for your safety, too."

"I know you do, Sadie, I worry myself. And Joe does, too. I sometimes wonder if he's spending time with me because he cares about me or because he's guarding me."

"Perhaps both," said Sadie.


The Monday after Thanksgiving started off with a troubled parent. Nell met me at the top of the stairs, now her method of warning me of some problem ahead.

"A Mr. Clark Cummings is sitting outside your office," she said. "And there's another man with him. Terrance something."

Terrance something turned out to be Terrance Magee, a local attorney.

Mr. Cummings was, of course, Celeste's father. I seated them both at the table and asked Nell if she would please bring some coffee.

Clark Cummings did not strike me as the typical helicopter parent who swoops in every semester to talk to the administration about how his child is doing. This was his first visit to the school since bringing Celeste up for freshman orientation. He had driven three hours from his home and his eyes were bleary above a firmly set mouth.

Cummings folded his hands together and leaned into the table. "Celeste came home for Thanksgiving with some very disturbing news," he began.

"Is Mr. Magee here representing you or Celeste?" I asked.

"I'm just here as a supportive family member at this point," said Magee, unbuttoning the jacket of what looked like a thousand dollar suit. Magee was in his fifties and well-tanned. His tone was friendly but his eyes were not. "Celeste's mother is my cousin."

"Celeste tells us you plan to expel her from the school," said Cummings, rubbing his short gray crew cut. He had the look of an ex-marine, a tired and angry ex-marine.

"I've already expelled her," I said. "She received formal notice of expulsion before the Thanksgiving break. By the way, did she give you her permission to discuss this with me? We have strict rules about student privacy."

Cummings grunted and handed me a note from Celeste that authorized both men to discuss her case. "She didn't show me any formal expulsion letter," Cummings said, "but she did tell me she would have to find a new major in another college and you were expelling her from this journalism school for a very minor infraction."

"I'm sorry, Mr. Cummings, but stealing someone else's work and claiming it as your own is not a minor infraction. It's plagiarism."

Magee put a restraining hand on Cummings' arm. "But isn't this sort of plagiarism rather common these days, Dean Solaris?" Magee had a syrupy voice.

I looked steadily, first at Magee and then at Cummings. "Regrettably, academic dishonesty does occur all too frequently at many universities, but that doesn't excuse it. All students are told from their first day here, that penalties for dishonesty are severe. Warnings are written in all the handbooks and in every syllabus for every course we offer."

"My daughter says she simply forgot to attribute in her presentation. She was exhausted after working all night on the project," said Cummings. He worked his jaw muscles and stared grimly at me as if he thought his stare would persuade me to change my decision.

"Did she tell you about her earlier infractions?"

"What earlier infractions?" Magee asked, the syrup gone.

"Plagiarism in English. Cheating on a test in Anthropology."

For a moment I thought the wind had gone out of Cummings. He lowered his head, but when he raised it up again, I saw a renewed anger and new purpose.

"My daughter wants a career in television. She is not going to be expelled from journalism," he said.

"Yes, Mr. Cummings, she is."

"If you expel Celeste, then I'm afraid your Dr. Worthington is in for some considerable trouble."

What the hell was this?

"He seduced my daughter," said Cummings. His eyes were hard as marbles.

"Clark, are you sure about this?" asked Magee, surprised by this turn. Or, on second thought, as I looked at him, pretending to be surprised.

"Worthington and my daughter have been in a sexual relationship for some time," Clark Cummings said.

Oh, shit. The dark thought.

# Chapter 14

"What were you thinking?" I asked.

Max sat in the chair opposite my desk, a slight and unexpected smile on his face. He looked oddly at ease.

"I won't deny it, Red. But the sex was totally consensual. Celeste is twenty-one. She wanted me. I wanted her. There was no pressure. She didn't ask me to change a grade or anything." His smile became that little rueful grin of his. "She didn't even ask me to talk to you about her expulsion. That was my idea."

"You're her advisor, Max. Consensual doesn't count in a professor-student relationship. You're twenty years older than she is. It was wrong, ethically wrong. You know she can use this against you, against the school. Her father is threatening to report you and go to the media if I don't reverse my decision to expel her. How could you be so stupid?"

Max sat up straighter in the chair. "I didn't harass her, Red. I didn't seduce her. She came to my office one day and, while we were talking, she casually unbuttoned her blouse. Sure I was aroused. I asked her to leave. But she walked over to me, knelt in front of me and unzipped my fly." Max reddened. I tried to remember Max was my good friend, my supporter, but then he said, "I'm sorry, I'm a lonely man these days, Red. Trudy's very pregnant and..."

My hands flew to my face. "Oh, Max. No more. No more. Oh God, you're terrible."

*    *    *

I dreaded seeing Stoddard after Max left. The provost's usually cheerful big face was grim when I described my discussion. He looked like an angry bear. "I don't believe it," he said. "You journalists are something else."

"That's not fair. This is not the first case of sexual exploitation of a student you have ever seen." I was flustered and angry with myself. Why I don't know. I was not my faculty's keeper.

"You're right, Red. I'm not being fair. It's just that for a small college...a small school of journalism, you guys seem to be making too many big, bad headlines these days."

"What's the next step?"

Stoddard stood up, shook his big shoulders and walked to the window. It was cold outside. The sky was gray again and promised snow. He shoved his hands into the pockets of his oversized tweed jacket and let out a long whistling sigh. Then he turned back to me and said, "You have a decision to make. You can give in to Cummings' threat and let Celeste stay in journalism and hope this problem with Worthington stays discreet. Or, you can expel Celeste and take the public exposure she and her father probably have in mind."

I ran my hands over my skirt. In spite of the cold, my palms were sweaty. "Celeste Cummings does not belong in journalism." I realized how naïve that sounded.

"And Max Worthington does not belong in education. He should be put on administrative leave, or at least brought to a hearing, but you don't seem to want to do that."

We were both silent for several minutes. Stoddard was not going to make my decision. At length I said, "I think I'll let Max suffer whatever happens. Celeste is out."

Stoddard nodded. "I agree. I should probably drag Worthington to see Phil Lewis, but we just received a fifteen million dollar donation from the McCloskey family for the med school and I don't want to spoil Phil's day. I was hoping to see this McCloskey story on the front page tomorrow. What do you think are my chances?"

"Elaine Morgan will run with it," I said. "Congratulations."

"And if Celeste or her father goes to the paper?" he asked as he walked me to the door.

"Elaine will still run with it. Fifteen million deserves more than equal time with a sex scandal." I tried to smile.

Stoddard just whistled another sigh. "Red, make sure Worthington knows you're giving him a break by not bringing him to a hearing. Tell him he's on warning about this. If I hear about another female student and him, I'll fire his ass out of here."

I left Stoddard and hurried back to my office. I still had to meet with the Faculty Senate. The senate meets on the last Monday of the month in a large paneled room at the back of the College of Liberal Arts.

Still reeling from my day with Celeste's father and Max and my meeting with Stoddard, I cobbled together a few comments about guest speakers we hoped to bring to campus next spring and prayed the senate would have a full agenda and not keep me long.

I need not have worried. Nothing so grips the academic imagination as a vigorous discussion of parking space on campus. They went on and on.

By the time they got to me, it was starting to get dark. I hoped that would work in my favor even though several senators still wanted the opportunity to express their condolences for the loss of Henry or inquire about the investigation into his death.

"According to the paper, there is some suggestion his death was not from natural causes," observed the senator from liberal arts.

"There is no evidence to suggest he died of anything other than a heart attack," I said, avoiding any speculative tone that might creep into my answer.

"Doesn't it make you nervous for your own safety?" inquired a blonde female senator who looked to be about twelve years old. The sign in front of her read, "Dr. Bridget Mason, Women's Studies."

I took a deep breath. "I have not been given much time to worry about my safety, Dr. Mason. Truly, I have too much else to do."

"Well, I'd be terrified," she said. So much for feminist courage.

An envelope was sticking out from under my office door. Nell had gone home and most of the school was dark. The envelope was plain and lined, an inner office envelope with no postmark. No name was written on the outside. Inside, the note was short and looked as if it had been typed on a computer.

*"You are totally unqualified to lead this school. You lack perspective. You are disorganized, overly emotional, and devoid of objectivity. You must resign immediately. Henry was mad to promote you. His motivations were regrettably transparent. You are intellectually and morally corrupt and do not belong in this university. Leave before something dreadful happens."*

No signature. My heart rate increased. Morally corrupt? Hell, I was an ethics professor. What did that phrase mean? Could this be Simon's work? Blunt, insulting. Controlling. George? I could see his beefy fingers on the keyboard. But George was an egotist. He would have signed it. As for Edwin, the style was a tad literary. It could be Edwin.

"Bring the note home. I'll meet you at your house." Joe's voice on the phone was flat.

I headed for the elevator. I had stopped taking the stairs. It was still too easy to visualize the landing where Henry's body had been sprawled, broken and bleeding. Had Henry received a note before he was killed?

As I drove through the snow, I tried to concentrate on not skidding. I wondered if I should be less worried about what had happened to Henry and more worried about my own safety. Should I take the dog to school with me for protection? Good God. I hoped Joe was already at the house.

\*    \*    \*

Joe arrived ten minutes after I got home. He looked flushed and irritated. He threw his coat over a chair and his woolen gloves on the kitchen table. Oh well. He'd warned me. This is the life of a homicide detective. They see all kinds of crap all day long. He pulled a pair of thin rubber gloves out of his pants pocket, put them on and took the note from me.

"So you think this could be from Simon?"

"It could be from anybody. But I suspect Simon or maybe George or even Edwin. Hard to tell. They're all so awful."

"That's why I want you to stay away from them," he said, carefully putting the note back in the envelope.

"Joe, I work with them. I'm their dean. It's impossible to stay very far away."

"Just be careful, then. I'll check this for prints tomorrow, but it's unlikely we'll get much. No signature means whoever wrote this took care to hide his identity."

I watched him pocket the note in its envelope. "Not a word about this to anyone. Even Sadie," he said.

"Can I make you a drink?" I tried to sound cheerful and ignore the fact that we both were distressed.

Joe accepted a beer and folded his hands around the cold bottle. "I interviewed Simon Gorshak again today," he said. "Christ, what a cagey bastard that guy is."

"Did you tell him what the blackjack dealer at Tahoe told us?"

"Only enough of Bingham's story to try to get Simon to tell me something. But it didn't work. When I asked about his wife he told me it was none of my business. When I asked about his finances, same response. When I asked him—again—where he was the night Henry died, he said he couldn't remember and challenged me to charge him or leave him alone."

"Simon knows how to stonewall."

"He knows we don't have any hard evidence in this case. That's what that son-of-a-bitch knows. That's what all your people know.

Henry had enemies. One of them probably killed him. Right now, my money's on Simon."

# Chapter 15

Tired of worrying and just plain tired, I was grateful when Joe called later that week and suggested we go to a hangout that served good hamburgers. On a Thursday night in a university town, the bar was smoky and crowded. Many of the students seemed to be drunk, or well on their way.

"Binge drinkers," Joe said, leading the way ahead of me through the crowd to find a table.

"They all looked over twenty-one," I said as we sat in a booth in back.

Joe fiddled with the menu. "Twenty-one or not, how can they get blasted on a school night? Don't they have classes tomorrow?"

"Upperclassmen are usually careful to schedule classes on Monday through Thursday. That leaves Friday open so every weekend is a three day weekend," I said. "For that matter, try to get professors to schedule Friday classes."

"I had Friday classes," Joe said. "I didn't drink until Saturday."

We ordered cheeseburgers.

After the waitress left, I caught sight of a familiar figure weaving through the room, taking the small baby steps of the seriously drunk. Celeste Cummings. She made it to a booth across the room from ours where she was loudly greeted by a boy and two others I could not see. Celeste did not look my way.

After we finished our supper, we lingered over coffee.

"You look wiped. I should get you back home," said Joe.

"I need the bathroom first," I said. I calculated a path to the restrooms that would avoid Celeste's booth. The bar was still noisy and crowded. On my way back I glanced in the direction of the booth. It looked empty. Then I saw a form lying under the booth's table. It was female. I called to Joe and we tugged Celeste out from under the table. She moaned but didn't open her eyes. Her clothes were stained and her hair tangled and oily. The manicured red nails that had drummed on my table were chipped. One was broken back to the quick.

Joe called 911 for an ambulance. It came screaming into the parking lot with two cop cars. The uniforms joined us to keep the curious away. The paramedics were somber as they worked over Celeste's barely conscious body. They put her on a gurney and got her into the ambulance.

"How serious do you think this is?" I asked, following them out to the ambulance.

"Don't know if she'll make it," said the medic, a gray haired heavyset man who shrugged and slammed the door. The siren sounded again as it raced away.

Joe turned on the siren and put the flashing light on top of his own car. We arrived at the emergency room in time to see Celeste on a bed with two nurses and a doctor in attendance. A nurse pulled a curtain around the scene.

We waited. We talked about our own experiences with drinking in college, although I gave him a somewhat sanitized version of my own. Joe had lost a good friend to drunk driving. His green eyes grew dark when he told me. "I still miss him."

"We thought we were immortal."

"My parents thought drinking was a normal part of college," said Joe. "My dad used to tell stories about how drunk he got at football games."

"Most parents are like yours," I said.

"I don't remember binge drinking," added Joe. "We got drunk but usually because we were stupid and careless. Now these kids drink to get drunk. Deliberately. I can't fathom their reasons."

Celeste may have had a reason, I thought, but kept it to myself. I knew that some of our students start binge drinking in high school. They may be unskilled freshman when they arrive at university but, as drunks, they're pros.

A doctor appeared from behind the curtain and we approached him. His eyes looked kind through rimless glasses.

"I'm the dean of her school. How is Celeste?"

"It's bad," said the doctor. "Probably the worst case of alcohol poisoning I've seen this year. Anyone know when she started drinking today? Or what she was drinking?"

"No idea. Two hours ago she was with friends, drunk but laughing. It seems her friends just left her, passed out. Then I guess she slid under the table." I felt a tremendous sadness for Celeste Cummings.

"Good thing you found her. We'll know more tomorrow," said the doctor, and turned toward another emergency bed.


In my freshman year at college, I learned to drink.

I'd assumed I'd never drink liquor at all, much less drink too much. Wrong. I'd been told the children of alcoholics are genetically predisposed to alcoholism. I learned in my first semester just how susceptible I was.

It started with Ivy, my roommate, who always managed to smuggle liquor into the dorm—usually tequila, occasionally vodka. Ivy was a tall, good-looking brunette who dated an upperclassman named Sid, the primary source of our booze. Ivy would mix the tequila with bottled orange juice we bought from the dorm vending machine. It tasted innocent enough so I tried it. After the first two months of school, neither of us went to bed completely sober.

Ivy hated her father, who showed up once and hit on one of the blonde twins in the room next to ours. Ivy claimed her father had tried to abuse her when she was fourteen but she grabbed a kitchen knife and went after him and he never tried again. Ivy started drinking in ninth grade.

Ivy was funny and brave and what people call wise beyond her years. She was kind and loyal to me. When we pledged sororities, she was invited to join three of the most popular. I received an invitation from one. Ivy stuck with me even though she could have gone to the top sorority at our university.

So when Ivy asked me to join her for a drink in our rooms, or to go with her to a bar or a frat party, I rarely turned her down. We always had a couple of drinks before we went out. To "arrive buzzed," as she said.

I discovered that, if I only drank heavily on Fridays and Saturdays, I could sober up on Sunday and make all my classes during the week. I worked on my homework until ten every night before drinking. During the week, I managed to get buzzed without getting wasted.

I didn't get behind the wheel of a car when I was drinking. But I rode in the back of cars while others drove drunk. One night, the car I was in skidded into a truck. I woke up in the hospital with a broken arm. The driver of the car needed four plastic surgeries on his face before he could return to college.

And still I drank.

In the spring of my sophomore year, I caught a bad case of flu. I was in the infirmary for two days and in bed for the week following. Ivy tended me like a nurse. Sometimes her boyfriend, Sid, would show up with fresh fruit as well as booze. I did not drink that week because I was taking too much medication and I felt like hell. On the sixth night, I woke up to find that Sid had removed my pajama pants. He was naked from the waist down and standing over me with a bottle of vodka in one hand and an erection in the other. I asked for Ivy. "She's out," he said and pushed my knees apart. He ran his fingers down the inside of my thigh. I was too weak to resist him and too loyal to Ivy to tell her later anything about what Sid and I had done.

The next day, I went back to drinking.

The last afternoon of February my sophomore year, Ivy and I went to a bar together after Friday classes. Sid was there, avoiding me and making elaborate declarations to Ivy. Clearly he had a good headstart on the drinking. I switched to ginger ale after one beer, but Ivy matched Sid glass for glass. After an hour and a half, I was ready to go home. A girl from our sorority offered me a ride. She and I got into her car and, as we were pulling out of the parking lot, I saw Ivy and Sid lurching toward Ivy's car. I rolled down the window and called out to them. "For Christ's sake, don't drive. You're too wasted. It's getting dark and the roads are wet."

I asked the girl if we could please follow Ivy and Sid and she agreed. We saw Ivy's car up ahead. As we approached the bridge spanning the river, Ivy was driving too fast and the car spun out in the middle of the bridge. It crashed into the bridge supports and plunged into the river below. It all happened in seconds.

The girl who was driving our car stopped abruptly and reached for her cellphone. I got out and made my way down the icy riverbank. I could see Ivy's car being buffeted by the current and sinking.

By the time I reached the river's edge, only the top of Ivy's car was visible in the fading light. I stood shivering until the police car pulled in beside me. I could hear the sirens of the ambulance coming from far away.

The next day, after I identified their bodies, the coroner's assistant told me the bones in Ivy's hands had been broken by her fierce pounding on the car window. Ivy's blood alcohol level registered three times the legal limit when she was autopsied.

I stopped drinking.

My junior and senior years were lonely but productive. My grades improved dramatically. I was accepted into two good graduate programs and didn't drink alcohol again until I went home to visit my father after my mother died. He offered me a glass of Bordeaux. I sipped it very slowly and decided I could probably handle wine in small doses. I never told him about my drinking at college. He had enough heartbreak with my mother.

Now, I don't drink hard liquor, only wine—cautiously. The children of alcoholics have to be careful.

\*    \*    \*

The next morning, I was due to meet with a major donor to the school of journalism. Benjamin Howard had given us five million dollars for computers and television equipment and had helped renovate the top floor of the building after a serious roof leak. He had talked of giving us more before the end of the year. It was a conversation I should not miss. But I called Nell and asked her to track him down and postpone the meeting. "Tell Mr. Howard we have a desperately ill student I need to see. Henry always described him as a good guy. I hope he'll forgive me for standing him up."

The morning was crisp and bright. Snow from last night's storm had melted on the street but still frosted the trees and bushes. Several houses were already decked out with Christmas decorations. The car radio, tuned to the university station, played medieval carols and, all the way to the hospital, all I could think about was the possibility that my decision to expel her was the reason Celeste drank too much last night.

She'd been moved to a private room. The sunlight streamed through the sheer curtain at the window washing the faces of those in the room. Clark Cummings stood by the window hands shoved deep in his pockets. It was obvious he had been weeping. A blonde woman with a tired face sat in the chair on the right of Celeste's bed, holding her daughter's hand. On the left side, a young man sat in a chair, the boy who had been with Celeste in the bar. His fingers played idly with the cord leading to the equipment monitoring Celeste. His eyes found mine and closed in pain.

"How is she?" I found the courage to ask.

Clark Cummings turned from the window. "About the same," he said sadly. He put his hands on his wife's shoulders. "Irene, this is Dean Solaris from Celeste's school."

The woman rose and came toward me.

I was sure all the guilt I felt about Celeste must show in my face and that she was going to scream at me. But instead she held out her hand and said, "You're the one who got Celeste to the hospital. The nurses told me you found her unconscious on the floor of the bar."

"Yes."

"Thank you for saving her life."

Clark Cummings stared at me. The man was devastated.

"Yes, Dean Solaris. Thank you," he said so softly I could hardly hear him. "This is Thad," he said, indicating the boy on the left. "Thad's the hero who left my daughter to die last night."

"I told you before," said the boy without looking at any of us, "Celeste told me to leave her. She told us all to leave. She said she never wanted to see me again and I should get the hell out of her life."

"Did she tell you how she planned to get home?" I said.

The boy looked at me. I recognized him as a journalism student, but I wasn't sure of his last name.

I repeated, "Thad, did she tell you how she planned to get home?"

He slumped to one side in his chair. Obviously, in addition to his grief, Thad was suffering a major hangover. "Celeste drove me to the bar," he said. "I left on my own and hitched a ride. Celeste had her car."

"And you were going to let her drive in that condition?"

Thad hung his head, "I was pretty drunk, myself, Dean Solaris. And I'd just been told I was an idiot and lousy in bed." He looked at Irene Cummings. "Sorry, Mrs. Cummings."

Tears streamed down Thad's face. "She said it was my fault she'd been expelled for cheating. She said I should have checked her stuff before she turned it in." Now he was shaking, "But she cheated all the time. How was I supposed to keep up with her?" He dissolved.

"Thad, go into the bathroom and straighten yourself up," said Clark Cummings. The boy obeyed.

"I feel so sorry about all of this," was all I could think to say.

Irene Cummings put her hand on my arm. "When Celeste recovers, if she recovers, we will take her home," she said. "And, I think we'll keep her home for a while. Celeste needs to be with us and we need time to help our daughter with some serious problems." Irene's voice was steady and her touch sure.

Thad emerged from the bathroom and stood next to me. "Sorry about that," he said, as if I was the one to whom he owed an apology.

I moved to the door. "Please let me know how she is and if there is anything I can do," I said. Irene nodded. Clark stared out the window.

Thad left with me. We walked together down the hall toward the parking lot.

"Thad, remind me of your full name," I said.

"Thad...Thaddeus Archer," he said.

"Thaddeus is my father's name," I said. I stopped and looked at the boy who returned my gaze. "He fell in love with the wrong woman, too."

Thad said nothing.

"I was a drunk in college," I said. I had never admitted that to anyone before. "I lost my best friend, I lost my dignity, and I damn near lost my mind."

He just looked at me.

"Stop drinking, Thad. At least stop binge drinking."

He nodded. Suddenly, he put out his arms and hugged me. Then, he walked away without a word.


When I told Sadie about my morning with the Cummings, my eyes watered. Sadie reached across the table and put her weathered, strong hand over mine. "You're being very hard on yourself," she said. "The girl didn't start drinking because you expelled her. She'd no doubt been drinking heavily for some time. You know that."

Wilson showed up with Sadie's iced tea and hot coffee for me. No wine today. Penance. I wiped my eyes. "I know. It's just that it's so damned awful to see a young girl that sick, even if it's self-inflicted. And her poor parents are so anguished."

"You're still in mourning," Sadie said. "This is another unhappy event piling on. It's not been long since Henry's death."

"I was happy on Thanksgiving," I said.

"It was a lovely Thanksgiving. I was happy, too." Sadie's hawk eyes softened. "Nothing takes away from good days like that one."

"I was happy and I was beginning to think I was doing a good job for the school..."

"You are doing a good job for the school. You're a good dean, Meredith Solaris. Know that."

"Everything feels tentative," I said. "Nothing's resolved. Henry's death. No doubt murdered by one of those ghastly men on my faculty. Then there's poor Celeste. Larry Coleman's tenure. Nothing seems to be working out. And, on top of that, I may have offended a major donor by canceling a meeting with him at the last minute."

Sadie sat back and deliberately made a slurping sound with her tea. "Has that cop taken you to bed yet?"

"What?"

"Well, I thought since everything else in your life is going to hell that he was probably disappointing you, too."

"Sadie, for God's sake, Joe is a very good friend and he trusts me to be useful on this investigation. That's all."

"Oh, I doubt that's all. I saw the way he looked at you at your Thanksgiving dinner."

"Maybe after he solves Henry's murder, we can begin some sort of...relationship."

"What if Joe never solves the murder? They don't all get solved, you know. Some cases just get colder and..."

"Sadie, stop. Are you trying to drive me crazy?"

"No, I'm not," she said, putting her hand back on mine. "I am just reminding you that your personal happiness depends on a lot more than solving this case. It also means knowing when you're well off. You have a distinguished job and a great career ahead of you. The administration and most of your faculty support you. You have a good man definitely interested in you. So you are, Queen

Red, in my estimation, very well off these days. Murder investigations notwithstanding."

I squeezed her hand. "Sadie, my rock. I love you very much."

# Chapter 16

One of the few good conversations I had with my mother was about hair. We both had dark, thick red hair that tended to curl. "Take good care of your hair," she advised, "it can be your best feature. Men will love it and women will envy it."

Maybe because I still cherish those few good times with her, I took her counsel seriously. After a year of searching my new city and trying all of Trudy Worthington's suggestions, I had finally found a stylist who knew how to give me a good cut. Tuesday after lunch, I headed to the salon. After the stylist was finished, I stared at myself in the large mirror above. My hair framed my face with curls, some dark as wine, some lighter and more golden.

For years, as a kid, I thought I was homely. But by thirty-five I had decided I was good-looking without being conventionally pretty.

Thirty-five was not past childbearing age, but also not a girl anymore, a woman to be taken seriously. Sadie was right. The hell with whoever had written that anonymous note. I was qualified and, given the events since Henry's death, I knew I damn well better be taken seriously.

Several faculty members who were coming up for annual reviews were due for visits to their classes to see how they were doing as instructors.

I promised myself I'd be diligent. I would start my evaluations with classroom visits to the people I liked least, hoping to avoid invidious comparisons with those I liked better. I decided not to bother with Simon's class.

In George's class, what the faculty saw as verbose and pompous, his students saw as dramatic and interesting. For the most part, George lectured, but all fifty students seemed engaged by his rhetoric, especially stories of his days as a young reporter and some of the celebrities he met when he became editor. After I left George's class, I headed for Edwin's.

Edwin taught writing with conspicuous concern for students who were having trouble. The students worked at computers. When they were finished writing or editing, they turned their chairs around and wheeled over to a long table in the center of the room. Edwin's critiques were thorough and useful. His students seemed eager to improve their work and present again. Edwin walked around, stopping to kneel down beside a student and offer more guidance. This was a kind and articulate Edwin. As I left his classroom, I knew this was the Edwin a young Mary Cartwell had loved all those years ago.

George and Edwin were difficult colleagues, but excellent teachers. I resolved to make a greater effort to understand the complexities of the two of them.

Especially if it turned out Simon was not the killer who had sent Henry down that flight of stairs.


Larry Coleman was a wreck. According to Nell he had been waiting for me in my office for over an hour while I watched Edwin's class. Larry had been pacing the floor and bugging Nell every ten minutes about my whereabouts.

As I approached my outer office, she stuck her head out of her office that adjoins mine. "Watch out, he's a mess," she said as she rolled her eyes.

Larry was standing by the window behind my round table looking out over the quad. "I'll pick you up at the airport. I love you, too," he said to his cellphone when he saw me. He closed his phone and sank into a chair facing my desk. "Oh, Red. It's getting worse."

"What's getting worse?" I tried to sound sympathetic.

"Simon and the Dynamic Duo. They've been visiting other members of the faculty. They trap each person in his or her office and then trash my tenure application."

"Tenure reviews are confidential," I said. "Are they breaking the rules?"

"They're not only breaking the rules, they're busting my balls. They're telling everyone who will listen that my research is irrelevant, my teaching sucks, and my student evaluations are awful. Lies, Red. Outright lies." Larry was slender with a delicate, almost feminine face. He had a short beard and a mustache, which I suspected existed to make him look more masculine. His eyes were awash. "And worst of all, Edwin and George corralled a couple of grad students yesterday and told them not to take my classes next semester."

My resolution to try to better understand Edwin and George dissolved. "That's outrageous. I'll deal with this, Larry. You go home and get some rest."

"No one to go home to," he said, starting to sob. "Karen's in Chicago on a business trip. I just spoke to her. She can't get home until tomorrow."

He pulled out a handkerchief and blew his nose just as I was reaching for a box of tissues.

"I'm sorry, Red. I know I should be handling this better. But I have worked so long and so hard." He cleared his throat and stood up as if to make it easier to talk without tears. "I'm filing a grievance against those bastards. And please don't even try to talk me out of this. I love the school, but if I can't file a grievance, I'll file a lawsuit for slander. I'll go to the media, and if all else fails, I'm going to get a baseball bat and break their kneecaps."

"Take a deep breath, Larry. And sit down," I said. "I'm not going to try to talk you out of anything. I'm going to tell you how to file a grievance."

"Maybe I should just see my attorney now," he said.

"A good attorney will advise you to go through the grievance procedure first."

"Shit. I'm starting to like the baseball bat idea better."

"I know. But these guys are not worth you going to jail, are they?"

I explained the steps he should take. He listened, then stood up, straightened his shoulders and strode out of the office. He left me to think about what I was going to tell Stoddard and what I was going to say to the gang of three when they received a formal notice of grievance.

Idiots.


Celeste Cummings survived. Irene Cummings called to say they were taking her home and withdrawing her from the university.

"Do you think she'll come back in the fall?" I asked. "I would be happy to help her find a new major in another college."

Irene was silent for a moment. "Thank you, Dean Solaris. That's thoughtful of you. But her doctors want to see if there's even slight brain damage," she said. "We'll have to wait and determine what Celeste can do in the next weeks. Also, she needs some therapy before she should come back here."

An hour later, I had a meeting with the university president. Philip Lewis was finally showing his age. His fine features were pale and drawn and his expensive tailored suit seemed to hang on him. He motioned me to a chair by his desk, then leaned back and put his fingers to his lips. I had telephoned him to alert him to Larry's predicament.

"You're having a tough go aren't you? Tougher than we anticipated."

"Do you want to appoint someone else?" I said, half hoping he would say yes so I could go home to my dog and back to my old teaching job and forget about all the assholes and their stupid bickering.

He smiled gently. "No, Meredith. You are still the best person. I don't know of anyone who could have done more or foreseen more."

I sensed a "but."

"But I wonder if it would help if I put the school of journalism into receivership?"

Receivership happens when an independent college is put under the wing of another college because it cannot function on its own or is too dysfunctional to govern itself.

Lewis went on, "The dean of the College of Liberal Arts tells me he would be willing to help out."

"I don't think we are at that point yet, President Lewis," I said, carefully choosing my words. "I'm working with the provost and hope to get this grievance matter handled with as little publicity as possible."

"Some of your senior faculty deserve to be spanked and sent to their rooms without supper," said Lewis.

"Yes, they do. Care to make that happen?"

"Regrettably I can't, Meredith. But I can put the school of journalism under Liberal Arts if things get any crazier."

"President Lewis, that punishes the entire school for the asinine behavior of a minority of the faculty. I'm sorry, sir, I think that's unfair and, frankly, I don't see how it would do much good. Also, please keep in mind we are all suffering a police investigation of Henry's death."

"I do admire your determination, Meredith." He played with a small stack of papers on his desk. I waited.

"I'll hold off for a while." A frown on his forehead, old eyes looking fierce. "But know this, Dean Solaris. I didn't put you in that job to see you whipsawed by a bunch of thugs. So call me right away if you need help."

"Thank you. I'm meeting with the provost in half an hour," I said. "Let me see what he and I can work out."

Usually decisions take forever in a university and events move at a snail's pace, but, as I walked downstairs to Stoddard's office I had the anxious feeling that, this time, events might run ahead of my ability to manage any of them. It was no longer just the quarrel. My school was in jeopardy.

"Are you willing to try to talk to these clowns again?" asked Stoddard. "I can be in the room with you this time."

I sat down in one of the provost's overstuffed chairs and moaned. "I tried before. I warned them Coleman would file a grievance if they didn't cease and desist. But they went ahead anyway."

Stoddard's office felt cold. No doubt a man of his girth kept the temperature down, but I shivered visibly and he rose and closed a window behind me.

"Yes, but things are different now. With Phil giving serious thought to putting journalism into receivership, you may find that your powers of persuasion have been enhanced," Stoddard said.

"Will they believe it?" I asked. "They're so delusional, I wonder if they'll think I'm making it up."

"That's why I'll be there to back you up. If they have any doubts about Phil's intentions, I'll make sure they get it. Are you game?"

"Yes, I'm game. Do you think President Lewis would really do it?"

"Oh, yes. Phil has the guts of a pirate captain when it comes to dealing with rogue faculty."

I left Stoddard's office and walked across the quad toward the school. It was getting dark early as we approached the winter solstice. The lights were bright in the three colleges facing me. Snow crusted the ivy that climbed on the larger buildings. A choir was practicing carols somewhere near. Voices high and crystal clear in the winter air. In two weeks, Mountain West would close for winter break and go home to celebrate Christmas.

God rest ye, merry gentlemen.

Let nothing you dismay.

It was thirty-three days since Henry Brooks had been found at the bottom of the stairs.

# Chapter 17

Joe was compassionate. "I'm sorry this investigation is taking so damned long and I'm also so sorry for Celeste, and for Larry," he said. "I know you feel lousy about all this, even if none of it was your doing."

He was wearing an old apron of mine and stirring spaghetti sauce while I sat, glum and tired, at the kitchen table. Joe makes terrific spaghetti sauce, not to mention fried chicken and meatloaf. I also figured he came not only to feed me and bring me up to date, but also because college basketball was starting and my television set was newer and larger than the one in his bachelor pad.

"I feel a sort of guilt about Celeste," I said. "I drank too much in college. I just didn't get into Celeste's kind of trouble. Now I wish I had known she was a heavy drinker when we talked in my office."

"How would that have changed things?"

"I'm not sure," I said. "I think I might have better understood the irrationality of her behavior if I had known more about her. I might have been a bit less angry and aggressive. I might have gotten her to talk more about herself."

"Maybe, maybe not," he said and put down his spoon. "I knew my best friend was an alcoholic and I talked to him all the time, but it still didn't change things. He would just make a joke about it. And, he was good at making jokes. He got more laughs than any of us. And, more girls, too."

"Oh, I doubt that."

"No. I was a little shyer in college than I am now. I didn't get to my full height until sophomore year and then I grew three inches.

That fall I tried out for basketball. I also hit the gym and tried to bulk up a bit."

"I would say you did very well at that."

He ignored my feeble attempt to flirt, and veered back to his friend.

"I can still see his face. One night before he died, we talked until about three in the morning. It was so easy to talk about yourself with him. He really listened, even when he was half in the bag, he listened. He had that way of looking intently at you when you were talking and making you feel like whatever you had to say was significant. I remember we sat in my room and I told him all about my parents and my sister and the girls I had lusted after and never dated."

I kept still. Clearly Joe was lost in his story.

"That night I told him about the day my mother died and how I found my dad lying on the kitchen floor after we came home from the hospital, just staring at the ceiling and refusing to get up until the next morning." Joe took a sip from his wine glass.

I kept still.

"He was supposed to be my best man. And he was the one friend I went to when I needed to vent."

Joe picked up the spoon, turned to the stove and resumed stirring the sauce. "Until I met you," he said to the wall behind the stove, "I didn't think I would ever find another person I could really talk to."

That picked me up. I resolved to learn how to shut up more often.


After dinner, Joe went into my living room to watch a game on television and I went into my home office. In preparation for the meeting Stoddard and I planned to have with George, Edwin, and Simon, I had taken home the still unopened suitcase Michael Brooks had left in my office. Maybe there was something in Henry's papers that would help me.

To my surprise, when I opened the suitcase at home, I discovered copies of the school's personnel files. Several had notes scribbled in the margins, Brooks' own private musings about his faculty, irreverent and in some cases irrelevant. Such as "Ardith is too uptight—needs to get laid." Really, Henry. One cryptic note on Edwin Cartwell's file read, "Get Sterling at Arkansas to recruit him for chair." So that had been Brooks' plan. Get Edwin to accept another more prestigious position at a university back east, and then steal the man's wife. Mary hadn't mentioned this plot.

Simon Gorshak's file was the first one I read thoroughly. Under marital status he had checked "single" and no one was listed as an emergency contact. There was no written reference to Henry's request for Simon's resignation. The comments about Simon's teaching were milder than I expected, given what I knew of Henry's true opinion. As I read though the draft of Simon's annual evaluation, I suspected Henry had caved into Simon's threats and was planning to give Simon a satisfactory rating. I put the file to one side so I could show it to Joe.

My file was at the bottom of the pile and offered a provocative note. Near the end of the marginal scribbles, I read, "If it weren't for M, I would like to have a go at R." What a sexy beast Henry had been. I was glad his children had left these files for me to examine. Phyllis and Max's files were missing and I made a note to ask Nell about them.

The folders had piled up on my couch and, by midnight, I had read as much as I wanted to for one evening. As I started to put the folders back in the small suitcase Michael Brooks had given me, I noticed a yellow slip of paper on the bottom, with the scrawled words, "Fucking thief. This warrants punishment. Call Shaw tomorrow." It was Henry's writing, but who was it about? Had it fallen out of one of the files? And, who was Shaw?

I showed the slip to Joe.

He stared at it. "What does it mean?"

"I don't know, but Henry wrote it and must have been angry with someone. Maybe this is a motive for someone."

"Someone on the faculty?"

"I think so, but I'm not sure."

"Could it be Mary Cartwell?" Joe turned off the television. "I dated a lady in Chicago who stole from me."

"You haven't mentioned her before. Were you serious about her?"

"Not after money went missing from my wallet and some credit card problems turned up."

"What did you do?"

Joe gave me one of his long looks. He was dressed in sweats and a t-shirt and looked very appetizing. I wondered if I really wanted a long conversation about another woman.

"I turned her in," he said quietly. "My partner arrested her."

"Josiah Morgan. What a rat. Did she love you?"

"I doubt it. Turns out my wallet wasn't her first theft."

"Did you love her?" My view of Joe was taking on a new dimension. Some tough emotional muscle inside this man.

"No, I liked her a lot. But she was, as Henry Brooks might have said, a fucking thief."

# Chapter 18

Three days before winter break we held the morning meeting with Stoddard and the three faculty members who had maligned Larry Coleman.

My objective was to persuade George, Edwin, and Simon to formally apologize to Larry in front of the whole faculty at the last meeting of the semester. I wasn't sure it would stop the grievance proceeding but it might stop the gossip.

It also might convince President Lewis to hold off on further thoughts of receivership.

Stoddard arrived first, bundled in an enormous camel hair coat and pale blue scarf. His big cheeks were bright with cold. "Coffee?" he gasped.

Nell was right behind him with a tray of mugs and milk. "Dr. Cartwell says he's running late," said Nell, putting the tray down on my round table. Nell wasn't good at concealing her contempt. "Do you want me to see if the others will be on time?"

"Tell them the provost has another meeting this morning and will be very disappointed if they miss this one," I said.

"Passive aggression. The hallmark of the dysfunctional group," said Stoddard, sitting down at the table and pouring milk into his coffee.

A cough from the doorway announced Simon.

He stared at Stoddard, his gray eyes as cold as the morning outside. "So you think we're dysfunctional," he said, taking a chair for himself.

"I do," Stoddard replied. "Also self-destructive."

The predictable stomach pain started. This was not going the way I had hoped.

If Stoddard antagonized Simon further, the likelihood of an apology to Larry Coleman seemed remote.

George entered, silent for once. He poured himself coffee, took a sip and looked steadily at the provost. "What brings you here to our little journalism school this frosty morning?"

Before Stoddard could reply, I stood up and said, as calmly as possible, "We are here to discuss the unfortunate campaign you two, along with Edwin, have been waging against Larry Coleman."

"He should not be tenured. We asked for your support on this," said Simon.

"And you did not get my support," I said. "You will recall, I said if you did anything to subvert the process, which you seem to have done, that Larry Coleman would file a grievance, which he has done."

"I look forward to making our case to a university grievance committee," said Simon.

"And if the media gets curious, I would be happy to accommodate them," said George.

Silence. Edwin entered while we were all contemplating the next step. "Sorry to be late," he said.

"You are here in time to hear the most important part," I said. "The president and the provost are considering putting the school of journalism into receivership."

"What the hell does that mean?" asked George, as usual uninformed and uncertain about academic procedures.

The pain sharpened. "It means we would lose our status as an independent school and be put under the management of the College of Liberal Arts."

"That's preposterous," boomed George. "We would lose all our benefactors, starting with me."

"You're being silly, Meredith," said Edwin. "Philip Lewis would never think of doing such a thing."

"Never," echoed Simon.

Stoddard remained silent with his hand under his chin as if forcing himself to remain quiet. As had happened before, the pain eased. I was beginning to believe that if I was willing to confront my opponents, my digestive system would cooperate. Maybe courage was returning.

I took a deep breath. "President Lewis has told me he would indeed do such a thing. I am the one trying to talk him out of it."

The three of them swiveled to the provost. "Your dean is right," Stoddard said.

"On what grounds would we be put into receivership?" asked Edwin.

Stoddard leaned in. "On the grounds that journalism can no longer justify its independence. Your fighting has spilled out into your classrooms. You have made the atmosphere so toxic the school is veering toward the unmanageable."

"It's our business," said George. "No one else's."

Stoddard barely glanced at him. "Not exclusively your business, since you were stupid enough to give an interview to the student paper. Not since your comments about Coleman have occasioned malicious and unprofessional gossip and involved his grad students. Now, thanks to you, it's everyone's business. Particularly since you three are facing a grievance hearing that will spread the gossip, further discredit the school and, quite probably, all of you."

Edwin sighed. "And how do we avoid these unhappy prospects?"

"I would start by listening to the advice of your dean," said Stoddard. "She's trying to make peace among you and she's facing a major re-accreditation visit next fall. Believe me, if you lose your accreditation, there's not much sympathy for this school maintaining its independence."

Stoddard rose and walked over to the coat rack. "Meredith's fighting for the school. Consider helping her." Simon and Edwin followed Stoddard to the elevator. I could hear their voices protesting to the provost.

After the others had left, George Weinstein lingered in the doorway and then came in and closed the door behind him.

"The meeting's over, George," I said. "I have another appointment."

"Cancel it," he said, standing in the middle of my office with his big hands clasped in front of him. His face was red and his eyes were beady with anger. "Now then, sit down and be very quiet while I acquaint you with a little reality."

He looked enraged and I was nervous about the closed door. Should I shout for Nell or tough it out with him?

"For starters, remember you are the interim dean, not the elected dean."

"I know that, George." I was trying very hard not to sound angry or frightened.

"Well, act like you know it. You can't go running to Stoddard and Lewis every time someone disagrees with you." George leaned on the chair that faced my desk. Sweat beads had broken out on his face. "You can't keep giving the administration the impression that the school is dysfunctional just so you can get your own way."

"I don't think I'm the one giving the impression, George..."

"Indeed you are. You are creating problems. You are behaving like a whining teenager and it's doing harm to the school." George's voice had risen and I wondered if Nell could hear.

"Lady, no one harms this school. Not while I can prevent it. No one puts us into receivership. No one. I'm not going to work in some pissant school that's just a department of a larger college. I came here to work in an independent school of journalism. And, that's the way it's going to stay."

"George, stop yelling at me."

"Then stop interrupting and listen. Meredith, I'm close to two members of the board of regents who govern this university and I am a personal friend of the governor's. I can get you fired. I know a lot of important people in this state and, if need be, I'll call on them. You may have won this round, but I will mow you down if you ever pull another stunt like this."

"Mow me down?"

"You bet your sweet ass, I'll mow you down. Remember that."

He wheeled and went out the door before I could think of what to say in response. I sat down, deep-breathing to calm myself down.

"Dean Solaris?" Nell was standing in the door. "May I have a minute?"

"Sure, Nell, come on in." I was grateful to see her solemn face. "Please call me Red," I said for the tenth time since she had become my assistant.

Nell took a deep breath. "Red, I heard George. I didn't mean to eavesdrop, but..."

"Sorry you had to put up with that, Nell. But you know as well as anyone how difficult George can be."

"More than difficult." Another deep breath. "I think there's something you should know about him."

"Oh?"

Nell cast her eyes down. Then she looked directly at me, and pulled a chair close to my desk. She smoothed her gray curls with her fingers. "I heard something about George years ago before you came," she said.

"Let's have it, Nell. This seems to be my day for difficult information."

"My sister's a nurse, you know."

I nodded.

"She told me one night some years ago that George's father-in-law had been admitted to her ward." Third deep breath. "The man was in his eighties and had been severely beaten. Bruises all over, two black eyes and a broken nose."

"Good Lord. Beaten? By whom?"

"Well, the father-in-law was living with George and his wife. I guess he had moved in after the mother-in-law died."

"Did he say George had beaten him?"

"Not exactly. And, a day or so later, when he was able to talk to the police, the old man told them it had been an intruder. But he couldn't describe the intruder."

"Maybe it was the truth."

"My sister didn't believe it. She said the day George came to collect his father-in-law and take him home, the old man wept and pleaded with her not to let George in the room. But the doctor said the old man was suffering from dementia and to ignore him and let George take him home."

"Did she ever see George's father-in-law again?"

Back to the fussing with her hair. "No. The old man died a month later."

"And you and your sister think George beat him?"

"My sister does. And, Red, I tell you this only to make you careful of George. I've seen him angry. You must not be alone with him and you must not trust him."


When Joe telephoned that evening, I greeted him with, "Any chance you can get evidence against George Weinstein for Henry's murder?"

I poured myself a second glass of wine and told him about my scene with George and his threat to "mow me down."

"Sorry, Red. I don't have any strong evidence pointing to George. But, I'd be happy to go punch him in the nose if that would help."

"George was so loud and so threatening, all I could think of afterward was what he might have done to Henry."

"Regrettably he has an alibi for that Sunday. He and his wife were at a dinner party in Reno and arrived at six o'clock according to their host. The medical examiner estimates Henry died between five and five thirty."

I inhaled and took another sip. "So George would've had to kill Henry and then jump into a car and drive incredibly fast to get to Reno by six."

"Drive to Reno through a snowstorm if you recall," said Joe. "But cheer up, alibis sometimes fall apart. The host who provided the alibi was his old college roommate and may have a faulty memory, or Henry may have been killed sooner. We won't take George off the list just yet, especially since he's been such a bastard to you."

"Why am I not more relieved?"

"Because he threatened you, Red. And, you're right, anyone who threatens you may have threatened Henry and may have killed Henry."

"There's more," I said, and I told Joe about George's father-in-law.

"Jesus. Be careful of him."

"Looks like we have Simon and George both as suspects?"

"And Edwin. And maybe someone we haven't considered yet."

"I thought Edwin was off the list."

"No one is off the list. Henry was sleeping with Edwin's wife and we only have her word that he didn't know. The fact that he reported the death could be due more to cleverness than innocence. Simon was worried Henry would find a way to fire him and refuses to tell us where he was that Sunday. And George…well, he has a bad temper and may be violent."

I hung up and decided I wasn't hungry for supper. I poured a glass of wine and went upstairs to take a shower. When I was putting on my robe, the doorbell rang. Who the hell? It was after nine. My hands shook as I opened my bedroom window and looked down at the front door. It was Joe.

"I thought I would come over and make sure you're okay," he said and walked in and went straight into my kitchen. He was wearing a dark green sweatshirt and jeans and carrying a large padded bag.

"I cooked lasagna and thought you could use some nourishment." He produced a flat covered dish from the bag.

My kitchen is small but efficient. Pale marble countertops and maple cabinets. I keep it neat.

As I watched, he turned on my oven to three hundred degrees, opened the cupboard and got out a baking sheet to warm up a loaf of French bread.

"You amaze me sometimes. You actually know how to find whatever you need in my kitchen."

"I'm a detective," he said.

"I should dry my hair."

"Don't spend too much time on your hair." His voice was husky.

I hurried upstairs, rapidly scrubbed my teeth and damp dried my hair and pulled it back off my face. The dinner was ready when I returned.

We ate in silence.

Then he said, "A professor goes duck hunting."

Here we go. I started to smile as he continued.

"The professor shoots a duck and it falls on the other side of a fence. So, the professor climbs the fence and goes to pick up the duck. But then a farmer appears and says, 'This is my land and that's my duck.' So the professor says, 'But I shot the duck.' And the farmer, who is big and beefy, stares down the professor and says, 'This is my land and that's my duck. But I tell you how we'll decide who gets the duck. We'll take turns. I'll kick you in the balls. Then you kick me in the balls and whoever lasts longest owns the duck.'"

Joe was grinning.

"So the professor agrees and the farmer hauls off and gives him one helluva kick in the groin. The professor doubles over and groans." Joe doubles over and rolls on the floor groaning. I was laughing.

"Finally, after ten minutes of agony, the professor stops groaning. He staggers to his feet and approaches the farmer, ready to take his turn. And the farmer says, 'You can have the duck.'"

I roared.

My kitchen felt cozy and warm. Very warm.

I hated to break the spell. "Should we talk about George?"

"Not now. Later, maybe."

I got up to refill our wine glasses and Joe was behind me in an instant. He unclipped my hair. I turned to him as he said, "You spent too much time on your hair."

"It's a bit wild."

"I like it wild." He ran his hand through my hair. "Your hair is beautiful. Thick and curly, the color of Cabernet." He kissed my forehead.

"I like your nose, too," he continued, "especially the freckles on the bridge." He kissed my nose. Then my mouth, a firm intrusive kiss.

I looked up at his face. He had shaved close and his skin gleamed smooth. His green eyes were dark and smoky. We both knew what was going to happen. His hands left my hair and traveled down over my breasts to the sash of my robe.

Making love had always been uncertain for me. At times warm and comforting, at other times an empty exercise that left me feeling alone and used. I was rarely aroused by the sight of my lover's nakedness and although my body responded to the right touch in the right place, my mind often drifted and I had to force myself to focus on the man, his weight, his smell, the sounds he made. I usually pretended to respond to overcome my passivity. I tried to be skillful at making men happy. I tried to seem passionate. Sometimes it worked. But, when I was being honest with myself, I had to admit sex was never so much a source of pleasure as the price I paid to feel closeness, to be the recipient rather than the giver of love.

For reasons I could not have explained, I knew that night with Joe Morgan would be different. As we climbed the stairs to my bedroom, I felt an excitement that was novel, a pure physical urgency to connect with him. No, more than connect, to merge, to be touched, to be tasted, to be known.

The first morning light found us dozing and warm together. Then we heard the bedroom door bang open and there was a loud thump on the bed.

My dog stood astride Joe, his golden head burrowing into Joe's armpit. Joe sat up and took the dog's head between his hands.

Looking deep into the dog's eyes, Joe said, "You need a name, pal. Charlie. That's your name. Charlie." The dog stared back, then looked down averting his eyes from Joe's insistent gaze.

"Charlie, go. Go downstairs and guard the house."

The dog jumped off the bed and looked back at Joe. "Charlie, go downstairs," said Joe, leaning forward and displaying impressive muscles in his back. The light from a bedside lamp played over his skin. The dog hesitated. "Charlie, go," he said. Charlie turned and went through the doorway. I could hear his toenails on the stairs.

"How do you do that?" I ran my fingers across his shoulders and down his spine. He turned to me and stretched his arm, sliding it under my back.

"Dogs are pack animals. You know that. You probably also know they defer to the largest male in the place."

"That would be you," I said.

"That would be me."

"I thought we had to wait until after the case..."

"I couldn't wait longer. And when you called tonight, I knew I would have to come over and be with you. Did I take you by surprise?"

"Yes. But I like your surprises."

He smiled and kissed me again.

I wanted nothing to break the mood. But my damned curiosity got the better of me.

"Have you ever been married?" I asked.

"Didn't Elaine tell you?"

Oh, God. He was once married, or deeply in love, and she died. Or still married? Please don't let it be that.

"No. Elaine never talked about your past."

"I was engaged in college. After my fiancée found out my roommate's father was a dot-com millionaire, I was no longer engaged to her. My roommate was, poor bastard."

"And others?"

"Yes, of course there were others. But no one I wanted to marry."

"Any regrets?"

He looked at me. "Hell, no." He leaned into me, kissing my neck, "If I was married to any one of them, I'd have to commit adultery with you."

"Have to?"

"Absolutely, have to."

He got out of bed and walked over to the dresser. A naked athlete with long sinewy legs, defined bicep muscles, and a sculptured butt was getting dressed in my bedroom. A thirty-seven year old cop still occupying the body of a college basketball player. Bliss.

"Do you have to go?"

"Will I be invited back?"

Bet on it.

At the last faculty meeting of the fall semester, Larry Coleman was wearing a suit and tie, looking like a man about to enter a courtroom.

He sat staring intently at what appeared to be a pile of notes. He didn't raise his eyes when Edwin started to speak. As Edwin worked his way through a statement he didn't want to make, it became clear that the fear of receivership had taken effect. Larry Coleman continued to stare at the papers in front of him and to make occasional notes.

"I am indeed sorry Dr. Coleman's graduate students took a casual remark of mine to mean that I did not respect Dr. Coleman and that I did not recommend his class," said Edwin. Larry said nothing and didn't look up.

"And if discussing Dr. Coleman's tenure qualifications with other members of the faculty was premature, I'm sorry. But I presumed we were all going to discuss the tenure application sooner or later." George simply can't admit to doing wrong so I guessed this was as close to an apology Larry was going to get from him. Larry continued to gaze at his papers.

"We discuss tenure matters in a formal meeting of the tenured faculty, not in the hallways," I interjected.

"Yes, we get that," said Edwin. Simon grunted.

The apologies were inadequate, but I hoped for the best.

"I trust this will suffice, Meredith," said Edwin, addressing me.

Larry was now staring at the wall.

"And that Dr. Coleman will forget about filing a grievance,'" said Simon.

I looked at Larry. His gaze did not leave the wall. The others in the faculty stirred restlessly in their chairs. Elaine took out her notebook. Phyllis rested her fingers on the edge of her open laptop. Max looked at Simon through hooded eyes. Ardith tried not to look at anyone. Her eyes darted from one window to the other. Still no one spoke.

At length, I said, "It's clear this is all the faculty meeting we're going to have today. Our next meeting will be at the January retreat. Be prepared to consider a presentation on the new courses to add to the curriculum. Nell will send out agendas before then. If I don't see you before the end of the week, I wish you all happy holidays."

The faculty rose and started to shuffle out of the room. Some murmured to one another as they gathered their papers and winter coats.

I waited until everyone except Larry Coleman had left. Then I said, "Well Larry, what do you think?"

His jaw hardened. "I think if I don't get a unanimous vote for tenure next month, I will do whatever it takes to bring those fuckers down."

# Chapter 19

Joe slept soundly, his head near mine. I could hear his breathing. Beside my side of the bed on the floor, Charlie breathed in perfect sync with Joe.

I eased out of the bed, trying to avoid the sleeping dog. I tried to keep my squeaking stairs from waking anyone, but Charlie hears everything and soon was padding down behind me.

A cup of tea later, I lit a fire and sat, wrapped in a heavy fake fur throw, trying to think my way through what had kept me awake.

Joe.

A great lover, an imaginative cook, and a thoughtful friend. What more could I want? Yet something nagged at me. Not about Joe—about me. My history with men was not promising. Every time I had gotten close to the possibility of a relationship, I'd screwed things up. My therapist back in Ohio suggested I was afraid of being deserted by men, so I always contrived to dump them first.

In my first semester of graduate school in New York, I'd fallen in love with an assistant professor who taught one of my courses. Unlike some of my current faculty, he was conscientious—he wouldn't date me while I was his student. The attraction was intense but we played by the rules.

The day of his last class we met at a hotel bar near campus. Fifteen minutes later we were in a room upstairs. We undressed each other in record time. The sex was not great, but the relief was tremendous. And, in the weeks that followed, the sex got better. I loved and admired him although I never felt the deep passion I expected to characterize my first adult love affair.

We got engaged the day before my mother crashed into a tree and killed herself.

I went home to Ohio and switched to a graduate program there to be near my grieving father. My fiancé came to visit several times; he was always kind and understanding. But, as time passed, I returned his kindness with complaints about his unwillingness to leave a very good position and move to Ohio. Six months later he called to say he thought we should start seeing other people. I didn't blame him. I blamed me. My therapist suggested that, sooner or later, I probably would have found some reason to push him away, and I agreed with her.

The attorney I went to bed with the following year was a different matter. He was fifteen years older than I, rich and self-centered. One night he made me so angry I threw a lamp at his head and left him sitting on the floor of his enormous bedroom nursing a significant cut on his forehead. After that, I never saw him again.

Since taking the job at Mountain State, I'd tried two relationships, one with a professor in biology and another with a man who wanted to be my stockbroker, but I ended both. I don't see a therapist anymore but I was sure my old friend in Ohio could have provided some sage insights into why I had so much trouble bonding with men. Even though I felt warm and safe with Joe, I felt surer of his feelings for me than of mine for him.

"What's the matter with me?" I said out loud to Charlie. The dog got up and put his head in my lap. "This is the first man I have been able to really talk to. We trust each other. Why am I afraid of messing up with the one guy who could be the right guy?"


Inevitably morning came and, even though everyone else had left for winter break, the dean's office would remain open until the day before Christmas. Nell was the only one in the outer office when I arrived at school. She and I had planned to catch up on all the work we had neglected during the semester.

For the first time since she and I had started working together, Nell actually looked relaxed and happy to see me. "Good morning Red," she said, smoothing the curls that frame her face, "there are messages on your desk. You might want to start with Mr. Howard who wants to reschedule the meeting you missed."

Benjamin Howard was our primary benefactor. I had cancelled our original meeting to go to Celeste's hospital room. He had been gracious at the time, according to Nell, but today his secretary had said this week before Christmas would be the last opportunity for a meeting until late spring. He had given millions to journalism schools all over the country, but Mountain State seemed to be his favorite. I returned the call and was put through to Ben immediately.

"I was wondering if we could have dinner tonight," he began.

I was surprised. I had thought lunch would be more convenient for both of us. "I know it's short notice, Dr. Solaris—may I call you Meredith? But my schedule is packed this week and I leave on Friday."

"I could meet for dinner. Thank you."

"Splendid. I hope you like Japanese food. If so, we can meet at seven at Kyoto's on Fourth Street. Would that be all right?"

"That would be fine," I heard myself say, thinking about the pot roast Joe had promised to make for us tonight. After I hung up, I wondered why I felt nervous. I'd met Ben Howard twice at school parties hosted by Henry. I recalled Ben as a big man with a ready laugh and a good sense of humor. He was tall and self-confident. His face was tan, his hands were strong and brown from sun. His suits were beautifully tailored. I found him appealing. Maybe that was why I felt uneasy about calling Joe to say I wouldn't join him for dinner.

"Of course I understand," Joe said. "Ben Howard's your biggest benefactor. You blew him off to see your alcoholic student. I hope you persuade him to give the school another big gift so the university will know what a sensational fundraiser you are. I'll meet you at your house later if you like."

Of course I liked. Intelligent, self-confident Joe. Why had I worried?

Another message was from a Dr. Alistair Shaw, a name that was familiar but I couldn't quite place it. Shaw answered on the second ring.

"I wanted to express my deepest sorrow over the loss of Henry Brooks, Dean Solaris."

"Thank you, Dr. Shaw. I appreciate the call. So will the faculty."

"I was also hoping you could help me with another matter but I wanted to wait a respectful time before asking."

"I'd be happy to accommodate you if I can," I replied, now remembering that Alistair Shaw was a distinguished retired professor who had taught at the top journalism schools in the country and had written several books, three of which faced me in Henry's bookcase across from my desk.

"Henry sent me some pages written, I think, by one of your faculty although Henry did not provide the author's name. He asked me to review the pages and give him an opinion as to their pedagogic value to the journalism profession."

"I see. Is there a problem?"

"Well, Dr. Solaris, it appears there is. About half of what I read, which I presumed to be part of a larger work, was—how shall I say this—directly taken from a book I have been writing over the past two years." Shaw paused. His voice sounded old. "Without any attribution to me, I fear."

"Oh, dear."

"Indeed. I don't know who wrote the document Henry sent me, but I do recall reading that same material from my book at a symposium last summer. Henry and several of your faculty attended and I handed out copies of what I presented."

"And you believe someone on our faculty plagiarized your writing in his or her work?"

Students are not the only sinners and Henry's little note in the suitcase now made sense.

"I don't know with any certainty that the person is on your faculty, Dr. Solaris, but Henry returned the pages to me with a note across the first page that read: 'Don't worry, Al. I'll put a stop to this. My apologies, Henry.'"

"I'm sure he was devastated by this discovery," I said, trying to cover my own anger with sympathy for the aging Alistair Shaw who, I thought, must have been close to ninety.

"Yes, well, Henry did try to reach me by phone before he sent this. I guess to prepare me for it. But I was in the hospital at the time and didn't open the packet until I came home. By that time, Henry was dead."

"I hope you're all right now."

"Oh, I'm fine, Dr. Solaris. But I would be most grateful if you could follow up on this. It's so distressing to think a colleague would copy my work and not give attribution. I would, you know, be happy to allow for the quote even though it runs to several pages of my book—if the writer had just asked."

I promised Shaw I would investigate.


Fortunately, the afternoon was quieter. Nell and I got through a small mountain of forms and paper procedures.

"Nell, do you know who on the faculty is currently writing a book?"

Nell looked up, again that small glimmer of contempt in her eyes. "Who *isn't?*" she said. "I'm aware of at least three of them because they keep pestering my student assistants to make copies and mail out stuff."

"Who are they?"

Nell squinted her eyes. "Hmm. Phyllis Baker, Edwin Cartwell, George Weinstein. Weinstein's the worst of all. Treats my staff as if they were here to work exclusively for him. Oh, and Dr. Worthington sent something out yesterday, but he tends to take care of his own copying and mailing."

"How about Simon?"

Nell blew out her lower lip. "That man hasn't written anything for fifteen years."

So, four books. When would I have time to examine four books? Maybe Nell could help me with a shortcut.

"Do you remember sending out any of the manuscripts or sections of manuscripts to Dr. Alistair Shaw?" She did.

"Did you make a copy of what you sent?" She did not. The envelope was sealed when Henry gave it to her. No point in telling her more. It would just upset her and, even though Nell is discreet, I couldn't risk faculty plagiarism becoming staff gossip.

"Please call Alistair Shaw back and ask him to send me the document Dean Henry mailed to him last month. I'm going home to change for my dinner with Ben Howard. "

"Have a good time," said Nell with an unusually merry smile. "Now there's a man I really like."

"The man or his money, Nell?"

"Nothing wrong with a man being rich *and* charming," she said. "You behave yourself, hear? That man has a way about him."

Well, how about that. Our very formal Nell felt comfortable enough to tease me. Maybe I was making progress.


Kyoto is dark and elegant. The center is devoted to a large dining room, with candles lighting the soft beige tablecloths. Along three sides are booths, several with pillows and tatami mats and low tables. I hoped Howard hadn't reserved one of those booths. I was wearing my good red suit and my skirt was too tight to sit on the floor.

"Mr. Howard is waiting for you," said the slender Asian man who led me to the back of the restaurant to a set of paneled Shoji doors. I entered a small room with a round table and a round sofa curving behind the table. Thank God, no floor pillows. Ben Howard was standing beside the table. He shook my hand. A firm, warm grip. "Delighted to see you," he said.

"Mr. Howard, thank you. This looks wonderful."

"Please call me Ben. I'd like to call you Meredith. Or do you prefer Red? Wonderful nickname for you."

"Red is the name my father gave me," I said sliding onto the sofa behind the table.

His knee brushed mine as he seated himself beside me. "I trust you won't think of me as your father," he said smiling. The sofa was curved just enough so we could see into each other's face. But small enough that our knees touched.

He had ordered an expensive sake. "I hope you like this. I can order some French wine if you prefer." I love sake. Usually hot. But this one was elegant and served cool.

The food was delicious and the conversation comfortable. I liked Ben immediately. Over small dumplings stuffed with pork, he told me about his college and how he had first started his business. Over a salad of cold cooked spinach dressed in a sesame sauce, I told him about my graduate education and how Henry had promoted me to his assistant. Over sashimi and a delicate scallop dish, we talked about the special vacations we'd each taken. My favorite was to the French side of St. Martin's in the Caribbean.

As we finished the scallops, the conversation turned to the school. "I'm thinking about endowing a chair in Henry's name," Ben said.

"That's very generous, Ben. Henry would have been honored."

"Well, Henry was a very good dean in my opinion and I'd like to do something that will keep his memory fresh in the minds of your sometimes difficult faculty." He smiled. "Perhaps, if you don't become the permanent dean, you could become the first occupant of the Henry Brooks Chair in Journalism."

"Oh, I doubt I'll ever be a dean permanently," I said.

"You are much too beautiful to be that modest."

I blushed but fortunately the waiter opened the shoji paneled door to serve tea so I didn't have to reply.

When the waiter left, I felt Ben's hand on my knee, "I'd like to get to know you better, Red," he said. His voice had changed to low and intimate. I was acutely aware of his smooth tanned face. A few wrinkles surrounded dark brown eyes. I shifted away slightly but his fingers remained on my knee. Gentle but warm.

"I hope we can become friends," I said, inching further away.

"I would like us to be more than friends," he said, shifting closer on the couch. I could feel his breath close to my face and his hand was once more on my knee.

"I'm involved with someone," I said. I could feel the heat coming off his body.

"So am I," he said. "I've been married for thirty-six years."

I moved to the end of the couch.

"Red," he said, smiling and leaning his elbows on the table. "I have a condo on the beach in Mexico just south of Cancun. It's not St. Martin's but I have a jet that can get us there in four hours and, after a day or so, back in plenty of time for you to spend Christmas with whoever he is."

"I'm sorry, I can't," I said, starting to rise from the couch.

"I'm sorry, too," he said, leaning back into the couch. "I'd love to see you in a bikini." And out of one, no doubt. His voice was still low and sensual without a trace of annoyance.

"I'm sorry Mr. Howard. If this means your offer of a chair in journalism is off, I understand. But I can't be more than your friend."

"Oh, my dear Red. Of course the journalism chair offer is still good. I'm not going to punish you for turning me down. I never negotiate with women I want to sleep with."

I was sure he didn't.

He got up from the couch and took my hand in both of his and raised it to his lips.

I could still feel the heat of him. My reaction was Joe's fault. He had awakened the fire in me, and my unavoidable response to a man's mouth on the palm of my hand.

For that moment I was tempted to give in to Ben Howard, married or not. Joe or not.

"Friends?" he said, smiling.

"Friends," I said, "and thank you for dinner."

"The pleasure was mine, Dr. Solaris." He returned to my hand and his lips were hot against my palm. Once again, it produced the desired effect and he knew it. "My office will call you about the chair in journalism. Have a Merry Christmas with your man. I hope he's good to you."

Oh, he's good to me, my Joe. That's the sentence I repeated to myself all the way home, trying not to wonder what Ben's Mexican condo would look like and how Ben's strong brown hands would feel on my suntanned body. Stop it, I said to myself. Joe Morgan is the best thing that ever happened to you. Slut.

Whoever said academic deans lived lives of contemplation and scholarship? What naive observer sees us only as elderly, distinguished men and women who commune daily with brilliant faculty and spend evenings at concerts and fund-raisers? Anyone knows a proper academic dean was not supposed to resemble a sweaty redhead driving home on a snowy night with her hands gripping the wheel, tears in her eyes and too much moisture between her legs.

Damn it, Joe. Be there watching television even though you knew I was dining with another man. Be there even if you're supposed to be out investigating a lead in Henry's murder. Be there even though you have good reason not to be there.

I opened my front door and heard the sound of television and the unmistakable cadence of a sports announcer. Joe was half asleep on the couch, dressed in sweatpants and an old gray t-shirt that was too small and thus stretched across the muscles of his remarkable chest. His beautiful green eyes opened and looked up at me.

"You look a mite flushed, my dear. I must say pink cheeks suit you." His voice was low and lazy. "Everything go all right?"

I collapsed on the couch and told him everything. Everything except the kisses on my hands and my sexual thoughts driving home.

Joe's powers of observation are acute. "I think this Howard guy turned you on a little," he said, smiling. I blushed. He reached over and started unbuttoning my jacket.

"I was flattered, I admit," I said, still blushing.

"Well, I'll try not to deck him until after he's given you the chair in journalism. Especially since, whatever feelings he inspired, you were sensible enough to bring home to Papa."

And then, right there on the couch and in front of my dog, this incredibly handsome cop gave me exactly what I wanted and more than I deserved.

# Chapter 20

Christmas was at Elaine's. She set a beautiful table and her husband, Vince, made a rich, overwhelming eggnog. Sadie brought two apple pies reeking of nutmeg and cinnamon. Joe spent too much money on a Bordeaux that we all agreed was delicious and probably much too subtle for the palates we had ruined with eggnog.

We didn't talk about Henry's death, the lagging investigation, the faculty fight over Coleman, or the politics of the university.

Joe gave me a jade pendant designed by a local artist I admired and I gave him a green cashmere sweater. The rest of us exchanged books and passes to movie theaters.

Driving home with Joe, I realized I was happy. Happy as I had been when I was little and could still tell my father everything. I was happy in spite of all the troubles at the school. Joe Morgan had transformed me. I thought as we drove through the snowy streets of Landry back to my comfortable house, that I had finally found a good man and hadn't messed up. I hadn't driven him away.

Making love to Joe that night confirmed my resolve to hold onto him. Afterwards, as he slept beside me, I rose up on my elbow and stared at his sleeping face.

Merry Christmas to me.


The glow lasted through the next day and stayed with me until I walked into the office two days after Christmas. The campus was cold and deserted and the school was empty. Nell was still away visiting her children and not due back until the end of the week. The office felt chilly. I turned on the overhead lights. My desk was clean, but a large FedEx envelope from Alistair Shaw was waiting on the counter in the outer office. Beside it lay another smaller envelope with the return address of a law firm in San Francisco.

I sat at my lonely desk and felt the glow of the holiday fading away. I opened the letter first, praying it was not about Celeste, or some quirk in Henry's files.

It wasn't. The attorneys represented Ben Howard and the envelope included a short, formal note from Ben and a more detailed letter from his attorney suggesting a meeting to discuss the specifics for the Henry Brooks Chair in Journalism. Ben had been true to his word. I looked at the letter and hoped he had enjoyed a good holiday with his wife of thirty-six years and however many children and grandchildren they had. I had recovered from our dinner meeting and was convinced I was now together with Joe Morgan and not likely to betray him. Maybe I was going to grow up after all.

Howard's offer was a generous gift from a famous benefactor. I knew I would enjoy telling Stoddard and Lewis and I would truly enjoy announcing the gift to the faculty at our retreat.

Some of the Christmas glow returned and then I remembered Shaw's envelope.

The pages inside were clearly from a book. Shaw had also included pages from his own manuscript, identified by a different font from that of the plagiarized. The thief, whoever he or she was, had even copied Shaw's footnotes.

I suspected whoever had done this, had accessed Shaw's work electronically and just copied and pasted it into his or her own work. Then, the thief had changed the font to fit his or her own manuscript. A note from Shaw was scrawled on the top of his pages. "Dr. Solaris, thanks for whatever you can do to find this scoundrel. Best, Al Shaw."

Shaw's material was from a book he planned to publish next year on the decline of printed newspapers and the rise of electronic media. Alistair Shaw was nationally renowned for his writing and, chances were, his book would outsell any others. I wondered how the plagiarist intended to get away with it.

I would have to look through the manuscripts of at least four members of my faculty and, because they were all on winter break, I would have to wait until after they had returned.

Maybe there was a shortcut. I wrote a note for Nell to find upon her return. "Before he died, did Henry have any faculty manuscripts in his possession?"

And then I left the cold empty journalism building and tried to focus on my kitchen in my warm home.

A door closed down the hallway. Who was here? Everyone should be on break. The hallway was dark, just barely lit with the emergency lights that stayed on twenty-four hours. I listened. The hall was carpeted so no footsteps sounded.

A figure appeared. He stopped when he saw me and stared. He said nothing but his eyes were dark and squinted, and I was intensely aware we were alone.

"Good evening, Simon."

"Nothing good about it, missy."

I walked to the elevator and glanced at the stairwell opposite. I hated that stairwell but the exit route might be safer.

I hesitated. Simon's bent figure moved toward me.

We stood probably two feet apart. His head jutted out from between his shoulders. His hands were clenched into fists, his thumbs moving across the knuckles of his forefingers. His mouth curved in a sneer and I could hear his breathing, heavy and uneven.

"I hope you had a good Christmas, Simon."

"I don't celebrate Christmas." His voice was low and menacing. "It's pretentious for anyone with half a brain to believe in it."

I stood silent, wondering if I could just walk past him.

"But then of course, you are pretentious aren't you, Solaris? An incompetent woman pretending to be a dean." His eyes flared.

"That's enough, Simon. I think we should both go home."

"You should go home, Solaris. Leave Nevada and go back to whatever shithole town you come from."

I froze.

I was sure he had written the note and was about to challenge him when he made a sudden turn and headed to the stairwell.

His footsteps were slow on the concrete stairs, the same stairs that had held Henry's body. I waited until the sound faded. Then I pushed the elevator button.

I took out my keys and thrust them between my fingers to form a weapon. I was ready for him. When the doors opened on the ground floor I expected to see Simon waiting for me.

But the atrium was empty. And mine was the only car in the parking lot.

Joe showed up two hours after I got home. He was excited about a small break in his investigation of Henry's death, so I decided to put off telling him about meeting Simon until after I heard his news.

The police had found a witness who saw a man crossing the parking lot early that Sunday afternoon. The new witness was a groundskeeper who had gone home with the flu and stayed home for a week. He remembered he'd seen a man late that afternoon. The groundskeeper was far down on the list of people to question and, when his illness kept him absent, the policeman checking grounds employees, never went back to the university office where the groundskeepers work.

Someone gossiping about the possible murder of the dean of journalism jogged the groundskeeper's memory and he called the police.

"So, we know now that someone besides Edwin Cartwell may have been in that building the afternoon Henry died."

We were sitting in front of the fire in my living room waiting for the stew to finish up in the kitchen.

"Any idea who the man was?"

"Not yet, but the groundskeeper said he was tall and he walked quickly. He didn't see the man's face, but he's quite sure the guy went into the journalism school by way of the side door."

"That's the way you get into the school on a Sunday when the rest of the building is locked."

"I know," said Joe, "but doesn't that also mean the tall man was a faculty member with a building key card?"

"Probably, but I can think of three tall male faculty—George Weinstein, Max Worthington, plus one adjunct male faculty. But adjuncts don't have key cards. Did the groundskeeper say any more?"

"No, he couldn't see anything but the back of the man. And the guy was dressed for winter and wearing a cap and gloves."

I got up and went into the kitchen to stir the stew. Charlie followed at my heels.

The image of Simon in the hallway flashed. I still hadn't told Joe about my encounter, but I certainly couldn't describe Simon as tall or a man who walks quickly. He didn't fit the description. Much as I would have liked it if he did.

Joe came into the kitchen. "Anyone outside of faculty who might have access to a campus building. An administrator or a janitor?"

"Our janitor is a woman." I tasted the stew. It wanted more salt.

"As for non-faculty, I'm sure there are a number of people who can access a university building for emergency reasons or maintenance work. Not to mention the people in the offices of the president and provost."

"Stoddard's a big tall guy," said Joe. Hmm. But what would have been Stoddard's motive? I wandered into the living room to collect our wine glasses.

"Do any of the faculty stay home on winter break like you do?" Joe was, at this point, setting the kitchen table.

"Some do," I said. "But I'll bet Weinstein goes south for some warm weather and golf. I know Max and Trudy were planning on visiting her parents. The others might be home but no guarantees. I'm only here because you couldn't get away and go to the Caribbean with me."

He kissed my cheek. "I thought work was your reason for hanging around."

Work was my reason, but it came in second. I had been daydreaming about Joe sitting with me on a beach in St. Martin's ever since my dinner with Ben Howard.

After dinner, Joe got on his phone to provide the names of possible tall and murderous men to another detective. He was visibly cheered up. At last, a break in the case after all these weeks of dead ends. The last time he had spoken of the investigation he had looked so frustrated. "We just can't get any hard evidence on anyone. The captain seems ready to dissolve my team and put us all on other cases."

"Can you give up on a possible murder?" I had asked. "You told me cases like this are only solved quickly on television."

That elicited a wry smile. "I remember. No, we won't give up entirely, but the problem is that, until today, the trail was getting cold."

At last, there was new evidence. A tall man. I eavesdropped on Joe's call for another minute and then went back to the living room. Telling him about Simon would come later. Joe was happy and I was safe at home.

For that night anyway.


I turned my attention to the folders from the suitcase Michael Brooks had given me. Most of what I found were more evaluations of various faculty. Nell had looked for Phyllis and Max's folders, found one for Phyllis but not for Max. She would have to make a new one. Had he lived, Henry would've scheduled meetings with all of us to go over our annual evaluations and tell us whether we were going to get merit raises. Would a bad evaluation have occasioned a fight, even a murder?

I focused on the papers before me and promised myself to read through more files tomorrow in the office.

Edwin Cartwell's self-evaluation was full of self-congratulations about his teaching, his strong suit. He wrote a number of defensive paragraphs about his last book and prophesied a home run with his next effort. Edwin's book was another historical effort and, although I did not yet have access to his manuscript, I doubted it would include the plagiarized text from Alistair Shaw.

Henry's evaluation of Edwin was still in draft form for Nell to type up and was generally flattering. Henry, you devious bastard. Edwin would get a good raise this year even as you stole his wife.

George Weinstein's self-evaluation was similar but longer. He may have been an editor in his past, but as an academic, the man could not write a short sentence. There was no mention of a book. Interesting. Odd. If George were writing a book, surely he would have included a reference to it.

I wasn't having any more luck tracking down my plagiarist than Joe was tracking down a tall male murder suspect. Too many people, too little evidence.

# Chapter 21

And then, as if we were all living in a movie, there was another unusual death.

On the second page of *The New York Times* was a story about Alistair Shaw. He'd been found dead in his living room in North Carolina. In spite of the professor's age, the local police suspected Shaw had not died of natural causes. The speculation was that he died of a possible drug overdose.

As Joe was quick to point out, if it hadn't been for my conversation and correspondence, neither of us would have connected the unusual death of a ninety-year-old professor in the southeast with the unusual death of a dean in the mountain west.

But we did, staring at each other across my table, silently putting the two events together. Shaw's death had taken place while all the universities were on break and our faculty members were free to travel anywhere. Was there a connection between the plagiarism, Shaw's overdose, and Henry's fall down the stairs?

"This makes matters more complicated," Joe said, and left for police headquarters to contact a source in North Carolina. I headed to my office at school.

"Happy holidays," I said to Nell as I walked to my office. As usual she was there before I was. I was glad to see her serious face again. It was lonely in the school without another person.

"I don't know how happy it's going to be," said Nell, looking glum. "Edwin Cartwell is in his office and wants to see you."

I pondered going down the hall to Edwin's office, but then decided it would be nice to summon him to mine.

"Hi, Edwin," I said when he arrived, without looking up from my desk.

Edwin sat in one of the chairs facing my desk. "Has Coleman withdrawn his grievance?"

"I hope so. But I haven't seen Larry since before Christmas."

"It's important he do so," said Edwin. "We can't afford the possibility of a new scandal or to have the school considered for receivership."

"Delighted you have developed some concern for the welfare of the school," I said. This time I did look straight at him.

"That's not fair, Meredith. I have always put the interests of the school first."

"How's your new book coming, Edwin?" I asked, hoping to befuddle him. It worked. He looked bewildered.

"It's fine," he mumbled.

"Any chance I could take a look at it?"

"Well, I suppose...it's not finished. I just have a few chapters so far."

"Great," I said, rising from my desk. "I'll walk you back to your office."

Edwin continued to look confused as we headed down the hall. "I'm trying to finish up Henry's annual evaluations and you made reference to your new book in your self-evaluation. It would help me to see what you've done so far."

"Well, if it would help," he said. He unlocked his office door and went to the bookcase behind his computer desk and pulled down a cardboard manuscript box. He opened the box and handed it to me.

"May I borrow this for a few hours, Edwin?"

"Well, I was going to do some work on it today. That's why I'm here." He studied me carefully. Suspicion glinted in his eyes.

"Oh, I thought you came in to find out if Coleman was still filing a grievance," I said. "But, if you could let me read through the introduction and some of the chapters, I'll bring them back later today."

It was evident Edwin was perplexed by my request, but he was also aware that I was now in charge of his evaluation and merit raise. He pulled about twenty pages out of the box and handed it to me.

"I haven't written an introduction yet, and I'm not sure this will be the first chapter, but read this if you like."

I took the pages. Practicing cheerfulness, I said, "Thanks, Edwin. I'll get this back to you as soon as I can, so you can work on it today."

Edwin's book was about nineteenth century journalists. His method of storytelling was windy and he wrote much of it in the passive voice.

In contrast, Alistair Shaw's writing was active and vivid. It seemed unlikely that Edwin would have had any reason to paste Shaw's discussion of new media into his book. The topic was wrong, the style was much too different and so was the font.

Edwin Cartwell was not the plagiarist.

Joe's source on the police force in Chapel Hill, North Carolina came up empty handed. There was nothing in Shaw's home or the forensic evidence that pointed to one of our faculty having been anywhere near the place.

Turns out Shaw had been suffering with terminal cancer and had, indeed, died of an overdose of potassium. The Chapel Hill police said it was a confirmed suicide albeit a painful death for a nice old man.

"I've instructed our guys to send the police in Chapel Hill all the relevant fingerprints we picked up here at the school plus photos of the faculty. And, I'm sorry...I know you wanted to keep a lid on this, but I did have to tell the chief about the plagiarism and the notes between Henry and Shaw."

I told him about my meeting with Edwin and gave him a copy of the twenty pages I had made while they were in my possession. "I guess he's not your plagiarist."

"I hope you're right about that. And, Red," his face was very serious and his hands were on my shoulders, "I am grateful for your help with the academic information on this case, but remember I don't want you putting yourself in jeopardy. Anything that pertains to actual evidence in the Henry Brooks case or the Shaw case, you leave to me, all right?"

"Copy that, Detective."

"I'm dead serious about this," he said. "I love your help when you're with me. But I worry about what you might do on your own."

"Joe, I'm not doing anything dangerous. I'm examining manuscripts for plagiarism. That's a legitimate activity for an academic. If no one had died, you wouldn't even be involved."

He leaned in and kissed me, a little harder than usual. "I couldn't stand it if anything happened to you."

The following night, Joe came to my house late, but this time with news about Simon. "We found out where Simon was the day Henry died. And I'm afraid our nasty Dr. Gorshak has an airtight alibi."

I pulled up a kitchen chair and waited.

"It seems," he began, "Simon was in Buffalo, New York that weekend."

"Buffalo? Was he seeing Doris?"

"Sort of. I've been trying to track her down or find her brother, but no luck, until this afternoon. I got a call from a buddy on the Syracuse police force who'd read a general email I sent out, looking for people named Gorshak or Jacoby, which was Doris Gorshak's maiden name. Seems a David Jacoby had been the victim of a hit and run in Syracuse in December. My friend tracked him down to a Syracuse hospital, but didn't interview him until yesterday."

"Jesus. And I thought academics moved slowly."

"Give 'em a break, babe. Syracuse is a big city. Their cops have too many cases and one inquiry from an old buddy in Nevada does not exactly rise to the top of the list."

"So how does Jacoby in Syracuse put Simon in Buffalo?"

"Because, before he was hit by a car, David Jacoby had been in Buffalo and saw Simon Gorshak at a memorial."

"On a Sunday? Whose memorial?"

"Doris Gorshak's. She died. Her brother held a small memorial at his home in Buffalo and her cousin David attended and spoke to Simon. He is absolutely certain about the date and that gives Simon his alibi."

"Wow. You took your time getting to the point."

"I'm training you to be a good detective," said Joe with a smile. "One thread at a time."

My Joe. What a beautiful pain in the ass. He looked particularly attractive in the sweater I gave him for Christmas.

"So, Mr. Master Detective, how did poor Doris die?"

"The cousin was vague, but I gather she was in rehab and had been in bad shape for a long time."

"And her dumped ex-husband went all the way to freezing cold Buffalo, New York in mid-winter to mourn her?"

"We've never found any record of a divorce here or in New York." Joe looked solemn. "Maybe he still loved her."

Maybe he did. But the Simon I had encountered in the hallway didn't seem the loving type.

"So, you think I should stop thinking Simon killed Henry and that I might be next."

Joe got up and came over and put his arms around me and his head next to mine. "Probably," he said into my ear. "But we still have to find the tall man who was seen entering the building that Sunday. So be careful of tall men. Okay?"

"Except for you. Right?"

His tongue caressed the edge of my ear and his hands moved down my back, slowly and suggestively. With this kind of foreplay, how was I supposed to concentrate on a murder case? Or a case of plagiarism?

"I need a few minutes to make a phone call," I said, pushing him toward the kitchen.

"A few minutes are all you get."

I pulled away from his seductiveness. I needed to call Phyllis at home. The final edit of Phyllis Baker's book had already gone to her publisher and was due out in three months. Phyllis was an expert on electronic journalism design and I knew I would have to check it out. I called her.

"I'm flattered you want to read my book." Her warm voice still carried a slight trace of her Nigerian birthplace. "I wouldn't have figured you for a fan of this stuff. You sure you don't want to wait for a published copy rather than reading an electronic version on your computer?"

I felt a twinge of guilt for even suspecting her of plagiarism but I had to be thorough. And I had to lie to a good friend. "I wish I could wait, Phyl, but I need to look at it to complete Henry's annual evaluation."

"Hmm. Henry saw the first draft last year. Not that much has changed." Phyllis' voice was a little flatter.

"Yes, I know, but his notes are incomplete. Do you mind sending it?"

"Happy to oblige, Red. I guess it will be nice to know what you think of it anyway."

I felt guilty. Phyllis was my good friend on the faculty—as supportive as Max and, in some ways, closer. Phyllis knew more of my secrets. We didn't see much of each other socially, but, before I became dean, not a day went by that we didn't exchange some observations about what was going on. She had been a stalwart ally since I became dean and I knew I could count on her.

Once, at a cocktail party we were enduring together, she told me she and her husband had a special needs child. Would a good woman with a sick child have had reason to steal? If she got caught, would she kill? My mind rejected the questions.

# Chapter 22

Simon came to my office the day after the New Year's weekend.

"Your cop came to see me this morning—interrupted my breakfast." Simon spoke with his usual sneer.

"Did he?" I pretended to be involved with paperwork on my desk.

Simon moved from the doorway to the front of my desk and tapped his bony fingers on my paperwork. His closeness was alarming. "I told you not to meddle in my affairs."

"I haven't," I said without looking up.

"Well, call off your dog then. I don't need your cop calling my wife's relatives and messing around with my family business."

That got me to look up at him. He was still too close to me. I wanted to say "sorry for your loss." But with Joe's warnings in mind, I said, "Simon, he's not my cop and Detective Morgan is— along with a lot of other police—investigating the possible murder of our dean. He has to check out everyone who had access to this building. And that includes you."

"I warned you, Meredith. I warned you that I would cause serious trouble for you if you didn't stay out of my business." There was a look in his eyes that made me want to call Joe right away. I reached for the phone. Simon left before Joe answered.

I waited a minute to be sure Simon was gone. "Joe, Simon was just here and quite threatening. Is there any chance he might have hired someone to kill Henry and then gone to Buffalo to set up an alibi?"

There was a long silence.

"It's possible," said Joe. "But his financial records don't suggest he had enough money to hire a killer."

"But, Joe, remember he was arguing with someone on the phone the other day when I went to his office. He mentioned sending a check."

"One doesn't usually pay hired killers by check," said Joe. "And the records we now have on Simon suggest he spent every dime, including all his retirement fund on Doris. He still owes the Buffalo people."

"Which is why he refuses to retire. But he still terrifies me."

"Me, too. Just stay away from him and hope we can get better forensic evidence to nail this case down."

Faculty retreats are held by departments of colleges and universities all over the country. Usually scheduled to occur during winter break before school reopens, the purpose of the retreat is to give the faculty a full day to plan next steps in the growth and future of the department or college. Retreats are good times to air complex issues like our dispute about the curriculum.

Our January retreat was due to begin at 9:00 a.m. and last until 5:00 p.m. I had rented the large private room at Gormley's.

Wilson's almost smiling face met me at the door at 8:45. "Coffee's ready," he said. "Want a shot in it before the others get here?"

"Thanks, pal. I think I'll try to stay sober at least until noon," I said, heading into the private room. "What did you decide on for lunch?"

"Salad, fried chicken, oatmeal cookies," he said, following me into the room. "I considered roast beef but decided red meat would be inappropriate for this gang."

"Wilson, you know too much about academics for a restaurateur."

"I've had years to observe the species." He turned to leave the room, then added, "I'm bringing in fruit, yogurt, and bran muffins for breakfast. At least the faculty colons will be relatively healthy even if their reasoning is clogged."

"That man has an evil streak," said Nell, who was busy putting copies of the agenda in front of each place at the U-shaped table.

"Why do you think I keep coming here?"

I examined the screen and hoped Phyllis and Larry would arrive a few minutes early to set up their presentation on new media courses ideas for our curriculum.

George Weinstein was the first to arrive. He was dressed in a heavy parka and a fur hat.

"Good holiday, George?" I asked, meeting him at the coat rack. I noticed he had a deep tan.

"Good to get away from all this," he said.

"George, may I ask a favor?"

"As long as it doesn't involve anything about Larry Coleman," he said, removing his parka. "Or about putting our school into receivership."

"It's not about Larry. I'd like to see a copy of your book."

He turned to look at me. "Why, Meredith? What's piqued your interest in old newsroom issues?"

He loomed over me. George tends to stand too close to people, especially those who are shorter than he is. It was 8:45 in the morning but, from the smell of his breath, I was sure George had been drinking.

"Well, George." I steadied myself for the fiction that had seemed to work on Edwin. "I am in the midst of finishing up Henry's evaluations and trying to learn as much as I can about each faculty member's productivity. That means looking at any books written last year."

George frowned. "Well, not much point looking at mine. I withdrew it from publication last fall. Cretins at the publishers wanted too many changes."

I tried again. "Nonetheless, George, it represents a large part of your creative output last year, and I should take a look at it. You can just email it to me."

"I deleted it from my hard drive. It took up too much memory. But I have a printed version. If you really need to see it, I'll bring it in tomorrow." He gave a conspicuous sigh of annoyance and sank into a chair at the table.

With books from George and Phyllis, I would have only Max Worthington's left to consider. I knew Max was writing about television network websites and online coverage of breaking news. Close to Shaw's topic, but I hated to think Max would steal anything. Max may have been a fool about Celeste, but he was too good a writer and much too proud to plagiarize.

Had I missed anyone? Was there another member of the faculty working on a manuscript?

Several faculty members came in at once and the noise reminded me that the retreat was dedicated to the hopes of the future, not the sins of the past. Henry had been dead for two months. It was time to move on. I began the meeting with a cheerful grin and an announcement of the gift from Ben Howard.

Max opened the meeting with a slide:

*The number of working daily journalists has already shrunk roughly 30-35% in the last five years, and will likely go down at least another 10-15%. That's half the labor force.*

Max paused to let the reality sink in and then turned the front of the room over to Larry and Phyllis who spoke clearly and with enthusiasm about the need for students to have access to online publishing and the exploration of new ways to present the news, verbally and visually, online and on air. Despite the occasional grunt from George, no one interrupted and the rest of the faculty seemed engaged and interested. Several applauded at the end of Larry's plea for new courses and Phyllis's for new equipment. Others smiled and nodded. And to my complete surprise, no one, including the three antagonists, took issue with the recommendations.

As we broke for lunch, Edwin sat with his chin in his hand. George joined Simon in the corner where they spoke quietly together. The rest of the faculty congratulated Larry and Phyllis on the presentation and piled on the fried chicken from the buffet table.

I followed Max outside for a breath of fresh, cold air. I was hoping to see some sign he had recovered from our last conversation about Celeste.

"Not bad, chief," he said, stuffing his hands into his pockets. "I expected a food fight from the three musketeers, but they seemed to have learned some manners over the break."

I felt relieved. He seemed friendly again and I realized how much Max's friendship meant to me. "We still have the afternoon discussion ahead," I said.

"You know about wounded water buffalo?"

"No, but I'm sure I am about to learn."

"The story's told by big game hunters. They say the most dangerous animal in the world is a wounded water buffalo. Most dangerous because, if you shoot and just wound the buffalo, the animal will seem to run away. But actually he just runs into the bush where he waits. The buffalo will track you for days, following your trail, and, when you least expect it, he'll charge out of the brush and attack. He'll try to gore you to death."

I smiled up at Max. He looked ruddy and handsome in his scarf and camel's hair coat. His blue eyes sparkled. No wonder female students found him so irresistible.

"So I should be prepared for three wounded water buffalo?"

"Your leadership skills could get a good workout this afternoon."

It wasn't like Max to try to alarm me. But, since my scolding about Celeste, I supposed he was still annoyed with me underneath all his cordiality.

"Hey, are we still friends?" I asked.

Max took my face in his cold hands and kissed my forehead. "Of course we're still friends." His eyes were large and his expression soft. "You know, for all my stupid fooling around, you and Trudy are the only women I really love."

Then, he turned to go inside.

"Max, one more thing," I said. "Could I see the manuscript for the book you just finished?"

Max put his hands up to his face to blow on his fingers. I couldn't see his expression, but, after a moment he said, "I heard you were asking for faculty manuscripts. What's up?"

For a moment I wished I could confide my reasons to Max, who was smart and could help me figure things out. But I stuck with the story about needing to see work for purposes of evaluating.

"Well, I sent off the final version last month before break. But, I think most of it is still on the drive. Could I send it tomorrow?"

"Tomorrow's perfect."

Max looked quizzical for a moment, then turned to go inside. "You better get something to eat, Red. I'm counting on a victory today, you know."

As I said goodbye to the last faculty to leave the retreat, Wilson met me and offered me a Pinot Noir "on the house." I smiled a refusal and went straight to my car.

Joe met me at the door, also with a glass of Pinot. "I see I am gaining a reputation as a wino," I said, dropping my coat on the back of the couch and collapsing into the armchair in front of the fire.

"How did it go?"

"Not bad. In fact, better than I expected. Simon was irascible, of course. George worried out loud about traditional benefactors from the industry losing interest in us if we 'went too radical,' as he put it. Edwin was unusually quiet and, when he spoke, surprisingly civil to Larry and Phyllis."

"And the others?"

"The others were positive. I really didn't have as much refereeing to do as I anticipated."

"How did it end?"

"Better than I had hoped. Max called for a vote to approve the recommendations and most of the faculty voted yes. The usual suspects did not vote no. They abstained...a bit of a shock, but better than another awful fight."

"A fight was what you were expecting?"

"That's what I was expecting. But I guess the threat of being put into receivership made the pit vipers calm down. And, while there may be some rough sledding ahead, I think I might even call this retreat an advance."

"You don't think the three of them are up to something, do you?"

"Shit. I hope not." I started to tell Joe the story about the water buffalo, but he stopped me midway.

"I know the story. And it's not just a story. It's been known to happen."

The announcement of the new Henry Brooks Chair in Journalism was held in the large auditorium of the Liberal Arts College next door. Phil Lewis beamed and Stoddard looked sunnier than I had seen him for weeks. Ben Howard made a brief appearance to talk about his friendship with Henry.

Michael Brooks made a special trip out for the occasion. As they walked to the door, I followed. "Thank you so much, Mr. Howard," I said. "And, Michael, it was great you could come."

Both men turned. Ben stopped, put his arms around me and gave me a bear hug and a kiss on the cheek. Michael smiled and gave me a gentler hug.

"Don't you think this gorgeous woman should become the first Brooks Chair?" Ben asked of Michael. Michael grinned agreement.

"A fitting tribute to my father," he said.

Sadie was at our usual table at Gormley's, reading, when I arrived for lunch.

"Good news about the gift of a chair," she said. "My spies tell me your retreat went well and no bombs went off."

"No bombs. The combatants treated each other with restraint if not respect and we got some good work done."

"So is all calm and sunny at the j-school?" she asked.

"Not really," I answered, "I have a new problem. A challenge, as they say."

"It never lets up," she said.

Over lunch I told Sadie about my conversations with Alistair Shaw and my plagiarism hunt.

"Is there no limit to the wickedness of the journalism faculty?" Sadie shook her head. "Do you need any help? I'm good at tracking literary thieves."

"I am dedicating the weekend to checking manuscripts electronically and reading through George's print copy."

"And Max Worthington's?"

"He hasn't sent his in yet, but I reminded him today and he promised to get it to me."

Sadie made good on her offer and came over on Saturday to go through both manuscripts. As I supposed, Phyllis' text had nothing to do with Shaw's. I called Phyllis that afternoon. "Your book knocked my socks off."

"I'm glad you enjoyed it," she said. "But I'm still not sure why you had to bother with it. Henry and I must have had two or three discussions about it before he died."

"I know, but I'm the one who has to complete your evaluation, so it was good for me to see it, too."

"How are you doing, sweetie?" Phyllis' kind voice almost made my eyes water.

"Some days are better than others but, most of the time, I don't feel I am getting anywhere at all."

"Isn't that typical progress for The Red Queen?"

I smiled. "Indeed, as the old girl said, it takes all the running you can do to keep in the same place."

"Hmm. A good metaphor for hard-working academics."

*   *   *

Sadie had taken on George's printed manuscript. We had agreed I would probably be less objective and more inclined to look for reason to believe George was our guilty plagiarist.

After an hour of reading, she looked up and grunted. "What drivel. This Weinstein is a dreadfully boring writer and not an inspired thinker. How did he ever get tenured?"

"He was close to the old dean, Simon Gorshak. Also, he's a genuinely good teacher. His students are crazy about him."

"Humph," said the former dean of liberal arts. "I haven't found anything plagiarized yet."

She was about a third of the way through George's manuscript. I picked up some of the remaining pages and started reading.

"Yuk. I see what you mean." George claimed to have fired his publisher because the editors bugged him about changes. No wonder. I wanted to write his editors a thank you note for saving the world from a truly tedious read.

I did find a few lines from Shaw, but George had put quotation marks around them and attributed fully on the page and in his endnotes.

"Much as I would like an excuse to hang George Weinstein by his thumbs, I don't think he's our villain," I said, after a run through the last third of his book.

"He can't get a merit raise for this work," said Sadie.

"No, but he'll get a compliment for teaching and a comment about how we hope to see a more productive next year in his evaluation."

"How will he react to that?"

"He'll be hurt. He'll be angry. He'll be loud. And, then he'll stomp off to figure out how to get even with me."

# Chapter 23

The Tuesday after Martin Luther King Jr.'s birthday was the first day of spring semester and a whirlwind of students trying to get into classes that were full, and faculty trying to get their syllabi copied by Nell's harried assistant. The copier broke down at eleven and the phones went out of order at noon. Nell's gray curls were a shambles by the end of the day. Her frantic tugging at her hair just made matters worse and she gave up on her comb. Promptly at five, she smashed a cap on her head and left.

I forgot to ask her if Max had said anything about emailing his manuscript. Her office was locked and I decided the hell with it.

Normally, I taught three courses in the spring, but this semester, Stoddard and I agreed I would devote all my time to managing the school. So, no ethics course, no students to brighten my day. On the way home, I recalled what Henry had said: management was "money and people, people and money" all day long. Although, unlike Henry, at least I did have a new curriculum to design with the faculty and an accreditation report to start.

Absorbed in the tasks ahead, I did not notice a strange car in my driveway until I pulled even with it. It was empty and I knew Joe was working late on a new case. I approached the front door with caution.

She was sitting in a corner of the front porch, her knees drawn up to her chest and her head down. Asleep or weeping or just resting, I could not tell. She wore a knitted wool hat, a parka, mittens, and heavy lined boots.

"Hello?"

Celeste Cummings lifted her head. Her pretty face was thin and pale. She wore no make-up.

"Hi, Dean Solaris. I hope you don't mind my coming to your home." She pushed off the floor of the porch and rose to her feet, dusting off her parka.

"I don't mind, Celeste. How are you doing?"

"Much better. I'm stronger and I'm in counseling for alcohol and other stuff."

I opened the front door. "You must be cold. Come in and get warm." She preceded me through the door. Charlie barked but came over to her and let her scratch his ears. She took off her gloves and hat and tugged at the snaps on her parka. She did not resemble the beautiful girl I had seen in my office, but she was healthier than the girl I'd seen in the hospital. She had lost weight. Her blonde hair had been cut short and framed her face. She looked much younger and so fragile. I looked away. I busied myself with starting a fire in the fireplace, I asked her to sit down and offered her tea. She seemed grateful to be given a moment to herself while I went into the kitchen.

"I'm just going to put on the kettle and feed the dog," I called from the darkened kitchen.

No answer.

When I returned with the tea, she was sitting, this time on the floor in front of the fire, her knees once more up against her chest.

Her thank you came in a whisper and the hand she extended for the mug of tea was trembling.

"I need to talk to you about something," she said.

"By all means."

"It's something you are not gonna want to hear, but my therapist says I probably should talk to you."

"Please go on and don't worry about whether or not I like hearing things. I was in therapy myself when I was your age and I know these processes are important."

She stared at her mug, took a sip and a deep breath.

"I'm sorry I called you a bitch."

"Apology accepted."

The firelight flickered across her face. Her skin was so transparent I could see a blood vessel throbbing at her temple. "I really want to go back to school, Dean Solaris. I am supposed to graduate this June."

I leaned down from my chair and put my hand on her shoulder. "I can't put you back into journalism, Celeste, but I will help you apply to another college for another major. With luck and good behavior, perhaps you can graduate."

"Thank you." She sniffed and reached for a tissue in her pocket. "I think I could get a degree in history. History was my minor and I think I could earn enough credits to graduate in another year and a half."

I reached for her shoulder and felt her bones through her sweater. Sympathy filled me. "I know the chair of history and I'll be glad to talk to him. But, I have to ask, any plagiarism or cheating problems in history?"

A wan smile. "No, Dean Solaris. I was a good girl in history. I enjoyed the classes and I did well."

"History is a solid major, Celeste. I'll make a call on your behalf." I sat back in my chair. It wasn't just her pitiable appearance that touched me. I identified with Celeste. I wanted to help this young woman who drank too much and got into trouble. I almost wished I could let her back in journalism, but then I would have had to deal with the irony of tracking a plagiarist on my faculty while forgiving one of my students for the same sin.

"There's something else," she said. "I have to get rid of Max and I need your help."

Puzzling. "What do you mean get rid of Max? Just avoid him."

She looked away and into the fire. "Max called me the night before last. He pretended to be some other professor calling about a sick student. He talked in a kind of code. I guess in case he thought my parents might be listening on an extension."

"I'm not sure I understand this. Why would Max call you at all? He assured me what happened was over and done with."

"I'm not sure it's ever going to be over with me and Max," she said. Her expression was tragic.

"Maybe you better tell me more about you and Max. I only have his side of the story and your father's accusation to go on."

She drew her knees up tighter under her chin.

"It started last September," she began.

"Last September?" I interrupted. That was much earlier than Max had indicated. "Maybe you'd better tell me the whole story."

"It was about the third week of school," she said, "and I went to his office to ask about an assignment I'd missed. It was one of those warm September days, so I was just wearing a t-shirt and a short skirt and—I'm sorry—I wasn't wearing a bra. I know I should dress more appropriately to go see faculty, but I was trying to get a boy's attention in class and usually no bra works."

"I can imagine."

"Anyway, I could tell by the way Max kept looking at my breasts that I was turning him on. And since he's nice and great looking I sat there and let him get turned on."

She took another sip of tea, got up and sat in the chair opposite mine.

"When I stood up to leave, he stood up too and I could see he had a...he was, you know, excited. He asked me not to leave and then he closed his office door and locked it. At that point, I got a little scared, because I let things go too far and I wasn't sure I wanted sex with him. I think I just liked the idea of turning him on."

"What happened next?" I remembered Max's story.

"Specifically?"

"Afraid so."

"Specifically, he picked me up, carried me over to the couch. Then he lifted my t-shirt and...kissed my breasts. Then he put his hand up my skirt and..."

"Okay. I think I get the picture," I said. I got up and paced the floor. "Max told me you had started this affair by performing oral sex on him one day in his office."

"I did. The second time I went to see him. The first time we had sex on his couch."

I looked back at Celeste. Her anxious eyes followed me.

"How often did you have sex with Max?" I tried to sound gentle and not too judgmental.

"All the time, Dean Solaris." She cocked her head to one side and closed her eyes. "At first, we had sex in his office, but then he got worried we'd get caught, so we used to meet at a motel on Grant Street."

"How many times a week?" My hands closed into fists.

"Three or four times a week—early in the morning before class or late afternoon before he went home. Sometimes, he'd sneak out on Sundays. Those times we went to his office because no one was in the building."

In the building? Sundays? "Did you ever get caught on a Sunday?" I could feel my fingernails digging into my palms.

"Never. Until I was expelled and went home and told my dad, no one ever knew anything about Max and me. We were crazy in love but we were still very careful. He was worried about Trudy, I mean Mrs. Worthington, finding out before she had the baby."

"Was she supposed to find out *after* she had the baby?" I collapsed back into my chair. How could Max have been so manipulative?

Celeste looked unhappy. "I'm not sure," she said quietly. "Max never promised me anything. He just said he adored me and I was the most exciting woman he had ever known. But he really didn't want his wife to get upset and have a miscarriage or anything."

"And you were all right with this arrangement?" Of course she had been all right with it. Max was so handsome, so smooth, so convincing. Damn him for what he had done to this girl.

"I had never had a guy as good at sex as Max. Never." Celeste stood up. "Dean Solaris, I know you're going to hate me for this, but one of the reasons I'm scared to go back to school is starting up again with Max."

"Am I supposed to talk you out of seeing him?"

"No. I thought maybe you could talk him out of seeing me. Or even calling me. You're his boss, aren't you?"

Celeste's request seemed extraordinary. I would have to think about this. I wanted to say yes to her sad little face, but I dreaded talking to Max now that I knew more about the affair. I needed time to think and get over my disgust.

And the girl looked starved.

"Hungry, Celeste?"

"No thanks, Dean Solaris," she said.

"Well I am. We'll have to finish this conversation in the kitchen."

Celeste followed me into the kitchen and sat in one of the kitchen chairs. I rummaged through the refrigerator and found some of Joe's lasagna. Celeste watched wordlessly as I scooped the lasagna into a glass dish and put it into the microwave. Avoiding the red wine clearly visible on the kitchen counter, I poured myself a glass of milk. Charlie came over to Celeste's side and nuzzled her knees. She patted him absentmindedly.

It was nearly eight o'clock when I dished up the warm lasagna, offered her a plate which she refused, and sat down at the table. I thought Joe was probably having a pizza with his buddies. Celeste clutched at her tea mug and patted Charlie, averting her eyes as if giving me some privacy to eat.

At length she said," Dean Solaris, do you think you could talk Max out of seeing me?"

"I don't know, Celeste. You said you were crazy in love. Was that just you or is Max in love, too?"

"I don't know about Max. I know when he called me night before last he was telling me in code to be at the motel tonight."

"Were you?"

"No. I came over here. I didn't think he'd look for me here."

"How did he tell you in code?"

Celeste shifted in her chair, perhaps ashamed to be revealing so many of her lover's secrets. "He said something like, I'd like to continue the conversation we started on Grant Street," she said.

"If you had the will to come over here instead of meeting him at the motel, why do you need me? Why can't you tell him it's over and you don't want to see him anymore? Tell him he's part of the reason you drank so much."

"He was part of the reason. I mean I drank before Max but, when I couldn't be with him, when I thought about him home with his wife, I would go crazy and head for the nearest bar."

"What about Thad? Couldn't you talk to him?"

"Thad was sort of a cover story for Max and me. Max said I should have a boyfriend, just in case people got suspicious. So, I slept with Thad a few times, but he was never important to me and he certainly wasn't a substitute for Max. With Max it was always fireworks and..." she shuddered, "and that's why I need you to make Max leave me alone, to tell him he can't just walk up to me on campus, he has to keep away. Honestly, Dean Solaris, if he starts after me again, I'll melt. I'll give in." Tears appeared and I went to the counter for a box of tissues.

Celeste sobbed, "I'm so in love with him, Dean Solaris. I have no resistance to him."

I gathered her in my arms where her sobbing increased. Charlie got up and went to the front door. I heard a car door slam shut. I expected to hear Joe open the kitchen door but, instead, the front doorbell rang.

I looked out the front window. Max Worthington was standing on my doorstep. "Stay in the kitchen and close the door," I said to Celeste.

I opened the front door a few inches. Max put one hand and his foot into the opening. "I'm sorry Max. Now is not a good time for a visit. I have someone here."

"I know," he said through his teeth. "Someone I need to talk to."

"Not now, Max. This is not the time."

His face was full of pain. "Red, I've been driving all over town looking for her. I just now saw her car in your driveway. I need to see her, just for a minute."

"Not now, Max. We'll talk tomorrow."

His eyes were moist and his breath was labored as if he had been running.

"Please, Red," his other hand was on the edge of the door, pushing. Max is a big man and I wasn't sure I could keep him out of the house.

Another car pulled up in front of the house. I could see Joe get out and head across the lawn. He was hurrying.

"Max, you have to leave," I insisted pushing against the inside of the door.

"I can't leave, Red. Not without talking to her."

With one shove, Max was inside the entry hall. Joe was right behind him. "What's going on?" I heard Joe ask. Max turned away from me to Joe.

"I need to see Red's visitor," he said. Sweat was streaming down his face.

"Red?" Joe asked, searching my face for clues.

"Celeste Cummings is here, Joe, and this is not a good time for Max to see her."

"Please," Max shouted. "Celeste, honey."

But there was no movement from behind the kitchen door.

"Let me help you to your car, Dr. Worthington," Joe said, taking Max's arm.

Max shook him off and stumbled out to the front step.

"I'll remember this the next time you need me to support you in something, Red. I'll remember. You can be sure of that." Max's voice was choked with tears. Of grief? Or rage?


It seemed best to have Celeste stay in my downstairs guestroom overnight rather than risk another encounter with Max. She accepted numbly, drank a glass of milk and headed into the room. I heard her crying at first, but then silence. I hoped that meant she was asleep.

"What was that all about?" said Joe.

"I'll tell you upstairs." I took his arm and led him to the stairs. "Although this is not a good bedtime story."

The next morning I insisted Celeste have a decent breakfast before she left us. Joe made French toast with maple syrup. I was hoping this would tempt Celeste and it did, a little.

I urged Celeste to go back to her parents' home for a day or so and said I would contact the history department on her behalf.

"Don't linger in town," I said. "Max is still looking for you."

"I'll follow her in my car," said Joe. "From here to the next freeway exit."

I watched as the two cars backed out of my driveway, turned down the street, and drove out of sight. The day was warmer than usual suggesting the possibility of spring even though we were still in midwinter. I took Charlie for a short walk and then headed to school, determined to confront Max and settle this problem with Celeste for good. Even if Celeste was unwilling to bring up harassment charges, I could make sure Max knew the provost and I would discipline him, even fire him, for having a sexual relationship with a student. That should scare him away. Max had a national reputation and a wife with three children and another on the way. He had much to protect from scandal.

But Max was not at school. And, no, he had not emailed the manuscript of his book. I closed my door and asked Nell for some time alone. Should I call Max at home?

I stared out at the yellow-brown grass that covered the lawn of the quad. I looked at the windows of larger brick buildings across the way. Did other deans have to deal with problems like mine? Was it possible to feel angry and depressed at the same time? I was suffused with ambivalence.

Max had been a warm, affectionate friend, a helpful friend. Was it possible Max truly loved Celeste? I had made a few sexual wrong turns of my own. Had I turned into a prudish bureaucrat? Nell interrupted my internal soliloquy. She had an urgent look.

"I have a Dean Lorenzo waiting on the phone. He says it's important. And, Stoddard wants to see you in his office right away."

Now what?

Manuel Lorenzo was a friend and recently appointed dean of a large journalism school back east. I had been meaning to call him. "Congratulations, Manny. Sorry to keep you on hold," I said.

"That's okay." Manny's voice came back, leaden and cheerless. "I have some troubling news, Red." Oh God. More trouble? So much for a peaceful week after the retreat.

"What's up Manny?"

"This morning I received a registered letter from a Simon Gorshak, one of your faculty."

"I hope he's applying for a job," I said.

"Sorry. He's not. He has written a five-page diatribe against your school. He insists you are indifferent to the value of scholarly research, that you have encouraged frivolous changes to the curriculum and, let's see, oh yes, you are romantically involved with a married professor and you and your lover are trying to get some unworthy fellow named Coleman tenured."

"Wow." Simon must have lost his mind.

"Yes, Red. Wow. He ends by saying he believes your school is at risk of losing its accreditation because of curriculum changes and weakness in research, not to mention your own questionable conduct."

"Jesus. None of that is true, Manny. I know Simon is unhappy about some of the changes we are considering, but I am surprised he would write anyone a letter denouncing his school. Especially since he knows we go up for re-accreditation next fall and we depend on the good opinion of others."

"Red, I don't think I'm the only dean who received this letter."

Oh, that would be why Stoddard wanted to see me. I thanked Manny and urged him to keep an open mind about the school.

Stoddard, a normally courteous man, did not rise from his desk chair when I walked in. His bald head shone, this time with sweat. He was furious.

"Sit," he said. No greeting, no how are you doing. Just the command.

He handed me a letter. "Read," he said.

I read through Simon's five pages.

"It's full of lies," I said.

"It went to the deans of every accredited journalism school in the country, plus copies to Lewis and me and, God knows who else." The Provost's voice was deadly calm, but he worked his huge fingers, tugging until the knuckles cracked.

"It's full of lies," I repeated. "Simon claims we're planning to abandon the teaching of writing and reporting in favor of teaching kids how to make websites. That's not remotely true. He says we have no important research being done, but I have a roomful of papers and presentations delivered just this past year, plus four faculty members have written books."

"What about you and a so-called married professor?"

"An absolute fiction. I swear. I'm seeing someone."

"Yes. I'm told you're seeing Detective Morgan."

"I am."

Stoddard stopped pulling at his fingers and leaned forward, his face cupped in his hands. "Dean Solaris, I sincerely hoped last week when you told me you had a successful retreat and we announced Ben Howard's gift, that the journalism school had turned the corner. But it would appear your faculty quarrel is alive and venomous."

"But none of what Simon writes is true."

"I understand, Meredith. But what in the name of God prompted him to denounce his own school to the entire world of academic journalism? What did he hope to gain?"

I sat silent. Indeed, what did Simon hope to gain by writing this? Stoddard stared at me, expecting some explanation. After an agonizing pause, I answered:

"Revenge."

# Chapter 24

I walked back to the journalism school, my ears ringing with Stoddard's final instructions. "Meredith, write a rebuttal—with facts, lots of facts—and get it to Phil Lewis and me before the end of work tomorrow. We will need it to compose a letter from Phil to all these deans and, especially, to anyone on the committee coming to re-accredit the school next semester."

There had been no sympathy in his face and no sense of the friendship he had always shown me. He didn't speak of my interim deanship, but his disappointment was palpable. I figured I was going to lose that job right after I handed in the rebuttal.

"Here's what I need," I told Nell, asking for detailed records for everything from faculty research in the last five years to records of student accomplishments. "I'm sorry Nell, I know this is a horrendous request, but I will need all this stuff to back up my rebuttal to Simon's letter. And, I'll need it by end of work this afternoon so I can write it tonight. Stoddard insists I have a rebuttal to him tomorrow."

"Simon's a lousy son of a bitch," said Nell. I had never heard her swear before. "I hate him."

"So do I Nell, but right now I have to diffuse the situation he's created."

I had one errand to do before I could go home to the comfort of Joe's arms. It took me to the other side of campus. As I drove through the still winter landscape I realized how much I wanted to keep my job as dean. I had been feeling wonderful after the retreat and after the ceremony accepting Ben Howard's gift. I had begun to enjoy being dean of journalism. I loved my students and my friends and this university. Now it was all in jeopardy. Now I had two faculty members in trouble, one who had to be disciplined and one who probably had to be fired. In less than three months, I had lost the confidence of the provost who had once admired me and the president who had appointed me.

It was a mess. And, heading out the back gate of campus, I wondered how much I wanted to go to Max's house and insist he see me and what? Get him to come outside, away from his wife, so I could talk to him about Celeste.

Get it over with, I thought. Deal with Max today because tonight you have to deal with Simon's betrayal.


The drive to the Worthington's took me through the main residential areas of Landry, a neighborhood that looks more like the towns I knew back east. In spring, maples, flowering plum, and linden trees bloomed in what had once been brown and barren high desert. Water from Lake Tahoe flowed downstream to nourish them.

Max and Trudy lived in an old Victorian in a section that had been the historical center of Landry and was still the most prosperous. The Worthington's house was gracefully proportioned and beautiful with a deep front porch and well-kept shutters at all the front windows.

Trudy Worthington met me at the door. Her face was haggard, her body heavy with pregnancy. Her usually carefully arranged hair was straggling down her back and about her face and looked oily from lack of recent washing. I could hear the shrieks of children playing in a back room.

"Hi, Red. Come on in. It's great to see you, although I'm a bit frazzled today. Hope you don't mind the clutter. Can I get you something to drink? I'm sorry about the noise and..."

"Thanks, Trudy. But I really just stopped by to see how Max was feeling and to see if he felt up to meeting with me."

"As far as I know, he's feeling fine," she said, brushing a stray lock of hair off her face. "But he's not here."

I was almost relieved, but Max's absence meant postponing a talk with him and I wanted to be done with it. I also wanted to be sure he didn't follow Celeste to her parents' home.

"Do you know where he is?" I asked.

"I thought he was at the school," said Trudy. "Is something wrong?"

"No. Not at all," I said. The last thing in the world I wanted to do was upset Trudy.

"How are you?" I said summoning up a smile.

"Oh, this pregnancy is driving me insane." She spread her hands under her massive belly. "But thankfully it will be over in a few weeks. Can I give Max a message for you?"

I paused. Might as well get something useful done. I remembered his book. "Uh, well I was hoping to get the manuscript of his book. He promised to bring it in last week but he keeps forgetting."

"Oh. He's been forgetting everything these days," said Trudy, sighing. "Last month he forgot Max Junior's birthday party. I know December birthdays are tough to remember, but really."

I decided to press on. "I wonder if I could trouble you to get the manuscript for me." I tried to sound casual and cheerful. "I really need to go over it this weekend so I can complete his evaluation for a merit raise."

"Well, we need his merit raise all right," she said. "Let's see if we can find it in his den."

We headed down the hallway to a room at the back. The door was locked but she reached up to grab a key off the top of the doorframe. "Have to keep it locked," she said, "or the kids get into it, and nothing upsets him more."

We entered a small cluttered room with a large desk in front of a back window and bookshelves on every wall. A computer sat in the middle of the desk and papers were stacked on either side.

"I know the galleys are in here somewhere," she said.

"Oh, I don't want to take his galleys. The final draft of the manuscript will do just as well, if he has it here."

"Well, let's see," she said, rifling through the piles on his desk. I spotted a large manila envelope on one of the lower bookshelves. It looked big enough to hold a book manuscript.

"Would this be it?" I said, picking it up and handing it to her.

She opened the clasp and looked inside. "Seems to be a draft of the book," she said. "Will this do?"

"It'll be fine." I took the envelope from her hands. "Thanks so much. I'll read this over the weekend."

As we walked back to the front door I noticed how slowly she maneuvered. There was a stain on the back of her sleeve. I had always seen Trudy as a pretty woman, neat and well dressed.

"Hope you feel better soon," I said as she opened the door for me.

"Oh, I'll be all right as soon as I unload this kid and as soon as I get my husband back from that big project he's working on at school."

"Big project?" So that's how Max accounted for his time at the Grant Street motel.

"Yes. Research on something. He's late most nights for dinner and he goes into work on Sundays. Sundays used to be family day around here. Do you have any idea when he might be finished, Red? I really need my husband back."

"I'll talk to him about it, Trudy. No research is worth missing your good cooking. Please tell Max I'll be at school and I do need to see him."

I walked back to my car praying Trudy would never find out about Max and Celeste.


The manuscript was thick and heavy in my hands as I put it on the front seat of my car. How could I look at this and also get Stoddard the data he needed to respond to Simon's letter? I decided Max's book could wait for another time. I drove away from his house but then my curiosity got the better of me. I pulled into the parking lot of an old church and started to scan the pages.

The book promised to cover the future of online journalism, a subject dear to Max and close to the topic Shaw had been working on. As I scanned the pages, I also prayed for Max. His affair with Celeste was enough trouble for him. Plagiarism would cost him his job.

In the second chapter, I spotted a familiar phrase. Then another. I turned on the ignition and put the car in gear. I would have to compare this chapter line for line with Shaw's and then search for attribution and hope to find something that would exonerate my selfish friend.

As I neared the entrance to the parking lot, I saw Max's car coming down the street towards his house. His eyes were fixed on the road. He did not look up. He did not see me. Just as well. Go home to your wife. Your world is going to hell soon enough.


Joe was in my kitchen. Corned beef and cabbage. A little early in the season but it smelled delicious.

"St. Patrick's Day is two months away," I kissed his cheek, warm from cooking.

"It's never too soon for corned beef."

I sat down at the table while Joe poured me a glass of wine. It was no good putting off the inevitable. I began, starting with Simon's letter and Stoddard's order for a rebuttal tomorrow.

"That's terrible," said Joe, abandoning his pots and sitting down next to me. He took my hand. "Why would a professor try to hurt his own school?"

I sighed. "Perhaps because he believes his school has betrayed him. Left him behind. Scorned him."

"How much damage has he done?"

"Maybe a great deal. It remains to be seen how much we can control it. I know Stoddard and President Lewis have been making phone calls to journalism deans all over the country. If Nell has pulled together enough evidence for me to write a refutation of Simon's letter, then we can send it on and hope for the best."

Joe read my copy of Simon's letter, a frown creasing his forehead. "Where did Simon come up with this idea of you having an affair with a married professor?"

"Who knows? He probably means to imply Max and it's just his way of combining his hatreds and creating a rumor that hurts us both."

"Max is a good-looking guy. No doubt that's how he gets pretty students to sleep with him. Maybe Simon knows about that."

"Max is an adulterous son of a bitch," I snapped. Joe looked startled. "And what's worse, I think Max may be the plagiarist Henry found."

"Jesus," said Joe. "Now I need a glass of wine." I told Joe about my visit with Trudy and my brief look at Max's manuscript.

"I don't know how I am going to talk to Max about this," I said, a lump in my throat. "He's been my friend for a long time."

Joe took my hands and looked steadily into my eyes. "You're not going to talk to Max about the plagiarism."

"I'm not? Why?"

"Because if Max is Henry's thief, that means Henry and he may have talked about it. I'm sorry, sweetheart but it gives Max Worthington a motive for..."

"Oh, my God, Joe. I can't believe Max would've hurt Henry over this. They were very close friends."

"Look, Red. We don't have any proof Max and Henry ever talked, or that they talked on that November Sunday. But I still want you to keep a lid on this plagiarism thing, until both you and I go over this manuscript." Joe picked up the envelope from the kitchen table and stuffed it into a cupboard. "This may be evidence of more than plagiarism."

I sagged in my chair.

I was close to exhaustion and even closer to tears. "I think I'll take a hot shower."

"Good idea. I'll have dinner ready when you come down."

I headed out of the kitchen and was hanging my coat on the rack by the front door when I saw a figure coming up the path to the front door. Max.

I called to Joe in the kitchen.

"Let him in," said Joe in the kitchen doorway. "But not a word about suspecting plagiarism. Tell him you haven't read anything yet."

"What if he wants the manuscript back?" I heard Max's footsteps on the entry.

"Tell him you left it at your office."

The doorbell rang. Max looked cold and upset. "I need a minute or two of your time, Red." He looked at Joe. "Alone, if it's okay with you Detective Morgan."

"I'm the cook tonight," said Joe, his voice casual. The kitchen door swung behind Joe. But I knew he would be on the other side, listening.

"Trudy says she gave you my manuscript."

"Yes, that was very kind of her. I plan to look at it over this weekend."

"Why couldn't you wait until I emailed it to you?"

"I could have, Max. But since I was at your house, hoping to see you, I decided to ask Trudy for it."

I stepped into the living room and poked at the fire. Max followed still in his overcoat, his hands shoved in his pockets. "Okay, what were you hoping to see me about?" he said. His brow was furrowed and there were circles under his eyes.

"You know perfectly well what I wanted to see you about."

"Did you tell Trudy?"

"No, Max. I hope Trudy never finds out about Celeste."

"Red, I told you it was consensual. All the way. Inappropriate perhaps, but not illegal. Celeste is an adult. You can't say anything about this to anyone. As long as you keep quiet, I can protect Trudy from knowing about this."

"Max, your relationship damn near destroyed that girl. Celeste is a wreck. You have to stay away from her from now on. You are not to see her or talk to her under any circumstances. That's what I came to your house to tell you."

"Knock it off, Red. You're my dean, not my commanding officer."

We heard the sound of pans rattling in the kitchen.

"You have to leave Celeste alone."

"Or what?"

"Or I will have to report you to the administration and put you on administrative leave."

His jaw hardened. "Do you really want to lose my support, Red? I could easily throw you to the wolves on this curriculum issue. I can rescind my support. I could vote against Larry's tenure. You seem to forget I'm a nationally known writer and I can make things very unpleasant for you."

I couldn't believe he was threatening me. "What do you want, Max?"

Max's face fell.

His hands came out of his pockets in a gesture of supplication. "I want you to forgive me, Red. Please." He took a step toward me. "I want you to forgive me and to forget about my affair with Celeste."

I had never seen this side of Max. Anger and flirtation, yes, but pleading, panic on his face?

"Can I trust you to leave Celeste alone?" I knew I was giving in.

"Yes, Red. I promise."

"I'm not sure I can believe you, and I have to protect your other students..."

"Please, Red. Please." Max's voice was louder. He put his hands on my shoulders.

"Everything all right in here?" Joe came into the room.

"Max is just leaving," I said, pulling away from Max's grasp.

Joe's eyes flashed but his voice was even. "I think that's a good idea."

"Guess what, pal. I don't give a shit what you think," Max said. "I only care what this beautiful woman thinks." Max turned back to me. "Red, sweetheart, remember our friendship, all the times I helped you."

Over Max's shoulder I could see Joe's scowl. Sweetheart? That didn't help. I had never felt so tired or so unhappy. "Okay, Max. I'll let it go for now. But if anything more happens..."

"Thank you, Red, Thank you," said Max, putting his hand back on my shoulders. "I knew I could count on you."

And then he turned and without a word to Joe, he rushed to the front door. I heard him running down the path to the street.

"You're not going to report his affair with Celeste, are you?" asked Joe, wiping his hands on a dishtowel.

"I guess I just agreed to that."

"You've got feelings for that guy," said Joe.

"He's been a good a friend."

"Red, I'm not just a detective, I'm a very good detective and my instincts tell me you do have feelings for Max Worthington, strong feelings that are interfering with your judgment. C'mon, the man seduced a student and still wants to sleep with her. And yet, here you are telling him you'll let it go. Forgive and forget. Jesus, Red."

"He's been my friend for years. I want to give him a chance to redeem himself."

"A slap on the wrist may not drive him to redemption."

"You think I should turn him in?"

"If he were anyone else but Max, I think you *would* turn him in."

"You're angry about this."

"I'm not crazy about your sympathy for Max. He's a bad guy, Red. You should be able to see that. You should actually fire him for what he did to Celeste. But you're not seeing him clearly. You're protecting him. I hate that." Joe bunched the towel into a ball and threw it on the floor.

"You're jealous of Max?"

"Should I be?" Joe's voice was almost a growl.

Silence and shock. Should he be jealous?

Do I have feelings for Max that I haven't acknowledged? But, before I could say anything, Joe was in the hall, putting on his coat.

"Damn it, Joe, you have no right to even think what you're thinking."

He stared at me. "No right? No *right*, Red? Now I'm *really* angry." His eyes and voice hardened. "Maybe Simon was on to something..."

"No, Joe. No."

"I think you need some time for yourself to figure what you really want. I know I sure as hell do."

"Joe, don't leave."

The door slammed behind him.

Gone. Really gone. I couldn't believe the turn this conversation had taken.

I went back into the living room and headed to my desk. Nell's data was piled beside my computer, but it was impossible to concentrate on it. How was I going to work on my report to Stoddard? I called Joe's cell but only got his voicemail. Maybe he would come back in an hour or so when he cooled off, when he realized he had been unfair. I had never come close to sleeping with Max. But, to be honest, there were times before Joe came into my life when I was drawn to Max. If Max had been single, I might have done something about those feelings. I realized that when Celeste had described sex with Max, I had felt a twinge of jealousy.

Joe Morgan was shrewd. Had he figured all that out?

I rifled though Nell's data. I had to write that report or lose my job the next day. But how could I concentrate? I worked a little, called Joe's cell, worked a little more, called Joe, and finally at midnight had a draft for Stoddard.

I went to bed exhausted. Too tired to weep. Too tired to wonder if I had been right to let Max off the hook about Celeste. But not too tired to know I'd hesitated at the wrong time, I'd denied Joe's concern and made him doubt me. I'd messed up the best relationship I'd ever had.

# Chapter 25

The next morning, Joe had not returned and still wasn't answering his cellphone. I stared out my kitchen window. What was he thinking? Probably that I had betrayed him. Probably that I was no better than the fiancée who had ditched him for his rich roommate, or the woman who had stolen his wallet. Just another colossal disappointment.

I had to stop thinking about him.

I flipped through pages of Max's manuscript and compared them to the pages Shaw had sent. The text was identical. I had found Henry's thief.

Now what? First things first. I had to edit a finished rebuttal for Stoddard or I risked my job. I called Nell. I went to the journalism school and spent the day in my office alone with additional records Nell had compiled for me to incorporate into my response to Simon's letter, all the while trying not to think about Joe's anger or about Max.

By mid-afternoon I had finished up my letter for Stoddard and Lewis. Then I called Sadie. I wanted her eyes on my response before I delivered it to Stoddard. I also needed my friend.

Sadie came to my office, read through the response, and said she thought it was effective.

"Can I fire Simon for this? I sure want to."

"Of course you do. But he's tenured and has been at the university for decades. He'd probably file a grievance and claim you were stifling his freedom of speech."

"But he trashed his school and his university."

"Regrettably, academic freedom means the freedom to trash your university."

"Is there any way I can punish Simon for this?"

"Oh, you can ignore him, assign him a smaller office, a less desirable teaching schedule. You can deny him funds for travel. But in the end you're just piling more punishment on someone who already feels aggrieved. That's why he wrote his letter."

"How do I live with him after this?"

"You outlive him, Red. That's what academics do when we can't be rid of a nemesis. We outlive the bastard. Actually, it works out more often than you might think. Simon knows he's done a terrible wrong to his university. He knows he is despised. Be patient, Red. He's old. Sooner or later he will leave or die."

Nell knocked and came to my office. I handed her the memo to Stoddard and the back-up data. "Please take this to the provost's office for me, Nell. I cannot bear to see him today."

Nell nodded. "I'm sure things will work out," she said and left.

"I'm going home," said Sadie, "and then I am coming over to your house."


Sadie shared supper with me and then we retreated back to the comfort of the fireplace. She asked about Joe and I told her what had happened the evening before. She was wrapped in a long lavender sweater. Instead of her conventional short ponytail, she had piled her gray hair into a haphazard bun on top of her head. She looked younger, softer. I hoped she was still wiser.

She had listened to me without speaking for half an hour. "Have you sorted out your feelings about Max...or for Max?" she said, looking into the flames.

"I think so."

Her face was sympathetic but her tone was admonitory. "Red, you are old enough to know better than to let a man like Joe, a man who cares for you, think for a minute you have yearnings for another man."

I groaned. "I know Sadie. I know. I've called Joe several times today and he hasn't answered or called back."

"He's hurt, Red. He may need some time away from you."

"But I want to tell him he was right about Max and I was wrong. I want to repair this thing."

"Joe isn't hurt because you were wrong. He's hurt because he suspects you have sexual feelings for Max and that's why you made the decision you did. Send him a letter. Give him some breathing room and some space. Let's talk again tomorrow. You'll get through this." Sadie moved forward in her chair as if to rise.

I must have looked as miserable as I felt. "So you don't think I've lost him for good?"

Sadie rearranged the bun on her head. She leaned down and patted Charlie, who was lying at her feet. "I don't know. I don't know how angry he is or how hurt. I do know you've been foolish with his feelings."

I had no defense against Sadie's pronouncement. After she left, I sat on the floor in front of the fireplace, hugging my knees with one hand and stroking Charlie's flank with the other.

My Ohio therapist had called it. As soon as I got close to committing to a man, I find a way to put him off. I replayed the moment I had hesitated when Joe questioned my feelings for Max. It wasn't exhaustion. It wasn't even some loyal impulse to save a friend who no longer deserved it. It was a test. Somewhere in the back of my mind, I felt Joe shouldn't have had to ask. He should have known me better. He should have believed in me. Joe failed the test.

No. I failed. I failed to trust Joe. I was a neurotic, self-destructive idiot.

Charlie looked up at me and made a soft whimpering sound. "You miss him, too," I said. "Sorry I drove away your best friend."

Friday morning the streets were wet from an early rain. The deciduous trees were still barren, but a few had started tiny buds.

That happens in Nevada when January warms up. No leaves were out yet. The first to bloom would be the pink flowering plum trees unless a deep frost bit the buds off. The big, bright sky stretched out behind the still bare limbs and over the mountains beyond. I loved Landry. I wanted to live here forever with Joe. But how long could I stay in Nevada with my heart so heavy?

I turned onto the campus road. There were still patches of snow under the tall pines near the north sides of the brick buildings.

I headed for Stoddard's office. He and Philip Lewis were both there and, oddly, both seemed pleased to see me. Perhaps they looked forward to relieving me of my duties as dean.

Stoddard held up the draft Nell had delivered. Lewis looked intently at me and a faint smile appeared.

"This is useful, Meredith," said Stoddard.

"I'll probably use a short version of it for my own note to the deans of journalism," said Lewis.

What? "Short version? Simon wrote a five page diatribe,"

"And it produced an interesting consequence," said Lewis, his smile broadening. "Believe it or not, at 6:00 this morning a messenger delivered a lengthy response to Simon's diatribe to my door. It was a copy of another letter that has been sent to all the deans to whom Simon sent his original letter."

"And the response came from the most unusual sources," said Stoddard.

I waited. Stoddard handed me a copy of the other letter. It totally refuted Simon's assertions about the journalism school. It contained facts and figures about our research I thought only Nell and I would have known, plus a glowing description of our graduates' success and the rigor of our curriculum. It was signed by George Weinstein and Edwin Cartwell.

Whoa.

"We were surprised, too," said Stoddard. "As best we can determine, Simon sent copies of his diatribe to Weinstein and Cartwell."

"Expecting their support?"

"Probably, but not counting on Cartwell's love of the students or Weinstein's fierce pride in the school's reputation and independence," said Lewis. "They both must have devoted considerable time to this and then had a messenger deliver copies of their letters to our homes early this morning."

"So you don't need what I worked on," I said.

Lewis put his hand on my letter. "Actually we do, Meredith. It will help us with a follow-up to those whom Simon wrote. The back-up material you gathered will also help you with your report to the accreditation committee next fall. You may have gotten a good start on the major part of the work."

I was still in a daze, when Stoddard said, "Red, we know how hard this must have been for you."

I fought the impulse to scream. What do you mean you know how hard this was? Don't you realize how often I have the feeling I have made mistakes and overreached, how often I have had major doubts about my ability to lead the school? How sure I was you both wanted me out as dean?

Instead, I swallowed hard and said, "I concentrated on developing a response to Simon Gorshak's letter. I didn't want to give you another reason to put us into receivership."

"Meredith," said both men simultaneously.

"My dear, you have to learn when you can count on our support," said Lewis.

Yeah, sure. Stoddard had forgotten the coldness of the instructions he had given me yesterday.

Lewis might never understand how I felt hearing his offer to put journalism into receivership and under the thumb of another dean.

"What about Simon?" I said. "I'm told I can't fire him."

"True, you can't Meredith," said Lewis. "But I have ways of dealing with treacherous faculty. If I can't persuade him to resign, well, I have put more than one faculty member on mandatory leave of absence for health reasons. Serious health reasons."

"Like the fear that I might follow him into the parking lot and tear him to pieces." Stoddard stopped with a grin, rubbing his massive hands together.

"I don't think you will see much of Simon this semester," said Lewis.


What a turnaround. I almost smiled as I walked back to the journalism school. The prospect of Edwin and George rejecting Simon made me giddy. Maybe Larry Coleman's tenure prospects were not so troubled after all. Maybe there was hope.

Except for Joe and me.

In spite of the white-haired woman's prediction, in spite of everything that had happened, I was afraid. Still afraid I would screw up the dean's job. Afraid I would never be with Joe again. Afraid to go back to my office and face the faculty. I wanted to go home and curl up under my quilt.

But I kept walking to the school. "Courage is not the absence of fear," my father had been fond of saying, mangling any number of quotes from Mark Twain and others. "Courage is acting in the presence of fear, even when you are scared to death. That's what you did when you took the driver's keys."

Fine. I liked the notion I had courage, but I still waited for the fear to diminish. As you get older, shouldn't you become less fearful? "It doesn't work that way," he had said. "Fear is just there. All the time." And I knew then that he was also afraid. Afraid of losing his wife. Afraid of diminished reputation as a result of old age and weakened effort. And then dementia came and took away his memory and his fear along with it.

Is that what was in store for me?


Phyllis was in my office, her arms spread wide, her beautiful face wreathed in a smile. She gave me a great warm hug. "You make me believe the impossible," she said.

Nell brought in mugs of coffee and a jug of milk.

"How did you ever get those two to write that letter?" Phyllis sipped her coffee.

"I had nothing to do with it. George and Edwin wrote it all on their own. How did you find out about this?"

"Oh, a copy of Simon's trash made the rounds. And a copy of George and Edwin's splendid rebuttal was in all our mailboxes this morning."

"Events overtake me," I said, feeling a surge of pleasure for the first time in days. "How nice."

"Maybe things will get better now," she said, putting her hand over mine. "Maybe the faculty fight will go away."

"Die of its own weight?"

"Die of its own stupidity."

"Maybe," I said. "After all, the essential argument was never over the new media courses. That became obvious at the retreat."

"It was always about Henry and the three stooges wanting Henry to be humiliated, wanting Henry to lose."

"Except that two of the stooges turned on the third."

"And you had nothing to do with their conversion?"

"I didn't even know about their response until this morning. Stoddard thinks it was all due to their love for the students and the school."

"Perhaps," said Phyllis. "But maybe because Henry's dead and Simon's been such a jerk, George and Edwin decided to step up and do the right thing. Maybe they think you're not so bad after all."

"I'm having trouble seeing George and Edwin as the cavalry, but I'll give it a shot."

I went looking for George and Edwin and found them both in Edwin's office looking as conspiratorial as ever.

"Thank you for the letter you wrote to the deans," I said.

"No thanks required, Meredith. We did it for the school," said Edwin.

"Simon's missive was incredibly stupid," said George. "There was no way I could let it go unanswered."

"Do you think Simon wanted us put into receivership?" I asked.

"Hard to say," said Edwin. "But it was clear he meant to do the school damage and sacrifice our reputation. He hates the idea of you as dean, but I think there was more on his mind. He's been angry at the university for years."

An unusually reasonable analysis from Edwin, but I took what I could get.

"Will he be fired for this?" asked George, who still looked gloomy. He was dressed in a large yellow ski sweater that emphasized his massiveness and reminded me of Nell's warnings about him.

"According to Phil Lewis, tenured faculty can't be fired even for this attack. But the president thinks he can encourage Simon to go away."

They looked at each other but neither spoke.

"Well, anyway, I appreciated what you did," I said. "The administration was impressed and that may help us keep our independence."

I walked back to my office. "Any calls?" I asked Nell.

"Several," she said, handing me a stack of messages.

Joe had not called, but almost everyone else had. I closed my door and wrote Joe a letter. I mailed it later that day—special delivery, overnight please.

I waited all weekend but no word from Joe. Four days without him. No calls. No response to my messages or my letter. I made some supper and drank a large glass of wine by myself. I left the dishes in the sink and sat in front of the fire, idly petting Charlie and feeling tired and overworked and very sorry for myself.

Around eight that evening, I resolved to do something. I took a shower, washed my hair, dressed in jeans and a soft red sweater, and headed over to Joe's apartment house. It was after ten when I pulled up to a complex of three story brick buildings a block away from police headquarters. Joe lived in the nearest building on the third floor. The complex housed mostly police and firemen who were single or married without children. The apartments were all one-bedroom look-alikes. Joe's was at the end of the hall. As I neared his door I heard music. That meant he was home and not watching television.

After a few moments of hesitation, I knocked on the door. No response. I knocked again. Joe opened it. He was barefoot, wearing shorts, no shirt. He looked incredibly desirable. I didn't see anyone else over his shoulders, but I sensed he was not alone.

"This is not a good time, Red," he said. His eyes were dark.

I said nothing.

"Sorry," he said, and closed the door.

I drove back home and returned to Charlie and the wine bottle. I spent that night curled around the dog on the floor in front of the fire. Sometime before dawn I woke and put my hand on Charlie's shoulder. His fur was still wet from my sobbing.

# Chapter 26

The meeting to discuss Larry Coleman's tenure application began at three in the afternoon on the last Friday in January. All the tenured faculty members showed up except for Simon.

"Anyone notice if Coleman came in with a violin case this morning?" I heard Ardith whisper to Phyllis.

"Probably not," said Phyllis. "It's too cold for the homicidal."

"Don't be too sure. Simon isn't here, yet."

I called the meeting to order.

Each of the other nine tenured members of the faculty were told to spend no more than a few minutes on their opening remarks.

After a half hour of discussion, Edwin made a surprising motion to approve Coleman for tenure and send our recommendation forward to the university Promotion and Tenure Committee.

"I had my doubts about Larry," Edwin began, "but since the retreat and reflecting upon the new media presentation, I have reconsidered. In fact, I plan to ask Larry to guest lecture in one of my writing classes later this semester."

A few jaws dropped. Good for Edwin. There's a man who knows when the train is leaving the station. The change in his attitude toward Larry was remarkable. But the look he gave me was icy. He cared about the school, but I wondered if he was just waiting for a better chance to punish me?

Phyllis seconded the motion. Everyone voted in favor. Even George muttered "aye."

The meeting adjourned.

On the way out I heard Ardith say to Phyllis, "Do you think Coleman will forgive those who trespassed against him?"

"Oh, I think Larry may seem to forgive but he will never forget the past months. He will carry a dagger for George and another for Edwin. But, for now, the weapons will be concealed."

Cynicism is the last refuge of the idealist but, sometimes, the first instinct of the academic.

Karen Coleman sat in a chair next to her husband in the hall outside my office. When I returned from the tenure meeting she gave me a tepid smile and left.

"I'll wait in the car," she said to Larry.

"Let's go into my office," I said, motioning him in and closing the door behind us.

I sat with him at the round table. "It went well," I said. "Your tenure application will go forward first thing Monday morning. I have every expectation it will be approved. I don't want to jump the gun, but I think you should feel good about this and take Karen out for a nice dinner."

Larry folded his arms across his chest and cleared his throat. "What was the vote?"

I could have claimed the vote as confidential, but the hallway gossip would make my discretion irrelevant.

"Unanimous. In fact, Edwin Cartwell made the motion to approve and both he and George voted aye with the majority."

"But not Simon?" Larry's eyes held the hardness I had seen before.

I sighed. "Larry, Simon didn't attend. But I do think it's important to note that George and Edwin both supported you."

He rose and shook my hand.

"Well, thanks Red. I appreciate your help in this and your leadership. I guess I won't keep Karen waiting any longer."

His eyes told me we were not out of trouble yet.

\*    \*    \*

A faculty meeting the following Monday confirmed my suspicion. It was not that anyone said anything antagonistic. In fact, on the surface, all seemed friendly. Simon was absent.

Coleman was quiet. George was expansive. Edwin was polite and the rest of the faculty seemed animated by the possibility that civil conversation was the order of the day and the year-long battle was finally over. But it was not over.

As I watched the group, I realized Coleman was also a wounded water buffalo. The quarrel may seem resolved but, in his heart, hatred remained.

George prattled on oblivious, too self-absorbed to realize how deeply he had injured his colleague. Edwin seemed indifferent.

Afterward, in the hallway, Larry offered courtesy to both George and Edwin, but I could see the unforgiving look in his eyes. The curriculum dispute would disappear but anger and a residual subterranean spitefulness would stay. More fighting was in our future.

When I got home Monday evening, I found a note in my mailbox. Like the earlier one, it was unsigned and created on a computer:

*"Now would be a good time to go back to Ohio before you get hurt. Henry Brooks ignored my warnings. Don't make the same mistake. I can promise things will turn out badly for you if you stay."*

My stomach lurched. I took the note into the house, holding it carefully by the edges. I knew I had to call Joe even if only to leave another message on his voicemail. There had been no sign of Simon at school, but I could still remember the menace in his voice.

A storm had been brewing since mid-afternoon. Suddenly the wind came up howling and tossing the trees outside my windows. I looked outside and saw snow falling heavily. When the phone rang, I thought it might be Sadie who lives near an unreliable power line.

Last year, she had spent a weekend keeping warm at my house after an ice storm had taken out her electricity.

The voice was very soft, but it was not Sadie's. It was Joe's. I had to fight back tears at the sound of it.

"I got your message. You okay in this storm?" he said.

"I'm okay. But, I wouldn't mind some company."

"I'm down the street. I'll be there in a minute or two."

I raced upstairs so fast it set Charlie barking with excitement. I brushed my hair and checked my sweater for crumbs from lunch. No time to change into the soft red sweater. Just as well. It was probably bad luck.

The doorbell rang.

Joe hadn't used his key. He stood in the doorway stamping his feet and brushing snow off his jacket and out of his hair.

No kiss. No hug. Just "hi."

Charlie was thrilled. He got lots of patting and rough scrubbing on his chest while I stood there watching the play between the man and my dog. Joe took off his jacket, walked with Charlie into the living room and sat on the hearth.

I sat in the chair facing the fireplace. Joe stared at the carpet. At length, his head came up. "I've been meaning to call you," he said.

"I'm glad."

"I know we should talk. It's just been hard to call your number."

I decided to get to the matter that had preoccupied me. "I'm sorry I interrupted you the other night at your apartment. I should have called first."

"You didn't interrupt anything," he said. "Because I...because nothing happened after you left."

Oh.

"I haven't been with anyone else," he said.

"Joe, I am so..." I started to move toward him but he held up his hand.

"Let me see the note."

I stopped, got up, and went to the hall table and picked up the note by one corner. He pulled a clear envelope from his jacket pocket. I handed the note to him and watched him read and then carefully slip the note into the envelope.

"We'll check it for prints." He resumed petting Charlie.

"Joe, I..."

"I know, Red. I listened to all the messages and I read your letter about Max and I understand you know you were wrong about him. And I know I was wrong about you *with* him. That was a stupid thing for me to say."

I sat still and quiet.

Joe breathed deeply and went on. "I need time to think this through, Red. I need to be able to trust you, and to trust us together. I can't worry about you having feelings for other guys."

"I don't have feelings for other guys."

Joe still looked troubled. "I share a lot of stuff with you. Stuff about myself and my work, and I need to be able to do that without wondering where your loyalties are. I don't want to be one of those cops who keeps it all inside and never talks about how he feels or what he did on the job."

I knelt down in front of him and put my arms around his neck. His mouth found mine, but the kiss was light, his lips closed, and it ended when Charlie pushed his head in between us.

Joe smiled at Charlie but not at me. "Okay, Red. I'm going to take this note down to the station."

He got up and went for his jacket.

"Aren't you going to stay tonight?"

Joe was silent. He put on his coat and took forever putting his fingers into his gloves. He looked at me. "I need to get back to work."

"I see." But I didn't.

"If anything happens tonight that scares you, call my cell. Otherwise, I'll call when we've checked this note for prints."

Out the door, into the snow now thick and wild around the front step. Then he was gone into the darkness.

*    *    *

I woke up late on Saturday. Snow covered the ground and the sky was pewter. More snow was due. My kitchen felt empty even though it was my favorite room in the house. Empty without Joe. Empty without croissants and jam and his arms around me. Even Charlie looked despondent. I made some coffee and then moved to the living room alcove to settle in front of my computer. Stacked on my desk were the personnel files for the entire faculty. Today I would have to re-read all the evaluations I planned to give next week. Nell had typed my notes and inserted them in each folder.

The phone rang. Joe's voice. "Sorry, Red, we could not get any definitive prints off the note that was left in your mailbox either. Apparently the writer wears gloves when he wants to threaten you."

"I see," I said, my heart in my shoes. "Is it possible to see you?"

Long pause.

"Maybe for a drink later tonight. Gormley's."

"Thank you." I hung up. Bad news. I felt sure the note was from Simon. I could picture Simon's cold bony hands in rubber gloves writing the note. I could see his wrinkled angry face, full of hate. I should feel sorry for Simon, but I was too frightened of what he might do, might already have done. But maybe it was from George. Big, beefy George so willing to try to dominate and intimidate. Did you kill Henry, George? Do you plan to hurt me?

That night Joe met me at Gormley's.

"You look good," said Joe, swirling the bourbon in his glass. If only he could believe in me again.

"Thank you for seeing me," I said.

"How's Charlie?"

"He misses you."

"You haven't mentioned your dad lately. How's he doing?"

"About the same as before. I rarely call now."

He sat back in his chair, stretching his long legs under the table at an angle to mine but not touching them. He looked inviting and sexy but I didn't dare move my leg to his.

"Tell me about your father. Did you love him?" Maybe if I could get him back to the subject of his own family, he would get comfortable with me again.

Joe looked away and pursed his lips. "I loved my dad. Maybe not as much as you love yours, but I loved him. So did my mother for all the good it did her. Sometimes I think her love for him is what ultimately killed her."

"What makes you say that?"

"She pined for him. He was unaware for the most part, but he was always leaving us to go off on hunting trips, poker nights, baseball games, football games. Sometimes he took me to a game, but Mom and Elaine were left at home. My mother spent years trying to figure out what she had to say or do that would make him pay more attention, make him love her more."

Joe shifted in his chair and looked at the duck prints above the bar. He spoke to the wall. "Mom even had a brief affair to try to make him jealous. But it didn't make him jealous. It just gave him another excuse to go out with the guys and keep his distance from her."

"Joe, you told me he was devastated after her death, that he lay on the kitchen floor all night."

Joe turned his gaze back to me. I could see the pain. "That's right. The night she died he realized what he had lost. For nights afterward I could hear him sobbing in his room—deep, heavy sobs I never thought possible from my father."

"Are you like him at all?" Please Joe, don't be.

Joe looked down at his hands. "I don't want to be," he said, and then looked back up at me. "I don't want to be like her, either."

That stung.

I wanted to touch his face and kiss his eyelids but I sat there, respecting the distance he had requested, watching his rugged face and the lines around his desirable mouth.

"If it's any comfort, I don't think you are like either of the parents you describe. You're a good friend and a great lover. I'm just sorry I messed up what I know was a terrific relationship."

He took a deep breath. "You're very brave, Red. And very independent. You've been through more hell than anyone I know and you're still standing, still fighting."

Somehow, perhaps to justify the compliment, I began telling him about my childhood, my mother and my own problems with drinking in college. It was so easy to talk to Joe and so hard not to touch him. He listened quietly, his eyes fixed on me. His green eyes softened when I described my mother's death.

"I think you may have had it rougher than I did," he said.

"I think I grew up skittish about serious relationships. My past has made it hard for me to commit to anyone or anything but work. I tend to push people away, especially important people. I test people to make sure they really care. I tested you, Joe. And I didn't have to. It was insane to let you believe for a single minute I'd ever had an affair with Max."

"Red, I was an idiot about that. I couldn't stand seeing you all upset and letting that son of a bitch get away with what he had done to one of your students. I couldn't bear your compassion for him."

"Maybe I was the idiot."

Joe shifted uncomfortably in his chair. "Face it. You were unquestionably wrong to let Max get away with having sex with Celeste. Even if he was your friend before, he's not worthy of your friendship now. And when this investigation ends and we know who murdered Henry, I trust you are going to do the right thing about his behavior and his plagiarism."

"When we know who murdered Henry," I murmured as Joe stood and put on his jacket.

"When we know."

Clearly, I was not forgiven.

I stared up at him, waiting for more. But there was no more and we went to our separate cars.

# Chapter 27

I carried the stack of faculty evaluation folders into my office. Nell followed with a cup of coffee.

"I think I'll start the evaluation meetings with the easy ones," I said. "I'm going to keep some of the more difficult for later next week."

Nell obediently pulled George's and Edwin's folders out of the pile and put them on the bottom. "You don't really have to meet with any of them just yet," she said. "Everyone knows you had a horrible time dealing with Simon's treachery."

"I need to work, Nell, but thank you."

After Nell had left for her office, I pulled out a new folder Nell had made for Max and put it on the bottom underneath the evaluation folders for George and Edwin. I dreaded the thought of having to confront Max even more than I dreaded Edwin's smugness and a nasty conversation with George.

The afternoon went quickly. Larry Coleman and Ardith Trent were easy on me. Ardith, overcome with emotions that made her pink and girlish, was grateful for a good evaluation and sympathetic for my distress. Then came Phyllis Baker, who read through my evaluation and then got up and hugged me. "Thanks Red," she said into my hair. "Now go home and take care of yourself. The rest of these can wait."

The drive home was slow and cold, the streets icy beneath my tires. I pulled up to my mailbox and collected the small pile. One envelope caught my eye. No stamp, just "Red" on the front. Oh dear. But, when I opened the letter inside, the handwriting looked like Joe's and it was.

*Dear Red,*

*I was so sorry to leave you at Gormley's. I wanted to take you home. But I couldn't because I am still much too vulnerable to you and I still have work to do to protect you. I hope you understand. I am determined to unweave some of this tangled web created by Henry's death and the notes you received.*

*You must realize you are now a target, probably have been for some time. Max Worthington has become a person of interest and may be a suspect along with George Weinstein, Edwin Cartwell, and Simon Gorshak. They are all bastards in my book, but I don't have an ounce of real proof against any one of them and, without proof, I can't keep them away from you. So I have to be sharp. And I have to be objective. And I have to work night and day to solve this thing.*

*So, please be patient with me. I am not seeing anyone else. I am working my ass off.*

*Joe*

I hugged the letter. I hugged Charlie and then hugged the letter again. I wanted to call him. But then I re-read, "please be patient with me." I took off my coat and sat down at my desk to write him back. *Dear, dear Joe. How I miss you. How I miss your understanding, your jokes, your spaghetti sauce, and the sight of your stunning bare back and shoulders in my bed.*

Charlie pressed his nose against my arm. He wanted attention and supper and here I was mentally composing a response to Joe I knew I couldn't send. I had to wait. I had to feed my dog and be patient.

More important I had to keep my wits about me. Joe was right. Both George and Simon had openly threatened me.

\*    \*    \*

I woke up the next morning and felt warm, unusually warm. I rolled over and found a golden dog's face on the pillow next to mine. Then the mouth opened and licked my cheek.

"Charlie, Charlie. You're not allowed in bed," I said, patting the dog's silky neck. Then I remembered the night before I had crawled into bed and invited Charlie to jump up and keep me company.

I had fallen asleep with my arms around Charlie, needing his warmth. Joe's letter was on the pillow above Charlie's head. I read it again. And again while I drank my coffee. And again just before I left for work, looking for clues he was more than a dutiful detective protecting a threatened source.

I spent the day in meetings with my faculty but I felt a renewed optimism. Someday, without all this business with Henry's murder and the threatening notes to me, someday when this was all over, maybe Joe and I could start over.

My reverie was interrupted. George Weinstein stood in my doorway. I had finished my last meeting of the day and was thinking about leaving early.

George's eyes were dark and unfriendly. "You and I have an evaluation meeting next week." His voice was flat; his big body leaned against the doorframe. I couldn't leave. He was blocking the door.

"Yes, George. We do. Nell will let you know the time."

"She'd better," he said, filling the doorway. "And you should know I expect you to recommend a significant merit increase for me this year. I trust you will not try to use our disagreements as an excuse to do otherwise."

Bile in my throat. I put on my coat and grabbed my briefcase. As I approached the door, he glared and did not move. "I have to leave now, George. I'll see you next week."

His jaw jutted out and he worked it back and forth. "I believe I have done a great deal for the school this year, Red. Saving you from the mess Simon made and voting for Coleman's tenure, just to name a couple of matters that should be acknowledged and rewarded."

I moved until I was a foot away from his beefy glaring face. I glared back.

"Let me pass," I said. I was furious. Good thing I wasn't evaluating him until next week. I wanted to challenge him, put him down. *Be patient, Red.* Joe's voice in my head.

George moved aside.


It was still daylight when I pulled into my driveway. I was unlocking the kitchen door when I heard a noise. It was Joe in his four-wheel monster Jeep instead of a police car. "Get the dog and pack your blue jeans. I'm getting you out of town. We're going to Graeagle." Joe had once promised we would go to his parents' log cabin in the mountains northeast of Reno in Graeagle, California.

I could hardly contain my excitement as I obeyed instructions and, fifteen minutes later, I was packed and we were on our way with Charlie in the back seat.

"Am I in danger?"

"Of course you are, but for the next two days only in danger from me."

"Oh. I'm a little surprised given your requests for me to be patient and wait until the investigation is over."

"I'm sick of patience. We both need to get out of Landry. My captain asked me to turn over my notes and let someone else work on the case for a while. He suspects I may not be seeing clearly."

"Does he know about us?"

"He knows I have been spending a lot of time with you."

"Are you upset he took you off the case?"

"Not really. It means I can now protect you by being with you. Hope you don't mind." A small smile flicked across his mouth.

"I don't."

\*    \*    \*

The drive to Graeagle from Landry takes about an hour and a half during the day when you can see the narrow roads clearly.

As night approached, I expected it might take longer, especially if there was snow in the mountains. Once past Reno and the outlying suburbs and industrial areas, the road was dark. Few houses, no lights.

"Ranch country," said Joe. These were the first words either of us had spoken in miles. I had a thousand questions but I was too tense and too excited to talk and terrified of breaking the mood of anticipation. I felt happy for the first time in weeks, glad to be with Joe and my dog in a big, warm car on a dark night driving away from troubles.

The cabin was large and comfortable with a huge stone fireplace and a generous kitchen. Walls of wood with family photographs surrounded me. A large bedroom was off to one side. I spotted a king size bed with an old quilt and a large fur blanket at the bottom of the bed. Joe put my weekend bag by the door of the bedroom.

I opened some wine I had stashed in my bag.

Joe lit a fire, opened up an ancient turntable, and put on an old record of Anita O'Day singing ballads from the forties.

I huddled on the hearth enjoying the warmth of the fire and letting the wine take effect. O'Day's throaty, rich voice filled the room.

*Spring will be a little late this year,*
*A little late arriving in my lonely world over here*
*For you have left me...*

Joe lifted the needle off the record. "That's probably not the right song for now."

I lifted my head from my knees. "No, Joe. That's exactly the right song for now. Let it play."

*Yes, time heals all things, so I needn't cling to this fear
It's merely that Spring will be a little late this year.*

Joe sat in a large worn leather chair in front of the fireplace. His rugged features were softened in the firelight. "We haven't left each other," he said.

"I hated it when you stayed away so long."

He rubbed his chin. "I came to your house three times and stood outside and watched through your window and then got back in the car and went back to my place."

"Why didn't you come in?"

"This is hard for me to say. But, as I wrote when I'm around you, I feel vulnerable."

I watched him for a moment.

He still looked away from me and into the fire. "I suppose vulnerability is not a good thing for a tough homicide detective," I said.

A smile, yet he still looked at the fire.

"But you brought me here anyway?"

He nodded. "You're safe here."

"Have you forgiven me?"

"For?"

"Letting Max off the hook, at least for now."

"I've decided you're smart enough—and decent enough—to take care of that problem when the time comes."

Change the subject, I said to myself. Now. "I loved the letter you left in my mailbox. It was stirring."

A smile, but he did not move toward me.

"I started to write you a response but then remembered you'd asked for patience and what I was thinking of writing would not have sounded patient."

At that he looked at me. "What would you have written?"

I still sat on the hearth with my knees under my chin, soaking in the warmth of the fireplace and dizzy with expectation. "I would have written about your kindness and your green eyes and funny jokes...and your body."

Joe's eyes twinkled and he shifted in his chair.

"And what would you have written about my body?"

I told him what I had planned to write about his shoulders and his back and his mouth. It was getting harder for me to sit still and keep hugging my knees.

A wicked smile creased his face. "Are those the only parts of my body you think about?"

I felt bolder. "No. Not the only parts. You should never have slept with a journalist because, one of these days, I will figure out how to describe that particular part of you I most desire." I could feel myself blushing but I kept on. "Suffice, it's the best—and the first instrument of its kind—that has ever made me come practically every time."

Now Joe was out of the chair. "Practically every time? How often have I failed?" He was standing over me. He leaned down, unlocked my hands from my knees, and pulled me to my feet.

"I'm going to take off my shirt." He was directly in front of me, inches away.

"That would be nice." I locked onto those dark, now smoky green eyes. He removed his shirt and I stared at the hair on his chest, daring myself to put my fingers into it.

"And now I'm going to take off your shirt."

"Oh, I love this part," I said, as he reached for the buttons and I shivered at the touch of his hands on me.

"What you just referred to as my instrument is tuning up, so to speak."

"It's a grand instrument, Detective Morgan." My shirt fell to the floor. He removed my bra and his hands rested on my breasts.

"And getting grander by the minute." He picked me up and held me in his arms. "You like the music?" he said into my hair.

"It's classic, Detective Morgan."

He carried me to the bed. "'1812 Overture' coming up," he said, and an ache grew at the base of my belly. Then our clothes were off and we were on the bed and his hands held my arms over my head and his mouth began its journey from my neck all the way down to the rest of me.

That night a full moon shone on the trees outside the cabin window. The moon was so bright you could see all the tall evergreens clearly, their huge branches laden with white. I felt safe. Even with Henry's killer still unidentified, I felt far away from the apprehension that accompanied me every day in Landry.

As I lay in bed looking at the window, I noticed a shape by the windowsill. Charlie was sitting on the floor looking out the window, too. Carefully sitting up, I got out of bed without waking Joe and walked over to stand next to Charlie.

"Lovely isn't it?" I said to the dog that leaned into my bare leg. "It's so bright reflecting off the snow we could take a walk without needing a flashlight."

"It's really cold out there," came a hushed voice from the bed. I turned to see Joe with his arms around the pillow. The moonlight turned his face to silver.

"Stand there for a minute. God, what a gorgeous body you have." He leaned up on his elbow. "I think I missed your body almost as much as your blazing intellect."

"Smart ass." I moved to the side of the bed. He put his hand between my legs.

"Come back to bed, beautiful. We'll go for a walk in the morning when the sun is up."

I crawled back into bed and put my head on his chest. I twirled his chest hair between my fingers. I loved the smell of him, musky and salty and male. "What made you change your mind?" I said into his chest.

"About what?"

I lifted my head and looked into his eyes. "You know what. About us being together before the investigation was over. About not wanting to feel vulnerable."

"Oh, that," he said combing my hair with his fingers. His eyes darkened. "After the captain took me off the case, I decided to stop going crazy staying away from you. I decided to risk vulnerability."

"I hate being away from you—I feel incomplete."

"Me, too. But I meant it about not being objective when I'm with you. I still worry I'll miss something important, not see or hear something that could put you in danger." He kissed me. "I want to protect you. But when I'm with you, especially when I am making love to you, the Iranian army could attack the house and I wouldn't hear anything but that little growling sound you make."

"Hmm," I snuggled into his neck. "No Iranian army in Graeagle at this time of year," I said. "Little growling sound? Want to hear it again?" and I reached for him just as he reached for me.


On the drive back to Landry, Joe told me more about his police work in Chicago and why he was glad he had returned to Landry.

"I like the police work in Nevada and I like the people. I like my captain. He's very smart and much more reasonable than my superior in Chicago."

"Did the captain really ask you off the case?"

"Yes. But not forever. Not because he was angry with me or even because of my spending time with you, but because my team and I weren't getting anywhere. And I think he was right. A new set of eyes may be a good thing for this investigation."

"What's the new team concentrating on?"

"Trying to identify the tall man who entered the journalism building on the Sunday Henry died."

George. I was almost sure. I told Joe about my last conversation with George. Joe looked thoughtful. "Maybe I should be there when you give Weinstein his evaluation next week."

"Joe, you can't be there every time I have to have a difficult conversation with a faculty member."

"I don't mean in your office," he said, smiling. "Maybe I could just be in Nell's office, visiting or pretending to read something."

"Oh yeah, a bodyguard no one would notice." I smiled back.

"Think about it," he said.

# Chapter 28

By the Friday following our weekend at the cabin in Graeagle, I had convinced Joe I could talk to George Weinstein about his annual evaluation by myself. Joe did not need to be in the building. Nell would be in her office next to mine and she would call Joe's cellphone if needed.

I had finished all my faculty evaluation meetings except the ones with George and Max and all of them had gone well. Even Edwin had been calm but then, thanks to Henry, Edwin's evaluation was stellar and he was due for a sizable merit raise. He had patted his thin, sandy hair as he sat in the chair in front of me. He was courteous and attentive and it occurred to me that, since the crisis caused by Simon's letter, Edwin had been cool but polite.

"Thank you, Meredith. This is most reassuring," he said. He was dressed in a pale blue sweater and gray slacks. Trim as ever, he looked slightly thinner as if he had lost some weight. As he rose to leave my office, I had one last question: "Edwin, the letter you and George wrote defending the school against Simon, did you write it together?"

"I wrote the basic letter. George edited," he said. "I was the one who had the data we needed in my office and mine was the better institutional memory."

That figured. Edwin was not only the better writer, he was probably the instigator of the response. For once, George just went along.

Nell came in to say Max was out sick with flu and would probably be gone for several days. I was relieved. George was due in my office at 4:30. I inhaled, tried to focus on the joy of seeing Joe later that evening. George was on time and tense as a cat—a big cat, stalking prey. He sat uneasily in the chair opposite my desk. He was wearing a white dress shirt open at the collar. His belly strained against the fabric. I could see sweat beads on the side of his neck.

I handed him a copy of the evaluation I had written and watched him read it. After a moment he looked up at me, his eyes bright and narrowed. "My overall evaluation says my performance has been satisfactory but not excellent," he said between his teeth. Excellent is the grade required to be eligible for a merit raise.

I braced myself, pressing my knees together and glad I was behind a desk. "Yes, that's so, George. If you look at the paragraph dealing with your research, you'll see why you didn't get an 'excellent' this year."

A sound emerged from George's mouth as he forced air out between his lips. "My research was my book and, as I specifically told you, Meredith, I fired my publisher so I haven't published this year. But I intend to do so. You've read my book, correct?"

"I have, George, and I think your publisher was justified in asking you to make revisions."

"What the hell do you know about my topic?" The sweat beads on his neck now seemed to have migrated to his chest, making his shirt damp.

Keeping my voice low and even, I said, "I may not know about your topic, but I do know good writing when I see it and your writing needs work before anyone will publish your book."

George was on his feet, his face beet red. "Says you, Meredith Solaris. Says you. What about my teaching?"

"As the evaluation reads, George, your teaching has been very good." My stomach muscles contracted but I kept control.

"What about my contributions to the school, my letter to the deans to refute Simon, my vote for that twit Larry Coleman's tenure?"

"Larry Coleman deserved tenure in spite of all your efforts to prevent it. As for Simon's letter, I doubt he ever would have written what he did if you and Edwin had not encouraged his mischief and his rants against Henry."

George sat down heavily. His voice still menacing. "I deserve better than this Red. I have given my life to this school and I deserve to be acknowledged. I have been a significant contributor."

"And you have also been a bully, George. And a huge problem, not just for me but also for Henry and several of the others. You started the argument over the curriculum to get back at Henry, not because you truly disagreed."

George opened his mouth but no sound came out.

I went on. "Your unending diatribes in faculty meetings were boring and unproductive. Your attacks on Larry Coleman were unconscionable."

George stood up and stared at me. His huge hands made fists and I thought about calling for Nell. I pressed my hands down on my desk to conceal any trembling.

"I'll go to Stoddard about this," George said between clenched teeth.

"Stoddard might relish the chance to tell you what he thinks of your behavior." My voice was steel.

"I'll file a grievance."

"Take your best shot, George. The faculty will not support you."

His breathing was heavier. "Goddamn it, no woman has ever..."

"Maybe it's time one did."

He stood, swaying back and forth on the balls of his feet, ready to pounce.

I stood up and glared back. "You don't deserve an excellent evaluation this year, George. You barely deserve the satisfactory I gave you. And you most certainly don't deserve a merit raise."

He looked as if I had thrown hot coffee in his face. His shoulders slumped. His swaying stopped. "I'll mow you down, Red," he croaked, falling back into his chair.

I cocked my head to one side. I was ready for battle.

"Take your evaluation and go home, George. Change your shirt and change your attitude. You are a good teacher and, if you work on your book, I am sure you'll do better next year."

He sat for several moments twisting the paper in his hands, staring down at the rug. The cage door slammed shut. Despair replaced anger and, suddenly, I knew he was no longer dangerous. George the loud, George the belligerent was now a scared, heavy-set lump in a chair in front of me.

He rose awkwardly and walked slowly to the door, an old man with a bad back. He opened the door and stood looking at me, his face moist, knees locked together and bent like a child who had to urinate. And then he turned and left.

I was exhausted but triumphant. I knew at that moment that George may have been angry with Henry but he wouldn't have had the guts to kill him. More than that, I felt certain, for all his threats, he wasn't going to hurt me. Under the bullying and bluster, George Weinstein was a coward. He knew it and I knew it.

I sat still, savoring my new insight, and wondered: if not George, who had been with Henry on November 6th?

As I walked out of the journalism building to my car, I saw the small green noses of daffodils poking up in the dark ground next to the parking lot. Driving home through the dusk, I saw a few more bits of green scattered on the straw colored front lawns, and, at a stop sign, the tall branches of a lone forsythia. In a week the forsythia would start to bud and, in a month, it would be gold. Maybe, by the time it bloomed, we would know what had happened to Henry Brooks and who had made it happen.

As I sipped hot coffee the following Saturday morning, I realized that, in spite of difficulties at the school, at home I was reasonably content.

Joe called or came over two or three times a week. He fixed the faucet in the powder room. He rebuilt the trellis for the rose bushes that would start to green up the first of May. Charlie was delirious.

Which may explain why, several days after Joe and I began to see each other again, on a Saturday morning when I was in the kitchen and Joe had gone to the bakery for croissants, Charlie heard Joe's car and raced out the kitchen door the moment I opened it.

It wasn't Joe's car, but Charlie kept heading across the lawn. I didn't see so much as hear what happened. The squealing of brakes. The dog's anguished howl. I raced out of the kitchen and tore across the lawn to the street. Charlie lay on his side. His front right leg was gashed and blood was all over his yellow fur.

The street was empty. Whoever had struck the dog had driven away without stopping, leaving Charlie to die. Coward. God, I was sick of cowards.

I knelt down beside the whimpering dog. He was breathing heavily but his chest seemed uninjured. His leg was a mess and his pain was obvious. I patted his head. "Stay calm, Charlie. I love you. You'll be all right."

Another car pulled up and the car door banged. Joe was kneeling beside me, his hands under Charlie's body. He lifted Charlie into his arms and carried him to the back seat of his car.

"Call the vet. I'll see you there," was all he said.

Half an hour later we sat in the waiting room of the veterinary hospital. Charlie had been taken into surgery before I arrived.

"I told them he was my dog," said Joe. "I didn't want to have to wait for you."

"He is your dog."

Our dog. No, at that moment, he was our first-born child and he was badly hurt. Neither of us spoke again until the veterinarian came out.

"He's going to live," the vet said. "I'm less sure about the leg. I've done everything possible to clean it up, but it's a deep wound and may infect. If that happens, we may have to operate. I may even have to amputate. I'll know more in a day or so."

That night Joe stayed over.

He slept fitfully. I didn't sleep at all. All I could remember was how I had curled up with Charlie the night I had gone to Joe's apartment. We held each other for three days while Charlie was in the hospital.

On the third day, we brought Charlie home in a dog crate. His leg was heavily bandaged and he wore a large white collar around his neck to keep him from fussing with the wound. His golden fur was dulled. Protest lit his brown eyes. He would spend the next week collared until his leg healed enough to let him walk around. Joe and I took turns caring for him. Sadie came over to help when we both had to work. Elaine got a babysitter for her children so she could spell Sadie. The next Saturday, Vince showed up at the door to help Joe give Charlie a sponge bath. Charlie began to heal. His gold shined again. The vet said he would walk with a limp for a while, but he would walk on four legs.

Charlie was the tie that binds.


The doorbell woke us. It was 6:30 on a Saturday morning and still dark outside. "I'll see who it is," said Joe, grumbling and getting out of bed. "It's too early to be good news." He grabbed his pants and a tee shirt and headed downstairs. The doorbell rang again, insistent.

I got up and went for my robe and slippers. As I padded down the stairs, I heard a woman's voice talking to Joe. It sounded tearful.

The voice belonged to Celeste. Her clothes were disheveled and her face swollen with a large bruise under her right eye.

I had hoped Celeste Cummings would stay sober, earn a degree in history, and graduate with honors. So much for hope. I hurried to her and put my arms around her. "Oh, Celeste. What..."

She clung to me. "Max found me, Dean Solaris." Her voice was low and depressed. "He found out where I lived. He came to my apartment last night."

"Were you alone?" said Joe and I simultaneously.

"Yes, my roommate is away for the weekend." She went limp in my arms. I led her to the couch in the living room. Joe went for a glass of water and returned.

Celeste looked first at Joe and then me. "Max was in pretty bad shape when he showed up last night. He'd been drinking a lot and hadn't shaved in days."

There was another pause. Joe and I kept still, waiting while she sipped the water.

"So I cooked him some food and got him to drink some coffee."

"And?"

"And, he was much too drunk to drive so I showed him to the couch so he could lie down. He passed out almost immediately and started snoring. I went into my bedroom and, after a while, when I could still hear him snoring, I went to bed."

"Then what happened?"

"I woke up. It was about five this morning and I heard a noise. I put on my robe and went out into the living room. Max had found a bottle of my roommate's vodka in the kitchen. It was on the coffee table in front of the couch and most of it was gone. He was drunk again. I should have known better but I yelled at him about drinking and wrecking his life and damn near wrecking mine and...and he started to cry."

Joe and I waited.

"So I sat and put my arms around him, just to comfort him."

"And?"

Her voice was choked. "He put his face into my breasts and sobbed and sobbed and said he couldn't live without me."

I found a knitted afghan on one of the armchairs and wrapped it around Celeste's shoulders. She shivered and knotted her fingers together.

"Go on," Joe said gently.

"I pushed him away and stood up. I told him he couldn't stay and he couldn't drink any more vodka. He wanted me to drink with him. I told him he had ruined my life enough and I wasn't drinking anymore." Celeste moaned and grabbed my hand. "I told him I didn't want him anymore and that I hated him drunk and I was disgusted by the idea of sleeping with him."

"I imagine he didn't care to hear that," I said.

"He went ballistic," said Celeste, her voice rising. "He said 'don't you dare minimize my feelings.' He called me a stupid little student."

"Did you ask him to leave?"

"No. I got mad about being called a stupid little student. So I told him he was a self-pitying drunk and it was time to pull himself together. That was a mistake because he stood up and punched me in the face. I almost passed out."

"Did you leave then?"

"I tried to, but he grabbed my hair."

Her voice quavered, "And then he forced me to the floor and tore off my robe and...and he raped me."

Her speech became rapid. "I mean I know it's hard to claim rape when you used to have sex with someone, but I *really* didn't want sex at that point and Max didn't care. He just forced me and it hurt. It hurt a lot."

"How did you get away from him?"

"I screamed and screamed and he finally got off of me. Then he just sat there on the floor while I ran to my room."

"Did you call the police?"

"No, I threw on some clothes and drove here. I mean, come on Dean Solaris. I'd been having sex with Max all last year. Who's gonna believe me?"

We both believed her.

"We need to get you to the hospital," said Joe. "I'll get dressed. Give me your address, Celeste. I'll send a police car to arrest Max."

Celeste collapsed into my arms and we sat together on the couch. "I can't believe he did this to me, Dean Solaris. I can't believe I let him into the apartment. I'm so terrible at saying no to him."

I rocked her for a few minutes and then said, "I'm going to dress and come with you to the hospital."

*    *    *

"I want to keep her here today and tonight," said the doctor, a young Japanese woman with a round face. "The swelling on her cheekbone concerns me. And she seems to get dizzy on and off. Have you called her parents?"

"Yes," I said. "They are on their way. Is Celeste badly hurt?"

"She may have a concussion and her vaginal area is bruised." The doctor pulled me to the side away from the others in the emergency reception area. "The man who came in with both of you?"

"He's a police detective," I said. "He's gone to look for the man who raped Celeste."

The doctor nodded. "Wish the detective luck for me," she said and left.

I reached for my cellphone to call Joe. The police hadn't found Max at Celeste's apartment or at his home. Joe had made calls to his captain. "I'm back on the case," he had said.

My phone buzzed. Nell's name appeared on the caller ID. "Dean Solaris, this is Nell. I'm at the school. Security called me when they couldn't reach you at your house."

"What's up, Nell?"

"Looks as if someone tried to break into your office. Whoever it was left the outside door open downstairs and set off the alarm."

"Did they get into my office?"

"No, looks like they failed, but the door handle is broken and the wood around it is chipped."

"Was anything taken?"

"Not as far as I can see, but you might want to come over and take a look."

Unbelievable.

# Chapter 29

My watch read 8:15 when I entered the school of journalism. I had to use a key card to open the door since it was the weekend. We had been warned when the card system was installed that if we didn't use the card on entering and on leaving, it would set off the alarm. So, whoever had broken into the school probably had a key card, had entered, broke into my office, and then left in a hurry without sliding his or her card.

I called Joe again on my cellphone. It went to his voicemail. I left a message to call me on my cell, but I didn't tell him about the break-in. He had enough on his plate finding Max.

Nell had unlocked the door to my office with the help of a security guard who managed to reset the broken handle. She was standing by the table.

The security guard was nowhere in sight.

"The guard said he was going to check the perimeter," said Nell. "I am baffled trying to figure out what someone would want."

I went through the papers on my desk. "And nothing is missing?"

Nell shook her head. "Nothing." She looked anxious and I remembered it was Saturday and she took care of her mother on Saturdays.

"You go on back home. I'll take a look around and see if I can figure out what our intruder was looking for."

"Thanks Dean Solaris. My sister works on Saturdays and I'm afraid this disturbance has made her late. I should get home as soon as possible."

I sat down and went through my desk drawers then spent a few more minutes looking through the papers on my desk. I heard a noise that came from the direction of the elevator. The guard returning I assumed.

I looked up from my desk. Max was in the doorway. He looked awful. A heavy growth of beard covered his mouth and chin, hair tangled and matted around his face. He was wearing dirty jeans and a plaid wool shirt unevenly buttoned and hanging out over his belt. His jacket and shoes were muddied. Only his eyes were clear—oddly clear. He was sober.

"I was hoping to find you here, Red." His speech was firm and precise.

"There's a security guard on his way up," I said. "I'm not sure you want him to find you looking the way you do."

"He won't." Max moved into my office and closed the door behind him. "He's been called to another building on the other side of campus. I guess another alarm went off." He smiled. His lips looked dried. There was dirt caked in the lines around his mouth and his eyes.

"I have to leave now, Max. I have to take my dog to the vet for a check-up this morning." That was true except Joe was supposed to take Charlie to the vet. Why hadn't Joe called? I reached for my cellphone.

Max stepped closer, grabbed my wrist, wrenched the phone from my hand and threw it across the room. It clattered against the wall. "We need to talk, Red. Without interruption."

I zipped up my jacket. I could handle this. "Sorry, Max but I can't be late. My dog was injured and he needs to see the doctor."

"Sit down, Red and listen."

"Listen to what, Max?"

Max's eyes narrowed. He moved silently to the other side of the room and picked up my phone, put it on the floor, and crushed it under his heel. He sat down in the chair opposite my desk. He pushed the papers off the desk onto the floor and put his hands, folded, in the center of the desk.

"Trudy left for California four days ago. Drove down to her mother's in Santa Barbara. Took the kids with her."

"In her condition?"

"I tried to talk her out of it but she said she wanted to be with her family when the baby was born."

"Not here with you?"

"Not with me. She says I drink too much."

"Judging by the look of you, I'd say she's right."

His hands on my desk formed fists and he banged on the desk so hard the lamp moved. "Don't judge me, Red. Don't judge me. I've had enough women telling me how to behave. I don't need it from you. Now sit."

I obeyed. I realized I was truly frightened. Max was glaring at me with eyes as icy as I had ever seen. He was calculating. What? How to kill me?

Joe had not returned my calls and didn't know I was at school. He would expect me to be home. If he couldn't find me there he might think I had taken Charlie to the vet. I was in my office in an empty building, alone with a man who had just raped a student. My mind raced. Max had been my friend for years. How could I get him to remember that?

"I won't judge you, Max," I said. My mouth was cotton.

Max sat back in his chair. He worked his jaw. He took a deep breath. "I came to get my manuscript back and to tell you I am with Celeste again. I know you don't approve, Red, but I need her now that Trudy has gone. I don't want any interference from you."

I reached for my lower desk drawer.

"What are you doing?"

I pulled up a bottle of water.

"Just getting some water, Max." I forced my hand to steady and took a deep drink from the bottle. "Want some?"

He reached for the bottle and I saw the dirt under his fingernails. He drank. It seemed to calm him. He sat back and rested his arms on the sides of the chair. "Celeste went out this morning. I was looking for her and wondered if you had seen her?"

I hesitated.

"Don't lie to me, Red. Did you see her?"

I nodded.

"Did she come to your house?"

I nodded again. My eyes teared up remembering Celeste's bruised face.

"So where is Celeste right now? I need her."

"I don't know, Max."

This brought him forward in the chair, his lips curled. "Don't lie to me, Red. Where is she?"

My mouth was dry again.

"She's in the hospital," I said. "Her cheekbone may be shattered." Maybe this would alarm him enough to want to go to her and leave my office.

He leaned back and stared at the ceiling, rolling his bloodshot eyes. "I guess I was a little rough on her last night," he said. "But I'll make it up to her." His calmness was terrifying. This was a Max I had never imagined.

I summoned my strength. "Leave her alone, Max. Please leave her alone. You're married. You're about to have another child."

A smile formed on his lips. "Oh, knock it off, Red. You're not a prudish woman. You know I'm never going to leave Trudy, no matter how many girls I fuck."

"Celeste Cummings is a mess, Max. She drank herself into a coma last semester. Now at least she's sober, but she's hurt. She needs you to leave her alone."

The smile disappeared. "I know. I'm sorry as hell for her. That's why I want to see her."

"Bullshit."

"Okay. Bullshit. I enjoy her body."

"Leave her alone, Max."

"Or what?" Max shifted in his chair and folded his arms. "You're going to shoot your mouth off? You're going to report me and Celeste, you're going to devastate my wife—your good friend— your kind generous Trudy?"

Amazing. The man had raped a young woman just hours ago and here he was cool and confident enough to think he could bargain with me.

I took a deep breath. I had brought George Weinstein down yesterday. Maybe reminding Max I was his boss would have the same effect. I decided to go for broke.

"I'm not planning to tell Trudy anything about Celeste."

Here goes.

"But your book is another matter. And, I wonder if I should talk to Stoddard about your second and third chapters and maybe even call your publisher. Or, better yet, you should."

His face transformed. He had probably figured he could back me off and probably talk Celeste out of filing charges. But my discovery of the plagiarism stunned him. I watched carefully as he realized my knowledge of the text he had stolen from Alistair Shaw could ruin him. He would be fired. No respectable journalism school would hire him. The media would denounce him.

His shoulders sagged. He seemed to weaken just as George had, so I continued, feeling surer.

"Why, Max? Why did you copy Shaw's text for your book?"

I tried to sound sympathetic. I wanted Max to remember we had once been friends. I wanted him to think we could talk our way through this, could come to a sensible solution. I needed to stall him. Sooner or later the guard would return. Or Joe would figure out where I was.

My question seemed to have some effect.

Max pulled his chair closer to my desk and leaned in, his elbows now on my desk. "First tell me what you know, Red. Or, what you think you know."

"I know you plagiarized because I compared the text in your second and third chapters to text Shaw sent here. I know what you did, but I don't know why. You're a good writer, Max. You didn't have to steal Shaw's work."

He leaned forward with his chin in his hands. "My publisher was hounding me for two chapters I couldn't seem to write. Then, I heard Shaw at a symposium and knew his text was what I needed. So...I borrowed it."

"And you copied it into your manuscript."

"It got the publisher off my back. It got me my final advance payment. I needed that money."

I began to feel in control of the situation. I glanced at the clock on my wall. Ten thirty. Joe would have discovered Max was not at home or at Celeste's. He could be looking for Max at the school. He could be looking for me.

"How did you think you were going to get away with it?" My voice was even, gentle.

Max pulled back and got up and paced the room. "I figured my book would be published long before Shaw's. I figured I could re-write it, but I didn't get around to it. Then, I figured maybe Shaw wouldn't even live long enough to finish his book. He was old and tackling a huge subject." Max took a deep breath and stepped toward my desk. "And, finally, I figured no one would notice."

"You know what this could cost you."

Max walked around to my side of the desk. His body odor was profound. "Red, I have three kids and another on the way. I had to re-shingle the entire roof of the house a few months ago and I'm still paying it off."

He put one hand on my shoulder and the other cupped my face. He leaned down, very close, his breath was rank, but his voice was calm.

Obviously, he thought he was persuading me.

"I need this book. You have to give me a break on this. I've always been on your side. Now, you need to be on mine." I pushed him away. His hands went back to his sides but he stayed close. "Red, Alistair Shaw is dead. None of this matters anymore."

"It does, Max. Using his text was unethical. You need to call your publisher."

"Goddamn it, Red. I can't risk it. They might stop publication. Even demand I refund the advance."

"Then you know that I'll have to call them."

Max's voice rose in a whine. "Why? Just to hurt me?" He raised his hand, palm out. I thought of Celeste's bruised cheek. I flashed on the memory of the driver of the car demanding his keys. Just as I was sure Max's hand would come across and strike me, I spun my chair around and bolted toward the door.

Max stood still behind my desk, staring at me. I opened the door and ran.

I heard Max's footsteps coming after me down the hall. No time for the elevator. I flew down the stairs, thankful I had dressed in jeans and sneakers. I sensed Max a few steps behind me. He caught my arm at the bottom of the stairwell.

"Damn you, Red," he shouted.

I brought my foot down hard on his instep. He cried out and I pulled free and veered down the back hallway toward the television studios. I turned a corner, pushed open a heavy wooden door and locked it behind me. Max pounded on the door but the lock held.

I was in the smaller of two television studios. The walls were thick and covered in dark material to keep it soundproof. TV studios have no windows. I turned on the light. A camera and some light stands had been pushed up against the far wall behind a small table that held a monitor and a telephone. I raced for the phone. No cord was attached. I was trapped. No sound. Max had stopped pounding on the door, but I sensed he was still on the other side.

I looked around the small studio for a weapon. One of the portable lights, perched high on a long pole might work, but it was top-heavy and unwieldy. I dragged it out from behind the table, gripped it with both hands and then leaned against the table waiting for Max to figure out how to break down the door.

I heard a thump. Then another. Max was kicking the door. I could see it tremble but the lock held.

Then silence. I waited. And waited. The studio was silent. Minutes passed. I felt sweat on my neck and under my arms. I had thrown on a jacket and sweatshirt before taking Celeste to the hospital. Still gripping the portable light stand, I moved toward the back of the room as far as possible from the door.

Then I heard the noise of metal scraping. Max must have found something he thought would break the lock. But the door held and the scraping stopped.

More minutes passed. I looked at my watch. Eleven. By now Joe should be really worried. He would know I was not home, not with Charlie.

Eleven fifteen. The air in the room was warm and thick. No one was going to come to help. Joe must still be out hunting for Max to arrest him. Not for me. I prayed Joe would think to come to the school.

A sound. A key in the lock. Maybe the security guard had arrived. No. My heart rate zoomed as the door opened and Max appeared with a set of master keys in his hand. He must have broken into Nell's office to find them. He was breathing hard.

I clutched the light stand. The lighting fixture on top was heavy and the stand trembled in my hand.

"Red, I don't want to hurt you. But I can't leave you until you promise you will keep this book problem to yourself." Max took a few steps toward me. I could see he was sweating even more than I. His teeth dug into his lower lip.

He took another step toward me.

I clutched the light stand. Another step. He was no more than a yard away. I inhaled and pushed hard on the light stand. Max dodged to one side. The light stand fell forward, grazed his arm and crashed to the floor next to him. He cried out, "Red, you bitch," and rubbed his arm. I had stopped him but only for a moment.

Weaponless, I shouted, "Stay away, Max. Stay away."

He lunged and then he was on me. I scratched his face. He grabbed my hands, pinned them behind my back and forced me to the floor. He grabbed a fistful of my hair and started to shake my head. "Promise me, Red, promise me."

This is the end, I thought. Max's breath was foul and hot and his face was dark red with exertion. My head hurt from his grip on my hair. He stopped shaking me, straddled me and put his hands on my throat.

I couldn't speak. I raised my knee up to kick his groin but he caught my leg and slammed it to the floor. Then he pulled up. He was still straddling me as he raised his hand and struck hard. I felt blood in my mouth and pain on my cheek and jaw. I felt his hands around my throat again but I was too dizzied from the blow to defend.

"You're a shitty friend, Red. You know that? I was always on your side and now you're trying to destroy me. It won't happen. I won't let you ruin me."

His grip tightened. I pushed against his arms but he was too strong for me. I started to lose consciousness.

In my darkness I heard the distant sound of barking. Were thoughts of Charlie going to be my last?

Darkness. Pain.

Then, from miles away, a familiar growl.

Less pressure on my throat.

I opened my eyes.

Charlie's jaws were firmly clamped on Max's arm and the growl was loud and low. Charlie wrestled with Max's arm, pulling and tugging.

Joe's voice was near. "Charlie, let him go."

Joe pulled Charlie off Max and I saw his fist strike Max's head. Max rolled off me and collapsed on the floor. Joe reached under my arms and lifted me to my feet.

He stroked my hair, ran his fingers gently across my face and throat and then sat me down on the table. "Will you be all right here for a minute?" he asked.

I nodded, my throat too painful for speech.

Max was on the floor holding his arm and moaning. Charlie limped over to my side and sat licking my hand—the scar and the shaved part of his front leg still visible.

Joe leaned down and handcuffed Max's arms behind him. "Maxwell Worthington, you are under arrest for the murder of Henry Brooks."

What? Henry's murder? Had Joe finally found evidence?

"I didn't kill Brooks."

"Your car was seen here the day Brooks died. And a man of your description was seen entering the building."

I was in shock. Was Joe bluffing or did he really have proof? I covered my bloody mouth with my hand. No way was I going to interrupt.

Max struggled to get up and managed to get to his knees. "Okay, shithead, I was here. But I didn't murder Henry." What looked like foam appeared at the corners of his mouth. "I saw him, but I didn't kill him."

Joe left me and took out his notebook. "Keep talking," he said to Max. "What did you see Henry Brooks about?"

"Henry was going to call my publisher and tell them I had plagiarized some text." Max seemed out of breath but he stayed kneeling on the floor.

Joe kept writing. He kept his eyes on Max, closing in on his target. "Details, Worthington," Joe said.

Max took another breath. His tone was defiant as he stared at Joe. "I don't have to give you details, Morgan. I didn't kill Henry Brooks and that's all you need to know."

Joe squatted down so his face was even with Max's. "That's not all I need to know. I can also charge you with the rape of Celeste Cummings and the attempted murder of this woman. You got nowhere to go, Max, so tell me about Brooks."

"I wasn't going to murder Red," said Max.

"Sure looked it." Joe reached for a fistful of Max's hair. He pulled hard. Max cried out. "Details, Max. Or I beat the living shit out of you right here."

More spittle came out of Max's mouth. "Henry was an accident."

I gasped. Joe shot me a look that said not to interrupt.

"Details," Joe said.

Max slumped down so he was sitting with his hands cuffed behind his back. He stared vacantly at the wall. Then he spoke. "Okay. That Sunday, Henry had telephoned me about two of my book chapters and demanded I come to his office and account for them. Demanded. Christ, he summoned me to his office like I was an errant schoolboy. I went."

Joe stared steadily at Max, notebook in hand.

Max inhaled. "When I walked into his office, Henry waved pages from my manuscript in my face. He threatened to report me to the administration. He threatened to call my publisher. He told me I had to resign."

"What did you do?" said Joe, now standing and writing.

"What did I do? For Christ's sake, Henry was my friend. I begged him to overlook the text I had copied, to give me another chance, to let me square things with Alistair Shaw and my publishers. I told him I couldn't resign."

"And how did Brooks react?"

Max looked at the floor, as if talking to himself. "Henry was so fucking arrogant. He said I was an embarrassment to the school and to him." Max gagged and stopped.

"Go on," said Joe.

"Henry was determined to humiliate me, to make me suffer. I had been his friend for years. I had backed him up in arguments with other members of the faculty, but he didn't care about that. He was so bloody self-righteous, so sure I needed to be punished." Max swallowed hard. "We argued and argued. Finally, I could see there was no changing his mind so I told him if he didn't drop the plagiarism charge, I would call Edwin Cartwell and tell him about the affair Henry was having with Edwin's wife."

Max looked at me. I could see tears forming in his dulled eyes. "And I guess that got to him because he stopped being so smug and he started yelling and he came at me. He was in a rage. Don't you dare tell Edwin anything, he screamed at me. Don't you dare talk about Mary. So I said okay, do we have a deal? I don't tell Edwin and you forget about Shaw's text."

Max seemed to run out of steam. He was barely breathing.

"So did you have a deal?"

Max looked at Joe.

His speech grew rapid. "At first I thought so. Henry was quiet for a moment. Then, he swung at me and I pushed him away. I was bigger and younger than Henry. I didn't want to hit him. Then he swung again and hit my chest and then he grabbed my jacket. I pushed him away. I swear that's all I did. I pushed him away and he fell back on his desk."

"And?"

"He lay on the desk for a minute and then he sort of staggered to his feet. His face was gray. He staggered away from me."

Max looked at me again. "Red, I wanted to help him. Honestly. I could see he was in pain. I could see he was hurt or something was wrong. But, I just stood there watching while he kept backing away from me. Then he turned and stumbled into the hallway. I saw there was blood on the back of his shirt. He reached the stairwell, looked back at me, and then pitched forward and fell down the stairs."

Max looked back down at the floor, breathing in gulps.

"What did you do then?"

Tears streamed down Max's face. "I didn't do anything. I just walked to the stairwell and stood there looking down at him."

"Did you think to go down the stairs to help him?"

Max sobbed. I thought he might pass out. "No, I stayed at the top of the stairs watching the blood pour out of his nose and mouth. Maybe I should have tried to help, but Henry wasn't my friend anymore. He was my enemy."

"What did you do next?"

"I went back into his office and collected my personnel folder and my book pages from his desk. I saw blood on that glass award and figured Henry had fallen on it. So I wiped the thing off and put it in a box under his desk. Then I left and went down in the elevator."

All I could hear was the sound of my own breathing. Max moaned and toppled over as two uniformed officers entered the studio.

*    *    *

"Sorry I neglected you," said Joe. "But I wanted to see if I could get him to talk."

"How did you find me?" My voice was raspy. Joe was examining my neck where Max's hands had been. The uniformed policemen had pulled Max up from the floor and half-carried him out of the studio.

Joe put his hands tenderly on the side of my head, avoiding my bruised cheek and jaw. He used his handkerchief to wipe the blood off my chin. He dabbed gently at my split lip. "I didn't find you. Charlie found you," he said. "When I came back to the house, you weren't there. You didn't answer your cell. I called the hospital and they said you had left. I took Charlie to the vet's to have his bandage removed and his stitches checked. I kept calling your cell." Joe kissed my forehead. "Now I'm taking you back to the hospital to have your neck checked over. That bastard almost killed you."

"But you said Charlie found me. How?"

"By the time we had finished at the vet's I was too worried to spend time taking him to your house so I brought him with me to look for you. I drove here and saw your car in the lot. I ran to the building—one of the doors was ajar. Charlie was right behind me. We started at your office, and then began to search all the other offices. Charlie sniffed every door in this building until he found you."

We drove to the hospital with me in the back seat, my arms around my dog. "Thank you, Charlie," I said over and over again.

The same Japanese doctor who had treated Celeste checked out my neck and face.

"You're going to feel sore for a while and you'll have a black eye and these bruises for several days, but nothing seems broken," she said. "You've had quite a morning haven't you?"

"How's Celeste doing?" I asked.

"Better. She's with her parents now," said the doctor. "Go home, put some ice on your cheek and get some rest."

On the way home, I sat in the front seat with Joe. Charlie took over the back seat. "Thank you, too," I said, my voice a bit cleared.

Joe squeezed my hand. "Just doing my job, ma'am." He raised my hand to his lips. Then he glanced at my battered face and bloodied sweatshirt and let out a huge groan. He kissed my hand again and kept my hand on his mouth.

I remembered I had a question. "When you arrested Max you said his car was seen on campus that Sunday. I didn't know that."

Joe squeezed my hand and released it. "I didn't know that either until I went to the station this morning. A rookie on the new team had been looking over a pile of automobile accident reports and came across it. It seems Max had a fender bender that Sunday. The roads were slippery and Max's car skidded into a student's car as they were both leaving campus. Max gave the student some money and never reported it. But the student's parents made him call it in the next day."

"So that made you certain Max was the tall man who had been seen going into the school. That Max had been with Henry."

"I wasn't certain until I saw him on top of you. Then I was certain."

"Were you bluffing when you said he was being arrested for Henry's murder?"

"Kind of." We came to the stop sign before my house. Joe turned and leaned toward me. "But, at that point I had two choices. To arrest Max Worthington for murder or kill him with my bare hands."

# Chapter 30

Six weeks after Max was arrested and charged with the wrongful death of Henry Brooks and the rape of Celeste Cummings, a huge field of daffodils bloomed on the quad outside my window. Edwin Cartwell knocked on the door.

"Hi, Edwin. What can I do for you?"

"Well, I wanted you to know I will not be able to teach any courses on the summer schedule this year."

"Oh?"

"I'm taking an extended trip to Venice." He sat and spread his hands over his lap as if warming himself in the anticipated Italian sun.

"That sounds wonderful, Edwin. I'm sure Mary is delighted."

"Mary will not accompany me," he said, still smiling and still looking at his hands. "We're getting a divorce."

"Oh, I'm sorry."

"I'm not."

"I see."

"I suspect you do see, Meredith. Mary tells me you knew about her affair with Henry."

I must have looked uncomfortable because he got up and walked over to the window. "Daffodils are beautiful this year. Worthy of Wordsworth."

"Edwin, I hope..."

He turned back to me. "I just wanted you to know why I'm away from this school for the summer."

"I understand."

"Yes, I am sure you do." His expression was wistful. "Henry was not her first affair, but I knew he was a real threat to my marriage." His eyes were bright. "And I knew what he was plotting. Did you know, Meredith, Henry actually recommended me for a chair at the University of Arkansas? Wily old Henry. He thought he could ship me off and then keep my wife for himself."

I knew, but couldn't bear to say so.

"I had my sources at Arkansas and I knew it, all right," Edwin said, his voice rising. "The night I found Henry's body face down in that stairwell, I almost danced a jig right there in his blood."

I must have looked shocked because he said, "Do I shock you, Meredith?"

"I was shocked when I heard you on the phone that night singing Ding Dong, the wicked dean is dead," I said.

"Were you? I had no idea."

"Who was on the other end of the phone?"

"Simon. I needed someone to help me celebrate."

"You hated Henry that much?"

"I hated Henry with all my heart and soul."

I didn't know what to say.

"There's one more thing, Meredith." The brightness returned to his eyes. "When do you plan to start the search for the Henry Brooks Chair in Journalism?"

"Don't have the date yet. Why?"

"I'm thinking of applying for it."

"That's wonderful, Edwin."

"Thank you, Meredith," he said and stood up. "How do you think Henry would have felt if I got the chair named in his honor?"

I laughed. "I think he would have been furious."

Biggest smile I have ever seen on Edwin's face. "Precisely," he said and was gone.


Edwin was turned, George was in retreat, and Max was in jail. But Simon was still out there. I shuddered to think of him. No one had heard from him, but Simon was tenured and knew he could come back at any time.

Sadie was waiting at Gormley's at our usual table. Her gentle smile reminded me that my world was coming back together. "How are things with you and Joe?" she said.

"Better."

"Better? But not perfect?"

"We're working on perfect. It's going to take some time."

"It's worth working on. Now, have your mysteries all been solved?"

"Not all, we still don't know who wrote the notes."

She frowned.

Sadie deplores untidiness. "It wasn't Max?"

"No. Max said he didn't write them and Joe believed him."

"So, we still have George and Simon to worry about?"

"I don't think George wrote the notes. Right now he is nursing his wounds and feeling somewhat marginalized. And, of course, Edwin has become positively friendly. But Simon, I don't know. He hasn't been on campus this semester. I'm still scared of him."

Sadie put her hand on mine. "Be vigilant my dear. You know better than anyone that the woods are dark and deep and the groves of academe can be especially dangerous."


On the last day of the semester, and quite unexpectedly, Stoddard walked into my office. "How's your dog doing?" He eased into the chair in front of my desk.

"He's fine now, all healed up. Thanks for asking."

"That's good. Red, I'm hoping for a steady stream of positive news from journalism these days. What are your plans for the summer?" Stoddard seemed in good spirits.

"I want permission to start the searches this summer," I said.

"Searches?"

"For the Henry Brooks chair and for the permanent dean of journalism."

"Well, I guess you can get started on the search for the Henry Brooks Chair, but not the dean's position."

"I thought I was going to lead the dean's search committee."

"No," said Stoddard. "I don't think you should even be a member of that committee."

I raised my voice. "Why not?"

"Relax, Red." He cleared his throat. "It seems several of your faculty members have expressed strong desires to see you apply for the permanent dean's position."

I could hardly breathe. "Several?"

"Yes, several, although I don't feel comfortable identifying them."

It took me a moment to recover. "Several journalism faculty members want me to apply for the permanent dean's position?"

A smile grew across the provost's sizeable face. "Yes. And that means you not only cannot chair the dean's search committee you can't, in any way, be involved in their work. If you agree to apply, you will have to stay a mile away from that committee." Stoddard paused.

"Oh, my."

"Feel good about this, Red. Your faculty apparently admires what you've done over this past semester. So do I." Stoddard stared at me for a moment and then winked.

Winked. For Christ's sake.

I walked out of the journalism building buoyant and excited. A man was leaning against a car parked next to mine.

"Up for an early dinner?" asked Joe.

"I'm not sure I have an appetite."

A big smile. "Red, you have more appetite than any woman I know."

Right.

# Bourne Morris

Bourne Morris began writing at Bennington College where she studied under the late poet laureate, Howard Nemerov. After college, she worked at *McCall's* Magazine and then went to Ogilvy&Mather, New York during the "Mad Men" era. David Ogilvy and his colleagues treated her wonderfully, promoted her several times and then sent her west to become head of their agency in Los Angeles. She had a splendid run in advertising.

In 1983, she joined the University of Nevada Reno as a full professor in Journalism where she taught until 2009. She learned about campus politics when she served as chair of the faculty senate. She retired to write mysteries in 2009 after an equally wonderful teaching career.

# Henery Press Mystery Books

And finally, before you go...
Here are a few other mysteries
you might enjoy:

# KILLER IMAGE

Wendy Tyson

## An Allison Campbell Mystery (#1)

As Philadelphia's premier image consultant, Allison Campbell helps others reinvent themselves, but her most successful transformation was her own after a scandal nearly ruined her. Now she moves in a world of powerful executives, wealthy, eccentric ex-wives and twisted ethics.

When Allison's latest Main Line client, the fifteen-year-old Goth daughter of a White House hopeful, is accused of the ritualistic murder of a local divorce attorney, Allison fights to prove her client's innocence when no one else will. But unraveling the truth brings specters from her own past. And in a place where image is everything, the ability to distinguish what's real from the facade may be the only thing that keeps Allison alive.

Available at booksellers nationwide and online

Visit www.henerypress.com for details

# MALICIOUS MASQUERADE
## Alan Cupp

## A Carter Mays PI Novel (#1)

Chicago PI Carter Mays is thrust into a perilous masquerade when local rich girl Cindy Bedford hires him. Turns out her fiancé failed to show up on their wedding day, the same day millions of dollars are stolen from her father's company. While Carter takes the case, Cindy's father tries to find him his own way. With nasty secrets, hidden finances, and a trail of revenge, it's soon apparent no one is who they say they are.

Carter searches for the truth, but the situation grows more volatile as panic collides with vulnerability. Broken relationships and blurred loyalties turn deadly, fueled by past offenses and present vendettas in a quest to reveal the truth behind the masks before no one, including Carter, gets out alive.

Available at booksellers nationwide and online

Visit www.henerypress.com for details

# DEATH BY BLUE WATER

Kait Carson

## A Hayden Kent Mystery (#1)

Paralegal Hayden Kent knows first-hand that life in the Florida Keys can change from perfect to perilous in a heartbeat. When she discovers a man's body at 120' beneath the sea, she thinks she is witness to a tragic accident. She becomes the prime suspect when the victim is revealed to be the brother of the man who recently jilted her, and she has no alibi. A migraine stole Hayden's memory of the night of the death.

As the evidence mounts, she joins forces with an Officer Janice Kirby. Together the two women follow the clues that uncover criminal activities at the highest levels and put Hayden's life in jeopardy while she fights to stay free.

Available at booksellers nationwide and online

Visit www.henerypress.com for details

# ARTIFACT

Gigi Pandian

## A Jaya Jones Treasure Hunt Mystery (#1)

Historian Jaya Jones discovers the secrets of a lost Indian treasure may be hidden in a Scottish legend from the days of the British Raj. But she's not the only one on the trail...

From San Francisco to London to the Highlands of Scotland, Jaya must evade a shadowy stalker as she follows hints from the hastily scrawled note of her dead lover to a remote archaeological dig. Helping her decipher the cryptic clues are her magician best friend, a devastatingly handsome art historian with something to hide, and a charming archaeologist running for his life.

Available at booksellers nationwide and online

Visit www.henerypress.com for details

# FATAL BRUSHSTROKE

Sybil Johnson

## An Aurora Anderson Mystery (#1)

A dead body in her garden and a homicide detective on her doorstep...

Computer programmer and tole-painting enthusiast Aurora (Rory) Anderson doesn't envision finding either when she steps outside to investigate the frenzied yipping coming from her own back yard. After all, she lives in Vista Beach, a quiet California beach community where violent crime is rare and murder even rarer.

Suspicion falls on Rory when the body buried in her flowerbed turns out to be someone she knows—her tole-painting teacher, Hester Bouquet. Just two weeks before, Rory attended one of Hester's weekend seminars, an unpleasant experience she vowed never to repeat. As evidence piles up against Rory, she embarks on a quest to identify the killer and clear her name. Can Rory unearth the truth before she encounters her own brush with death?

Available at booksellers nationwide and online

Visit www.henerypress.com for details

# SHADOW OF DOUBT

Nancy Cole Silverman

## A Carol Childs Mystery (#1)

When a top Hollywood Agent is found poisoned in the bathtub of her home suspicion quickly turns to one of her two nieces. But Carol Childs, a reporter for a local talk radio station doesn't believe it. The suspect is her neighbor and friend, and also her primary source for insider industry news. When a media frenzy pits one niece against the other—and the body count starts to rise—Carol knows she must save her friend from being tried in courts of public opinion.

But even the most seasoned reporter can be surprised, and when a Hollywood psychic shows up in Carol's studio one night and warns her there will be more deaths, things take an unexpected turn. Suddenly nobody is above suspicion. Carol must challenge both her friendship and the facts, and the only thing she knows for certain is the killer is still out there and the closer she gets to the truth, the more danger she's in.

Available at booksellers nationwide and online

Visit www.henerypress.com for details

Made in the USA
San Bernardino, CA
08 April 2015